With all the attention focused on celebrity hookups and breakups these days, we thought it would be exciting to publish a series of novels about love and the pressures of Hollywood fame, which we call ROMANCE IN THE SPOTLIGHT.

In this year's summer series, we asked some of romance's bestselling authors to pen stories of love, intrigue and sizzling romance set against the backdrop of tabloid media and Hollywood. This month kicks off the summer entertainment series with *Just the Man She Needs* by Gwynne Forster, which tells the story of two high-profile yet private people, who reluctantly find themselves the subjects of intense publicity. In *Celluloid Memories*, the July title from Sandra Kitt, a savvy screenwriter finds herself on the brink of success as she tries to unravel a family secret. In *Love, Lies & Videotape* by Kayla Perrin, a young actress on the verge of big-time success is plagued by an unseemly videotape from her past. And in Donna Hill's *Moments Like This*, an established actress looks to make the ultimate comeback.

We hope you enjoy *Just the Man She Needs*, and be sure to look for the other titles in the ROMANCE IN THE SPOTLIGHT series. We welcome your comments and feedback, and invite you to send us an e-mail at www.kimanipress.com.

Enjoy,

Evette Porter
Editor
Arabesque Books

GWYNNE Forster

Just the Man She Needs

ARABESQUE®

JUST THE MAN SHE NEEDS.

An Arabesque novel

ISBN-13: 978-0-373-83013-8
ISBN-10:   0-373-83013-0

www.kimanipress.com

Printed in U.S.A.

ACKNOWLEDGMENT

To my agent, Pattie Steel-Perkins, whose wisdom, guidance and support are invaluable to me. To Carole Smith, Mary Sheffield and Jeannetta Harris, whose kindness and thoughtfulness continue to amaze me; and to my beloved husband, who is my solid rock and comfort and never-failing support; and my thanks to Almighty God for my talent and for the opportunities to use it.

Chapter 1

Felicia Parker stared at herself in the full-length mirror of her bathroom, dazzlingly seductive in the red-silk ball gown that she'd bought that morning at Saks Fifth Avenue. "Damned if I'm going by myself to the most fashionable event of the season, and in the Willard Hotel, no less." Felicia lived and worked in New York City where she had more friends than she needed, but she didn't want to ask any of her men friends to go to Washington, D.C., to escort her to a gala. She had learned the hard way not to obligate herself to a man. Men had a way of collecting debts. Too bad she couldn't put a label on herself that read "reporter on duty" and go to the gala unescorted. She laughed at the thought. As one of the most popular society columnists, she could get away with it.

She twirled around before the mirror. "This dress deserves to go out in style," she said, pulled it off, hung it up and put her mind to work. Minutes later, she sat in front of her computer, surfing the Internet. After an hour, she found what she wanted: Capitol Gentlemen, a male escort service on Connecticut Avenue in Washington, a service that promised gentlemen. She telephoned the service, spoke with a man whose voice and manners she liked, and placed her order.

"I want a tall, handsome, neat, intelligent and elegant man to escort me to the Sterling gala at the Willard Hotel." In response to his question—which she thought a bit sarcastic—she told him, "I'm Felicia Parker."

"The columnist?"

"Yes."

"Give me an hour, Ms. Parker, and I'll see if I have someone for you. I assume that's the only service you need."

She knew he had a right to ask that question, but she was miffed nonetheless. "You assume correctly." She told him that she lived in New York, but would be staying at the Willard.

As he'd promised, the man called her back within the hour. "Ms. Parker, at eight forty-five, Friday night, Ashton Underwood will call for you at the Willard. Mr. Underwood's references are impeccable. The service is five hundred dollars, and you should give the check to him."

She thought that strange, but since she'd had no previous experience at hiring a man for personal service, she didn't let her mind dwell on the matter.

Felicia arrived in the nation's capital around noon that Friday in late March and went directly to the Willard Hotel. After hanging up her dress, she showered and took a nap. At seven o'clock, she ordered a light supper in her room, for she didn't snack, and she didn't expect that the food would be commendable. At eight-thirty, she finished her ablutions, sprayed her body with Fendi perfume, brushed her hair and slipped on the red ball gown. She added black-satin, elbow-length gloves, slipper sandals, and diamond studs decorated her ears.

"If he's tall and knows how to acknowledge an introduction, maybe I shouldn't expect more," she said to herself as she took a last look in the mirror. The telephone rang and, with her heart racing, she rushed to answer it.

"Felicia Parker speaking."

"Good evening, Ms. Parker. This is Ashton Underwood. I'm waiting for you by the registration desk."

Good Lord, what a voice! "Thank you, I'll be right down."

"May I ask what color you're wearing?"

"Of course. Red."

"And I'm wearing a red boutonniere."

A few minutes later she stepped off the elevator, trained her gaze on the registration desk and nearly swallowed her tongue as Adonis himself moved away from the registration desk and headed directly toward her. *Get yourself together, girl. This guy is used to having women eat dirt when he shows up. Don't fall on your face.*

He had the most contagious smile, and it bloomed as he approached her, seemingly becoming increasingly spellbinding. She automatically smiled in return. And then he stood within inches of her, smiling down at her.

"I'm delighted to meet you," he said.

"Thank you for agreeing to spend the evening with me," she said. "Would you mind if we take care of the money right now, so we can enjoy the evening?" she asked him.

She didn't miss his quick shrug. "Not at all. Make it to Habitat for Humanity."

She stared at him. "Are you sure? I mean—"

He interrupted her. "Very sure. It's my favorite charity."

She didn't bother to hide her bemusement, which he ignored the way a small child ignores a parent that it doesn't intend to obey. "Excuse me for a minute, please," she said, went to the ladies' room, wrote out the check and went back to him.

"That was fast and very considerate," he said when she handed him the folded check. He put it into his pocket without glancing at it, and it occurred to her that he was either very good at pretense or wasn't much concerned about money. She doubted the latter. He was an escort, wasn't he?

"Let's get this one thing straight," he said, staring down into her face, his own unreadable. "You want me to accompany you to some social events, and nothing more?"

Miffed and not bothering to hide it, she raised her head with as much haughtiness as she dared and said, "Nothing else occurs to me, nor is anything else likely to." He shrugged with such nonchalance that she would have enjoyed smacking him. It didn't require genius to know he was telling her that, although she'd paid for his services, she hadn't purchased him. Tension crackled between them like sparks from green logs on hot coals. But he immediately dispersed it with a smile that nearly made her lose her balance.

As they walked up the stairs to the grand ballroom, she stole glances at him and thought, *This is the man they had in mind when they invented tuxedos.* Somewhere near six-feet-four inches tall, she guessed, and with long-and-silky-lashed large, dark brown eyes. Sleepy eyes. She felt like fanning. He's an escort, she repeated to herself, hoping that fact would burn itself into her brain.

In the anteroom, couples milled about with drinks and hors d'oeuvres. She didn't want the snacks and figured that with such powerful temptation close to her side, she'd better not drink.

"Would you care for a drink and whatever else it is that they're serving?" she asked him.

He declined, saying that he didn't eat hors d'oeuvres and wouldn't drink unless she did. A point in his favor.

In the ballroom, the band struck up one of her favorites, and she itched to dance.

"My feet don't like to remain still when I hear Duke Ellington's 'Satin Doll,'" she told him. "Do you dance?"

Both of his eyebrows shot up. "Of course I dance. May I have the honor?" With his finger at her elbow, he led her into the ballroom, held out his hands and let her decide how close to him she would move.

"This is not as easy as I thought it would be," she said to herself as she moved into his arms. And the brother could move his feet. There wasn't anything stiff about his hips, either. "This was a mistake," she told herself.

At the end of the dance, he splayed his fingers at her back and guided her off the dance floor. She had asked for elegance and manners, and by damn, that's what they sent her. All evening, he didn't ask her a single question about herself, yet she wanted to know everything about him, and not as a reporter but as a woman. In her endeavors, she had many male acquaintances, but none was more self-assured than Ashton Underwood and not one carried himself with such grace. She began to wonder why he took the assignment and whether the fee she paid was so small compared to what he received from rich women that he could afford to give it to charity.

At the end of the evening, she had enough material for three columns, but more importantly, she'd spent five hours with a man who'd spun her around as if she were a top. He'd poleaxed her, but had showed no interest in her, merely exhibited the grace and charm that she imagined one should expect of an escort.

"I've enjoyed the evening and your company," she told him, standing at her door.

Looking her in the eye, he thanked her and added, "Would you like…anything else?"

She knew her face registered her surprise, but he didn't react. "No, thank you." His question disappointed her, and she let her tone of voice tell him that.

"Great!" he said. "It's been a genuine pleasure, Ms. Parker. Good night."

Ashton got on the elevator, inserted his card key in the penthouse slot, got off at the twelfth floor and went to his suite. It could have been worse. Much worse. He went straight to the bar, selected a miniature bottle of scotch whiskey, poured it over a glass of ice, shook it and drank every drop. He was forty years old, a father, and the survivor of a rotten marriage, and he should know better than to let a woman in a tush-hugging red ball gown poleax him. But that was precisely what she'd done, and there was no other way to describe it. With his libido primed to rear its ugly head, he stripped, hung up his tuxedo and slid into bed. Thanks to the whiskey and his empty stomach, sleep claimed him immediately.

He awoke at six o'clock as he usually did, showered,

dressed and made a cup of coffee in the Mr. Coffee machine in his room. A glance at his watch told him that it was only a quarter of seven, and he'd have to wait a little longer. He ran his hands over his tight curls and drew a long breath. What he wouldn't give to wake up and discover that the previous night had been a dream. He could see no place in his life for a glamorous, newspaper society columnist. He shrugged. What the hell! He was moving too fast; she hadn't shown an iota of interest in him as a man.

It gave him considerable satisfaction that he'd shocked her when, as they'd stood in front of her room door, he'd asked her if she needed anything else. *An escort would do that, wouldn't he?* Thank God, she'd said no. He laughed out loud at the thought of himself making love with a woman for a stated sum.

Seven o'clock arrived, and he dialed his brother's phone number. "Hello, there," he said when Damon answered. "Listen here, brother, you're in my debt, and I mean big-time."

"What?" Damon's voice had the sound of one slowly regaining consciousness. "Considering what she required in a date, I'd have thought she'd be…well…very special."

Ashton rubbed his chin as a smile altered the contours of his face. "Oh, she was special, all right. A knockout. She's also a famous society columnist for a chain of newspapers."

"I know. Was that bad?"

Damon could be dense when it suited him. He operated on the principal that if your adversary thought you didn't understand what was going on, you wouldn't be drawn into the fray. Damon soiled his hands only when doing so netted him a proper return.

"She was a perfect lady," Ashton said, "and I owe you five hundred."

"Why? Didn't she give you a check?"

"I told her to make it out to Habitat for Humanity. Damned if I was going to let that woman pay me to spend the evening with her."

He heard Damon grumble under his breath. "Like that, huh?"

"Yeah. Next time you need that kind of favor, call Cade or take the job yourself."

"Me call Cade for that? You're joking."

"Oh, he'd complain like hell, but he'd do it rather than see you lose business," Ashton said of their brother. "Can't you get some of your university pals or frat brothers to step in occasionally?"

"You can't be sure about those guys, Ashton. I have a dozen men who'll be and do whatever the woman wants, excluding sexual favors, but they're not for women like Felicia Parker. As for the frat boys, sophisticated women can't stand college jocks."

"No. I suppose not. Why didn't you take the job?"

"I had a class that I couldn't afford to miss, but I also don't want to be seen as competition for my employees. One more semester, and I'll sell this business. I can't wait to try my first case."

"You really want to be a trial lawyer?" Ashton asked his youngest brother.

"It's one of my options. Corporate law is the other."

"I'm getting the nine-thirty shuttle back to New York, so I'd better get out of here. I'll send you the check tomorrow. Keep the faith."

"Right on. You do the same," Damon replied.

Once seated on the plane, he opened the *Wall Street Journal,* checked his companies' stocks on the New York Stock Exchange, opened his briefcase and jotted down the order of his day. At eleven o'clock he put his key into his front door, and as he opened the door, his ears welcomed the sound he most adored—the noise of four-year-old Teddy bounding down the stairs. His son had adopted the habit of meeting him at the door, and he had to find a way to circumvent the likelihood that Teddy would manage to open the door for the wrong person. Ashton held out his arms to his son as he knelt to enjoy the child's warm and excited embrace.

"What did you do in Washington, Daddy?"

He never got used to the miracle of his son in his arms. He held the boy close for a minute. "I went to a very nice party."

"Did they have any children at the party?"

"It was an adult party. If it had been a party for children, I would have taken you with me."

Teddy kissed his cheek. "Why do adults need so many parties? Miss Eartha said all some women do is shop and go to parties. How does she know that, Daddy?"

"Beats me. Why didn't you ask her?"

"She says I get too smart sometimes."

"I imagine you do. Remember to obey her and to be respectful at all times. Do you understand?"

"Yes, sir, but she talks so much I don't listen."

He put Teddy on his shoulders and went to find Eartha, his housekeeper. "Is everything all right?" he asked her.

"We been just fine, Mr. Ash, except Teddy has started to use tricks on me. I want you to teach him that blackmail is punishable by law."

He put Teddy on his feet and hunkered in front of the boy, careful not to show his amusement at the child's latest crime. "You are not to bargain with Miss Eartha. If you do, I'll punish you. Got that?"

"Yes, sir, but that means I'll have to eat spinach and stuff."

"Spinach and stuff are good for you." He went to the stove, poured a cup of coffee, added milk and sat down to drink it. "What did you do yesterday?"

"I painted in my book."

"Good. What did you do that was bad?"

"I wouldn't eat my dinner till Ms. Eartha told me I could watch Dipsy and Doodly on TV."

"That was blackmail. If you do that again, you'll be punished."

"Yes, sir. You told me."

Ashton raised an eyebrow at that, but didn't comment. As a child, he also hadn't liked being told the same thing repeatedly. "I have to get to work. Be a good boy."

Teddy followed him to the door, reached up for a kiss and, as he thought back to his rocky relationship with Karla, Ashton couldn't help being amazed at the joy he found in his son. He wondered how he would explain to Teddy that Karla hadn't wanted to be pregnant or to have a baby after she became pregnant, and that she'd agreed to deliver the child only after he swore in writing that he would raise the child himself, without any assistance from her. All she asked at the divorce hearing was a ticket to Rome, Italy, and one thousand dollars for pocket money, in case she ever got broke. He hadn't heard from her in over four years, and though he bore her no ill will, he had no desire ever to see her again.

He walked down to west Sixty-eighth Street, got the crosstown bus to Second Avenue and Forty-eighth Street, and walked a block to his office at Third Avenue. In spite of his other concerns—his child and the fate of his companies—his mind invariably shifted back to Felicia Parker. The woman impressed him at a deep level, but he hoped it would prove to be a temporary fascination.

After Ashton left Felicia, she went inside her room, turned on the light, walked over to the window and looked down on Pennsylvania Avenue. A solitary figure crossed the empty corner, bringing to her mind that she'd never seen such desolation in a business area of New York City where lights flashed and human beings paraded twenty-four hours of every day. She didn't see Ashton Underwood, but perhaps he'd left by the Fourteenth Street entrance. What had she been thinking? Nobody told her that she had to wear a ball gown; a simple evening dress would have sufficed. But once she had the dress, going to the gala in the company of an eligible man was an absolute must.

"I'd give anything if I'd had the guts to go to bed with him," she admitted to herself, "but then, where would I be?" Vowing to forget about Ashton Underwood, she took out her laptop, wrote her story of the affair and faxed it to her wire service. Then she crawled into bed, too exhausted, too aroused and too excited to sleep, and flipped on the television. A local cable news station ran its story of the gala, and she had a chance to see herself with Ashton, to observe from afar his unbelievable good looks and the attention women paid him, his courtly manners, charisma and the way in which he showered her with attention.

"It's a wonder I didn't wilt right on that dance floor," she said out loud as she stared at herself moving her body to the beat of his rhythm. Undeniably, they made a striking couple. She didn't remember ever having met a man and wanted him on sight…until that night. She longed to see him again but had no intention of calling the escort service and asking how to reach him. For all she knew, he'd used an assumed name.

Felicia returned to New York Saturday around noon. While walking through the terminal at La Guardia Airport, she bought a copy of the *Brooklyn Press* for the purpose of reading that paper's society column written by Reese Hall, her rival.

"Your fangs are showing, girl," she said out loud when she read the first paragraph of Reese's column. Finding herself the subject of the gossip columnist's acid pen surprised Felicia, for she rarely rated mention. But Ashton had piqued Reese's interest and her speculation as to why the handsome stranger was in the company of Felicia Parker annoyed Felicia. She knew that Reese wouldn't stop digging until she discovered Ashton's identity. *God forbid she should learn that he's a professional escort!*

At home, she found the red light blinking on her answering machine. The phone rang, startling her. "Hello, this is Felicia."

"I would ask how it's going," her brother's deep masculine voice said, "but from what I saw of you on TV this morning, I expect you're feeling no pain."

"Hi, Miles," she said, sat down and kicked off her shoes. "You saw that on the local station?"

"No, ma'am. I saw it on ABC. Who's the guy? He makes quite a figure."

Being questioned by Miles was tantamount to an interrogation by a prosecuting attorney. A professor of law, Miles had a habit of carrying his profession over to his personal relations, at least with respect to her.

"I'm not sure you want to know who he is," she said. "I wouldn't want to put your avowed liberalism to the test."

"If he isn't an alcoholic or a crackhead and didn't vote Republican, I can probably handle it."

"You don't ask for much," she said while she decided how little to tell him. "I met him last night."

"You're joking! The two of you danced as if you'd done nothing but that for the last decade, and the way you looked at each other suggested something that's not my business." But that wouldn't stop him. "Where did the two of you go after the gala?"

"I'll fix him," she said to herself. To Miles, she said, "To my room."

"What?" he yelled. "Didn't you just tell me you met that man last night?"

She buffed her nails on her skirt. "Uh-huh. I sure did."

"Stop playing with me, Felicia. You didn't… That's not like you. I mean, you wouldn't be that foolish."

"No, but I can dream, can't I? He took me to my room and left me at the door. I've been kicking myself ever since."

"Oh, come now. I admit he could win a prize in a room full of men, but—"

It had gone far enough. She interrupted him. "He's more than what you saw. I've waited a long time to react to a man as I did to him, but I'll probably never see him again. That's life."

"I'm sorry, sis. I've been there, so I know how you feel. You're doing a column on that gala, I presume."

"Yes. I haven't seen the paper, yet. Reese Hall wrote a piece on it, too, but a good quarter of her story was about me and my date. She can bet I wouldn't give *her* that much coverage."

"I don't want to read it. Reese is too bitchy for my taste."

"It's not too bad, except she doesn't seem to think I deserve a date with that kind of man. I didn't see her. Maybe she got her information from the television. I wouldn't put it past her. By the way, why weren't you at the gala?"

"Have you forgotten how I hate those things? Nothing bores me quicker that small talk with strangers."

"I know. Talk to you later." She hung up and wondered why she hadn't told her brother that she'd used an escort service. She pondered, too, the awful emptiness that she'd never felt before. He couldn't call her, because the service rules probably forbade it and wouldn't give him her number. How she wanted to talk with him, to see him again, to assure herself that what he sparked in her wasn't real and would quickly pass!

Ashton had hardly settled in his chair when problems forced his thoughts away from Felicia. He had once faced the possibility of bankruptcy, and the lesson he learned from it was the importance of diversification, of owning more than one product and different kinds of products. Underwood Enterprises had bounced back from the brink of financial disaster when its flagship company, Dream, a cosmetics company, produced a popular, fast-selling, makeup for very dark women. Within a year, the company catapulted him into the ranks of multimillionaire. He and his two brothers added to their holdings a riding school that catered to the rich and an intracity sightseeing bus line. A few weeks back, he began negotiations to acquire a family of newspapers. Although it was of no relevance then, he wondered now if he wanted to own the Skate newspapers, in as much as Felicia's column appeared in one of the papers. He shrugged it off; the chance of his seeing that woman again was practically nil.

He knew that Felicia didn't connect him to the owner of Dream, for he was known in business circles as John Underwood. Ashton was his middle name. With an M.B.A. from Harvard, his management skills had made him a wealthy man, and he felt secure in his ability to oversee a group of unrelated companies, although his brothers served as managers of all but Dream. That one was his baby. He pulled himself out of his musings and answered the phone.

"Underwood speaking."

"This is Damon. I just got some news that you won't like. That is if it's true. A client told one of my escorts that Barber-Smith is planning to take over Dream."

"*What?* Who was this client?"

"Kate Smallens. She's Smith's mistress, and he's promised to give the company to her."

"Yeah? Over my dead body! That's all I need right now. Just as I'm about to clinch that deal with Skate newspapers, I get this. Not to worry, though. I'll handle it."

"Sure thing," Damon said. "Did you speak with Cade today? He told me he's going to Houston to a big conference and that he's giving a workshop. How about that?"

"He's working it, all right. I'll call him." He hung up and called Cade, the middle of the three brothers.

"Underwood speaking."

"Hey, brother," Ashton said, "get it through your head that *I'm* Underwood. Damon said you're going to Houston. What's your lecture about?"

"Ashton! What's up, brother?"

"Just checking on you."

"Right! I need that. After all, I've just learned how to get along without diapers. Thanks for your concern. China's churning out new chips. It's all about the competition, and believe me there's plenty of it. Who was that honey you were with last night? Man, she's a knockout, and when she looked at you, she definitely liked what she saw. Way to go!"

Ashton didn't want his brother's hopes raised. Ever since his disappointment about Teddy's mother, both of his brothers had hoped he would find a woman who suited him. He wouldn't mind their meddling, if they weren't so transparent with it.

"Nothing there, Cade. All I know about that woman is her name and occupation."

The sound of his brother's laughter always amazed him; if you didn't know Cade was amused, you wouldn't guess it from his laugh. "Get busy and do some research then. I have a feeling that you don't want to pass that one up, Ashton. At least not until you've sampled the goodies."

Ashton shifted in his chair, uneasy with that level of talk about Felicia Parker. But why? He and his brothers always joshed each other about women. "Listen to who's talking," he said, aware of the lameness of his response.

"Whoa. Like that, is it?" Cade said. "Forgive my loose tongue. You'd better get to work on it."

Ashton closed his eyes and leaned back in his chair.

From their childhood onward, Cade had been able to read him correctly, and to interpret his moods and manners with ease. First his parents and then their grandfather, who raised them, would ask Cade, "What's wrong with Ashton?" and he would invariably give him the correct answer. Yet it was to Damon that he felt closest. But then, everyone seemed to feel close to Damon. He reflected upon Cade's astuteness about people, thinking that that talent made him successful in everything he undertook.

"Aren't you going to pursue this relationship?" Cade asked him. "I sure as hell would."

Ashton explained to Cade how he happened to meet Felicia. "If I've got a problem, I can thank our brother. But I don't think this merits discussion. It's history."

"That's not the way I read it. How's Teddy?"

"Growing and getting clever. He's begun to match wits with Eartha, and he has her thoroughly charmed."

"Like father, like son," Cade said. "Damon told me about Dream, and I figure we're in for a rocky ride. It wouldn't hurt to have a nice soft and supple cushion to relax on. A warm, sweet woman can make the flu seem like a treasure, if you get my drift."

"Oh, I get it, all right."

"I hope I'll have some good news for Underwood Systems when I get back from Houston. Our software business is primed to take off. Incidentally, are you going down home this weekend? I'd promised Granddad I'd see him, but this conference came up and I can't afford not to take advantage of the opportunity to hold a workshop and spread the name Underwood."

"You're right. I'll call him, and if possible I'll be there at least Sunday."

"Thanks, I don't like to disappoint him. See you in about a week."

"Neither do I. Good luck in Houston."

Ashton hung up and pondered his moves. On Monday morning he would increase his shares of Dream, and he would encourage Cade and Damon to do the same. A good financial blow would serve Smith right for cheating on his wife and discussing his affairs with his mistress. He had a stockholder's meeting coming up, and he'd better be well prepared.

In the ten months that Dream had been listed on the New York Stock Exchange, its value had more than doubled, but with such growth came the risk of parasitic takeovers. Ashton stuffed a few papers into his briefcase, locked his desk and headed home. It was a perfect day for a stroll with Teddy in Riverside Park.

Tuesday morning came at last, and Felicia arrived at the Waldorf Astoria Hotel for Dream's stockholder's meeting, her first. She had purchased the stock four months earlier on a tip that it was a high flier, and her investment had nearly doubled in value. If the meeting became interesting with feathers flying and tempers heated, she might get something for her column. She took the elevator to the hotel's grand ballroom, presented her credentials and found a seat on the second row aisle.

At precisely nine-thirty, the tall, nattily dressed man stepped up to the podium, and her belly did a complete somersault. *It couldn't be!* What an incredible similarity! Ashton Underwood was not chief executive officer of Dream or of anything else. He was a good-looking charmer who made a living escorting unattached, lonely women.

"Good morning," that unmistakable voice said. "I'm John Underwood, CEO of Underwood Enterprises and Chief Operating Officer of Dream."

Her bottom lip dropped and she could feel her eyes increasing in size. But before she could restore her balance, his gaze, roaming the audience, settled on her, and although his eyebrows shot up, he kept his aplomb in tact. Hmm. *So Ashton Underwood led a double life.* She took out her writing pad and pen and noted that fact.

At the mention of a takeover, her antenna shot up. Was he in trouble? She hoped not. Without asking herself why, she silently prayed that the stockholders would stand with him. And with their investment having doubled in so short a time, they voted to retain the management that was working well for them. From the murmurs she heard at the end of the meeting, she understood that many of the stockholders would buy more stock in support of the CEO, and she would do the same.

"The meeting is adjourned," echoed in her mind while she remained seated trying to digest what had taken place, but especially getting herself attuned to this different Ashton Underwood. After thanking them for their support, he remained at the podium, and she realized that he was staring in her direction, waiting for her move.

"This is my chance," she told herself, "maybe my only chance, and I do not intend to blow it." Many of those present went up to the podium to speak with him and to shake his hand, and he wanted to speak with her, she saw, for he glanced her way from time to time. At last she saw an opportunity, walked up to him and extended her hand for a handshake. She hadn't planned what she would say, so she went with the woman rather than the reporter.

"Good morning, Mr. Underwood. Have we ever met?" She was leaving it to him, since he was the one at a disadvantage, and she could tell from his reaction that she'd said the right thing, for he almost smiled.

"Yes, we have. Last Saturday night, to be exact. How are you, Ms. Parker?"

"Relieved. I thought I might be hallucinating. I spent the last three days thinking about you and what an intriguing man you are. I wanted to phone you, but I confess I didn't have the guts to call that agency and get your number. Are you leading a double life?"

"I was on Saturday night, and I'd appreciate it if you wouldn't put that in your column."

"So you know who I am."

"Yes, and I knew from the beginning. I just wasn't prepared for the shock you gave me in that red ball gown, though I confess that, dressed as you are now, the effect isn't much different. Saturday night is the only time I've ever worked as an escort."

"Thanks for the compliment. Asking a reporter not to print something is an enormous request. How do I know you're telling me the truth?"

His eyes seemed to plead with her, and nobody had to tell her that pleading was not a part of his character.

"My younger brother owns Capitol Gentlemen. He knew who you were, and although he runs a legitimate business, he decided that he didn't trust any of the men who work for him to escort you. He called me, frantically, asking for a favor. I am not in the habit of saying no to my brothers when they ask me to do something for them. After meeting you, I wished I had said no."

"I want to meet your baby brother. If he convinces me

that you were helping him out, nothing about your exploits of last Saturday will go in my column."

Both of his eyebrows shot up and his skepticism was as obvious to her as his hand. "Do you mean that? Seriously? He's in school, so I doubt he'll have time to come up here, but if you're willing, we can go to Alexandria tomorrow. The trip's on me."

She thought about it for a long minute, mindful of her policy of avoiding obligating herself to a man. "I don't know. I like to pay my own way and foot my own bills. That way, I don't have to take 'what for' from any man."

Fire seemed to shoot from his olive-brown eyes, and there was no mistaking it: she had insulted him. "Haven't you ever met a decent man?" he asked her.

How was she to answer that question truthfully? It had been years since she'd given any man an opportunity to show her whether he was or wasn't *decent.* She resisted the temptation to shrug, lest he gain the impression that she didn't care what he thought.

She looked him in the eye and said, "I don't know," in what she figured was as honest an answer as she could give.

She realized that her answer took him aback, for she could see him softening until, finally, a grin warmed his face, exposing his natural charisma and turning him into the Ashton Underwood with whom she had spent a fairy-tale evening.

"I'm trustworthy," he said. "How about taking the nine o'clock shuttle down to Washington tomorrow morning? It's a short taxi ride from the airport to Alexandria. And so that you won't think I'm playing games with you, suppose you phone his office and make an appointment for ten-thirty. His first class on Wednesdays is at one-thirty. Give him any reason you like."

"No," she said on an impulse. "You make the call, and you pay for the trip."

He gazed into her eyes. "Why the change of heart?"

"I want to know who you really are."

His gaze didn't waver. So intense was it that goose pimples popped up on her arms. "Does it matter?" he asked at last.

You want this man, girl, so you had better start it right. "Yes, it matters."

After a long silence during which he continued to look at her, he said, "If you'll give me your address, I'll have a car at your place tomorrow morning at seven." She gave him her address, but not her phone number. If he wanted that, he'd have to ask for it. "You don't live far from me. I'm on Riverside Drive at Seventy-fourth Street."

He stared down at her until she began to fidget. "I'm sorry if I made you uncomfortable," he said. "I didn't mean to. Are we going to continue this formality? My friends call me Ashton. Mind if I call you Felicia?"

"No, I don't mind. I was going to ask you how you happened to be Ashton on a Saturday and John on a Tuesday."

That breath-robbing smile again. "My name is John Ashton Underwood, but my brothers and my granddad call me Ashton. Our mother started that, because our dad was also named John. They've been gone since I was seven, lost when a ferryboat on which they were passengers sank off Hong Kong. My paternal grandfather raised us."

"I'm sorry. Mine are gone, too, but I have my older brother, a law professor at George Washington University."

"Really? I'm sure my brother Damon knows him." He

looked at his watch, exposing the hairs on the back of his wrist and bringing her attention to the long lean fingers that had sent shivers down the naked flesh that her ball gown exposed.

She looked up at him and knew at once that he saw her staring at his hands. What kind of expression had been on her face to precipitate the hot arousal that she saw in his eyes?

"I've kept you too long," he said with a half smile that she knew he didn't mean. "See you in the morning?"

She nodded. "I'll be ready."

Ashton walked out of the Waldorf Astoria feeling as if Felicia Parker had his number. A few minutes with that woman and he had begun to burn for her all over again. Not that the attraction had subsided since Saturday. It hadn't. But the intensity of his desire for her had become more manageable. Now, it was once more on the rampage. He couldn't imagine what to expect of his feelings for Felicia in the future, and he didn't believe that having her once would appease his appetite for her.

When he'd glanced down to size up his audience, seeing her had almost knocked him for a loop. But it shouldn't have surprised him that a professional woman would own stock in a cosmetics company, though it did seem like an odd coincidence.

The next morning he called for a limousine and arrived at Felicia's apartment promptly at seven o'clock. She was ready, as she'd promised, and he considered her promptness a strong point in her favor, because he thought it inconsiderate of individuals who allowed others to waste their time waiting for them.

"Do you have time for a cup of coffee?" she asked him, and he hated to decline, because he hadn't had a drop that morning, but they had barely enough time to get through airport security and catch the shuttle.

"I'd love some," he said, "but if there's heavy traffic, it may take us an hour to get there. Thanks for being on time." She locked the door, and they walked in silence to the limousine.

"Is this your car?" she asked of the stretch limo.

"It is until we reach the airport. I don't engage in conspicuous consumption, Felicia. I remember when I cut grass, sold shoe strings, bussed dishes in S&W cafeteria and shoveled snow to get through college. I ordered a car, and this is what the limousine company sent me." From his peripheral vision, he noted her raised eyebrows and wondered if that information would find its way into one of her columns.

As soon as the car pulled away from the curb in front of the apartment building in which she lived, she turned to him and asked a question that he hadn't bothered to entertain. "Why is assuring my correct understanding of your relationship to that escort agency so important to you?"

He eased his trousers at the right knee and crossed his knee. "The answer to that ought to be clear. I don't want anything about it to appear in your column."

"I see. So you don't care what I think of you personally, right?"

"You couldn't be farther from the truth. I do not want you to have the mistaken impression that I lead an exotic double life, and definitely not as an escort."

"Mind telling me why your brother started a male escort service?"

"This is off the record. Ours is a family business.

Although we were doing well before Dream put us over the top. My middle brother, Cade, is COO of Underwood Systems, a software design enterprise. My grandfather manages our riding school with Cade's help. Damon joined ROTC in college and consequently spent three years in the navy, one of them in Iraq. He managed the riding school until he decided to return to school and get a law degree. He'll finish that in June.

"Damon entered George Washington University law school, noticed the unbalanced ratio of men to women in Washington, D.C., even at public functions, and started his escort service. Once word got around that sex wasn't part of the deal, the service became very popular. He could use twice as many escorts as he has, but he doesn't have time to supervise more than the sixteen he hires. Those men are busy every night of the week.

"When Damon sees an opportunity, he makes the most of it. I don't know whether he'll want us to retain the service after he passes the bar. I doubt it. If one of the escorts broke the rules and got caught, that could cause a lot of trouble for a lawyer, and for Underwood Enterprises. We own some real estate of which Damon is COO and general manager."

She had been silent while he spoke, but he noticed that she hadn't taken any notes, and he appreciated that. He'd said it was off the record, and she evidently intended to respect his request that she not print his remarks. But her mind had been busy.

"Back up a minute, Ashton. If Damon has a no-sex rule that escorts aren't supposed to break, what would you have done if I had replied 'yes,' when you stood at my door and asked me if I would like anything else? Suppose I'd said I wanted you to make love to me?"

"If I hadn't fainted, I probably would have replied that I'd love to, but that it was against the rules and that, in any case, I didn't have reference to sex."

She appeared skeptical. "I'd like to believe that. What was your motive?"

Before he could stop himself, he began rubbing his chin with his forefinger, a signal that he was about to do or say something that he'd rather not reveal. "You interested me a great deal, and I needed to know how you would respond in those circumstances to such an overture from me or any other man. Your reaction reassured me."

Her left eyebrow rose just enough to indicate her disapproval. "Well, when you left me, I was certain that I would never see you again. If I interested you one bit, you must be a phenomenal actor, because you neither did nor said anything to indicate it."

He lifted his right shoulder in a slight shrug. "Neither did you."

They boarded the shuttle and found seats. "Would you like to sit inside or on the aisle?" he asked her.

"You're taller, Ashton, so you need the aisle seat more than I do."

If she wanted to defer to him, she should find a more plausible reason. He guessed her height to be around five feet nine, so she would be nearly as cramped as he would.

His smile carried a glow that she could definitely get used to. "What you say may be true, but I'll be happier knowing that you're comfortable." His stares were usually sufficient to command compliance from those who worked for him so, having said that, he slid in and took the seat next to the window.

"How did you decide to become a columnist, Felicia?"

"I'm a journalist. I hated my assignments on Cub Scouts, trends in skirt hems and similar earth-shaking matters, and I wrote a piece questioning why an unmarried congressman who has no children would be eating ice cream with a teenage girl in a shopping mall. To fulfill the space requirements, I added information about people I saw at an Urban League gala. The part about the congressman caused quite a stir, and the editor loved the piece and rewarded me with column space. My dream is to write a widely read political column, and I'm laying the groundwork for that right now."

"I know. I read your column daily, and I'm aware of the gradual and subtle changes."

His leg accidentally brushed hers, and she didn't move away. The contact heightened his need to know how she felt about him, but he decided to let the incident slide. However, he didn't move his leg, and when she still didn't move hers, arousal slammed into him. He reached down, grabbed his computer out of his briefcase, put it on his lap and prayed for a blessing. Felicia Parker was either a gambler or very daring, he couldn't tell which, because her facial expression had not altered one bit.

Chapter 2

Felicia wondered if, by leaving his leg against hers, Ashton was trying to find out what she was made of. She wouldn't say he deliberately stroked her leg with his, but he knew where his leg was, and he should have moved it by now. If he was testing her mettle, he wouldn't discover a thing about her except that she'd meet danger head-on if it suited her to do so. She was damned if she'd blink first, but his warmth began to seep into her, and she had to resist squirming as the blood started a mad telltale race to her loins. If the position of his leg bothered him, he didn't let her know it.

From the changes in the plane's engine, she realized that they were about to land in Washington. And still he didn't move his leg. The plane came to a halt, the pilot turned off the seat belt sign, and all around them passengers scrambled for their luggage and crowded the aisle. He didn't move his leg.

"Aren't we getting off?" she asked him.

"Of course," he said as matter-of-factly as if he hadn't created the tension between them. "I'm waiting on you."

She looked him in the eye, saw what looked like a smirk, and said, "Have you ever wanted to smack an adult?"

He raised his shoulder in a shrug. "Plenty of times. Right now, in fact. One of these days, I'll have the pleasure of seeing and hearing you say uncle, and trust me, Felicia, I am going to relish every second of it."

She had to laugh. She couldn't help it. Wanting desperately to trail her fingers down the side of his face, she said, "All right. I work with men, and it's their daily sport to try and make me acknowledge their superiority. They try all kinds of tricks on me. I never let them win. I apologize if I overdid it just now, but you were no better."

"I know, and I paid for it."

She let a smile express her feelings about that. "I'm glad to know it."

They got out of the terminal and his fingers at her elbow steered her to a silver-gray Lincoln Town Car. He opened the door for her, fastened her seat belt, went around to the other side and seated himself behind the wheel.

"Now that we know we can heat each other up," he said, driving off, "let's try to be friends."

Nothing would suit her better. "Works for me," she said, and settled down into the comfortable leather seat, open for whatever came next.

Ashton parked in front of a four-story, redbrick building, got out of the car and walked around to the front passenger door. "Why didn't I know you'd be standing here by the time I got around the car?" he asked her. "Would it kill you to let me open the door for you?" He liked independent and successful women. Indeed, his experience with Karla had taught him that any other type of woman was not for him. Nonetheless, his feelings about Felicia Parker made him want to emphasize the gender difference between them. It seemed foolish, but he didn't want her to forget that he was a man, a man with whom she had to contend.

"I forget," she said. "I get out of cars all the time without help when I'm by myself or in a taxi, so I hope you'll forgive me."

"For not being a clinging vine?" he asked. "There's no way I could make the mistake of putting you in that category."

Her hand clasped his wrist, surprising him with her soft touch. "I'm sorry, Ashton. I'm not often around a man like you."

"What does that mean? I don't know how to take that."

"You're gracious, yet you don't have an ax to grind, you're not currying favor, and you're not hitting on me. You're just being yourself. That takes some getting used to."

"Thanks for the compliment. Frankly, I thought you were being cantankerous. This is where Damon lives." He took her arm, nearly withdrew his hand, then remembered that after what she'd just said about him, she'd probably trust him for at least the next hour.

He rang the bell at the door of apartment 3-A and waited. After a minute, the door swung open and his brother stepped out, opened his arms and clasped him in a warm embrace.

"Damon. You're looking great. School's obviously good for you. This is Felicia Parker."

"You didn't have to tell me. I'm delighted to meet you, Ms. Parker. You're even more beautiful in person than on television. Come on in."

"Thank you. We're disturbing you, I know, but Ashton wanted this question cleared up today, so here we are."

Ashton had often seen demonstrations of Damon's charm, but he hadn't seen it in so practiced and polished a manner. "I'm sure that after seeing us together, you won't doubt that we're brothers," he said to Felicia, "although he's a few years older than I. I thought he made the perfect escort. Didn't you?"

She looked from one man to the other one. "What are you telling me, Damon?"

Damon took her arm and guided her to a seat in his small but attractive living room. "Have a seat, Ms. Parker," Damon said, "while I get us a little something." He left them and went toward the kitchen.

"I should have told you that Damon has an odd sense of humor, Felicia, and I suspect he's about to demonstrate it."

She didn't respond to his comment. "If it wasn't for the age difference between you and Damon—or maybe it's the difference in experiences—you two could be twins. You look just alike, right down to size and height. Does your other brother resemble you and Damon so strongly?"

He sat across from her where he could see her reactions. "It's been said that 'you always know an Underwood when you see one.' Cade looks pretty much like Damon and me, but his personality sets him apart."

She crossed her knee, and swung the shapeliest leg he'd seen in years. "From my limited observation, you and Damon have strikingly different personalities, though there's one trait that I suspect runs in the family."

"I figured you didn't get anything on the plane except coffee," Damon said, returning with a large tray of food and coffee, "so I toasted some bagels, scrambled a few eggs and cooked some bacon. That and coffee will have to do."

Felicia sniffed in obvious appreciation for the food before her, took a small plate and helped herself. "You're a thoughtful man, Damon. Mind if I use your first name? Mine's Felicia."

"No, I don't mind. I think I'm thoughtful, too, because after you told me who you were, I wanted to make the sale, but I was afraid that my guys weren't suitable. Felicia, the qualities you asked for are not found in escorts. I can promise that all of my guys are handsome and charming, but you wanted elegance and intelligence, good conversationalist, plus something else. That kind of man does not work as an escort, unless perhaps, he's a student. Students lack the sophistication one needs in an escort.

"If you hadn't been a journalist with access to newspapers, I'd have said I didn't have anyone available. I phoned Ashton and cried help. I didn't ask Cade, because he'd make me pay for the remainder of my life, but Ashton always does whatever he can to help Cade and me, so I asked him. Ashton didn't dance with joy when I told him that I wanted him to escort you, but I have a feeling that he thanks me now."

"Suppose I have to attend another fashionable party in Washington, what will I do for an escort?" she asked Damon. Ashton didn't doubt that she was pulling his leg.

Damon lifted his shoulder in a leisurely and deliberate shrug. "Ashton will be delighted to escort you wherever and whenever you wish. No charge."

"He didn't charge me last time, either," she said. "He asked me to make a contribution to his favorite charity. I should have known then that there was something irregular."

Ashton finished chewing his bacon, sipped his coffee and sat forward in his chair. "Felicia, I can't imagine that any man, seeing you and the way you looked in that dress, would have let you pay him for his company." He turned to Damon. "And would you please not talk about me as if I wasn't present. And another thing. No matter what Damon imagines, I am not applying for the position of Felicia Parker's escort."

A frown marred her features. "Have we made you angry, Ashton? I hope not. I'm just beginning to enjoy this. I wouldn't insult you for anything."

"Are you satisfied that I'm not an escort?"

"Yes, and I can't tell you how much I appreciate the honor. I put you to a lot of trouble today, and I'm sorry. Personally, I wouldn't have cared what you did for a living. I knew you were honorable. As a journalist, I'm always on the lookout for a good story, but there's no story here. Okay?"

"Thanks," Ashton said. "Now that that's settled, why don't we make the most of the rest of the day? Alexandria is one of the most historic cities in the country, and it harbors a gold mine of information about the lives of eighteenth- and nineteenth-century African Americans. Also, if you haven't been to Arlington Cemetery and Mount Vernon, now's your chance."

Felicia leaned against the back of the sofa and scrutinized him. "I would have thought you'd be rushing back to the airport. You're a very busy person, and I put you to a lot of trouble and caused you to waste a lot of time. Yet you're willing to blow the rest of the day making the trip down here rewarding for me."

The more he saw of her, the more he wanted her, and when he added honesty and intelligence to her feminine assets, his reticence weakened the way water dilutes wine. She wasn't to be toyed with, and he didn't have time for games anyway. *I'm going for it,* he said to himself as he watched her smile bloom beneath the steadiness of his gaze.

"Don't I deserve an answer?" she asked him, causing him to wonder whether she was brazen or unusually courageous.

"You do," he said. "I won't be wasting my time. I've decided that I enjoy your company, and that I'll have as much of it as you'll allow me."

"Wait a minute," she said, seemingly aghast. "Haven't you skipped some important considerations?"

"You have much to learn about Ashton, Felicia," Damon said. "When he sticks his toe in the lake, he already knows the precise temperature of the water. I was planning to go sightseeing with you two, but prudence dictates that I study for my exams."

He thanked Damon with his eyes. He wanted to get to know Felicia, and the sooner the better, for she was already growing on him like mushrooms on tree trunks after a spring rain.

"I'm sorry you can't join us, Damon," Felicia said, but he'd swear he'd never heard a happier-sounding statement of regret.

"No problem here," Damon said. "Ashton will take good care of you. Say, Ash, why don't we go home to see Granddad as soon as Cade gets back? He was complaining yesterday that he never sees the three of us together anymore."

Ashton let his gaze drift to Felicia, saw that she'd been focused on him but looked away as soon as he caught her at it. "Work it out with Cade," he said, "and let me know when. Granddad wants me to leave Teddy down there with him, but I can't do that. If I walked in my house and Teddy wasn't there, I can't even imagine how I'd feel."

Felicia's eyes seemed to narrow, but he hoped it was his imagination. "Who's Teddy?" she asked him, and he wouldn't describe her voice as friendly.

"Teddy is my four-year-old son, my pride and joy," he answered, making certain that she knew his son came first in his life.

"And where is Teddy's mother?" she asked, obviously ready to push the issue.

He looked her in the eye. "I have no idea, I am not the least interested in locating her, and she is not interested in Teddy." Felicia's bottom lip dropped, she moved her head slowly from left to right and didn't say a word. Speechless.

He walked over to her and extended his hand. "Hadn't we better get started on our tour? I promised Teddy I'd read to him tonight, and that means I should be home by seven."

Still, she didn't speak, but reached for his hand, took it and rose to her feet almost as if she were unaware of her moves. Without examining his reasons or considering his right to do so, he wrapped an arm around her waist and looked down at her. "I rented the car for the day. Let's go."

She was about to enter the car when she stopped, turned and said, "I forgot to tell Damon goodbye."

"I know, but it's all right. I didn't tell him goodbye, either."

"Could we see Mount Vernon first, since it is farthest away?" she asked him after he drove several blocks. "I've never been there, and I hear it's beautiful, so I'd like to be uplifted before I look at depressing slave sites and other gruesome reminders of slavery."

"We don't have to go to those places, and they are depressing. But they're also very enlightening. It's wonderful to see what slaves achieved while staggering beneath the weight of the white man's boot."

"I'm sure of that, but right now, I want to see something that makes me feel good."

"Why?" he asked her.

"Because knowing that your son won't have his mother's love and nurturing is as much as I can handle right now."

A strange and unfamiliar feeling gripped him in the region of his heart, and he wanted to park the car and hug her. He hadn't thought about her in the context of motherhood, but now he wondered whether a beautiful, accomplished and sophisticated woman had genuine maternal instincts.

Felicia glanced at Ashton from the corner of her eye. The chemistry between the two of them could lead them into an affair on that basis alone, and she did not want to be a slave to a man's prowess in bed. Besides, the more she saw of Ashton, the more she wanted him for reasons other than chemistry. Besotted though she was, she meant to retain her wits.

"I should have known that you were or had been married," she said. "Tell me what happened." He could say she didn't have the right to know, but did he have the right to make her feel as if she were the only woman in the world?

"I dated Karla a number of times and had a casual affair with her. I thought I did everything possible to prevent her from conceiving, but it happened anyway, probably from a broken condom. She told me she was pregnant and asked me for the money to get an abortion. I begged her not to do that and signed an agreement relieving her of all responsibility for the child if she would marry me and give birth to it. We stayed together until Teddy was two weeks old, and she asked for the divorce, a ticket to Italy and one thousand dollars pocket money in case she ever got completely broke. She did not want money. She wanted her freedom from motherhood. I have not seen or heard from her since the day I drove her to Kennedy Airport and handed her an Al Italia ticket to Rome."

"I see. Well, I don't see. Did you love her?"

"No, and I never told her that I did. But I cared for her, and I tried to make her life as pleasant as possible during her pregnancy. Actually, I thought we became friends during that time. I took Lamaze classes with her and helped her deliver Teddy, but none of that moved her. She did not want any children, and I'm sure if she hadn't been Catholic she would have had the abortion in spite of my pleadings."

Felicia would never have suspected of a corporate bigwig what she had learned about John Ashton Underwood. "Something tells me that Teddy is a lucky little boy. Who's with him right now?" she asked, but she'd bet anything that Ashton Underwood did not leave his son with a girlfriend.

"I have a housekeeper, who lives with us, but he's

learned how to wrap her around his finger, and he black-mails her, too. Furthermore, he's proud of it. I've told him that I'll punish him if he does it again."

"Will you?"

He glanced quickly at her. "Certainly. I always keep my word, especially to my child. What about you? Do you have any children, and have you been married?"

"No to both. I want a family, but I need to get married first, and I haven't gotten around to that."

He shifted lanes to exit onto the George Washington Memorial Highway. "The men in your circle must be out of their minds. I'd like to get to know you. May we see each other in New York… Uh, will you have dinner with me tomorrow evening?"

He didn't plan to waste time and she didn't want him to. "I'd love to have dinner with you, Ashton, but promise me we can go someplace where we won't be a spectacle."

"What do you mean? Oh, I get it. Not where the celebs hang out. I'll do my best." His right hand suddenly covered hers, and his touch seemed…well, experimental was the best way she could describe it. She turned her hand over and let her palm caress his.

"You're getting to me," he said. "What are we going to do about it?"

She didn't feel like answering that. "I'd say we take one day at a time, but you seem to be moving on a faster schedule." She didn't think Ashton Underwood was a player, but you could never tell about a man. She was on the verge of deciding that she wanted him, and she in-tended to begin by playing according to her rules, not his.

He squeezed her fingers. "You will find that I am a very patient man, but when I see the need to move things along, I don't hesitate. Just be sure you don't toy with me, Felicia."

"That's not my style," she said, and immediately wondered if she'd told the truth. What would happen if she simply went with her feelings without regard for the consequence? No, she couldn't do that. Hadn't experience taught her not to let her body rule her head?

He turned into George Washington's Mt. Vernon estate, paid the parking and admission fees and parked the car. "Let's go see the slave quarters, storage house and smokehouse before we go up to the mansion," he said.

"You're the guide, Ashton. I'll go where you lead."

She paid little attention to the rueful expression that claimed his face. And when his right arm eased around her shoulder as they headed for the smokehouse, she moved closer to him, because her heart dictated it.

His arm tightened around her shoulder. "What a simple life this was," he said. "It's so peaceful here. The only stress I feel emanates from the bustling, rushing tourists. Could you live without the frills to which we New Yorkers accustom ourselves?" He looked down at her, his expression intimate and very serious.

"My Lord, this is moving too fast," she said to herself when he stepped closer and she realized that she wanted him even closer. She gazed up at him and saw in his eyes the answer to her most intimate dreams, and her nerves seemed to splinter. She had to do something to straighten out her head.

After backing up a step, she said the first thing that came to her mind. "How old is your housekeeper?"

Although he seemed taken aback by the question, he said, "Eartha's sixty-one. Why?"

She couldn't find fault with that. "When had you planned to tell me that you have an ex-wife and a four-year-old son?"

He stared at her with considerably less warmth than she'd seen on his face minutes earlier. "You haven't been so forthcoming about yourself. Why did a woman in your position, and who looks like you, need to pay an escort to take her to a formal affair?"

If he'd stabbed her, it wouldn't have hurt worse. But she tossed her head in a defiant manner and told him, "Because I do not allow myself to get into any man's debt. That's why."

"Really? You work with a bunch of small-minded men who you delight in outsmarting, and you think you can back every man you meet into a corner. Not this man, baby."

"Your problem is you're used to having women fall all over you. Well, not this woman, baby," she said, parroting him.

"What's this?" he said, his face a mask of incredulity. "You deliberately picked a fight with me. Any contact would do. Well, I can give you a better outlet for your frustration. Just say the word."

She poked her right index finger in his chest. "Isn't that just like a man, defining everything in terms of himself. I am not frustrated."

"Stop fooling yourself, and quit stabbing me with your finger. What you want is for me to…to—"

"What?" she asked with her flat palm now against his chest, almost daring him to say it. "To do what?"

His hands grabbed her shoulders, and she'd never seen such fire in a man's eyes. Eyes burning with desire. "Don't dare me, Felicia," he said, his expression thunderous. "You think if you provoke me into doing what you want me to do, you won't share in the responsibility. That it?"

Her gaze drifted from his eyes to his mouth, to the full bottom lip that she longed to feel on her lips, her nipples and all over her. She bathed her lips with the tip of her tongue and didn't bother to hide her thoughts and feelings.

"Damn!" His mouth came down hard on hers, and she parted her lips, shamelessly wanting him inside her. He locked his arms around her, pulled her tight to his body and drugged her as he unleashed his passion. He loved every crevice of her mouth until, exasperated, she pulled his tongue into her and feasted on it, loving him. His fingers gripped her buttocks, and his breathing shortened almost to a pant as he lifted her and held her to his body. His heat seemed to fire up her nerve ends, and her blood raced to her loins. Her nipples tightened, and all she could think of as his tongue plowed in and out of her mouth simulating the act of love, was how she wanted him inside her. She undulated against him, rubbing her left nipple and moaning her frustration. He let the wall of the two-hundred-and-forty-year-old building take his weight and grabbed her knees as she pressed herself to him.

Suddenly her feet touched the floor and he was no longer kissing her, but leaned against the wall and held her close. "What on earth got into us?" he asked. "How did we forget that we're in a public place?"

When his mouth touched hers, she hadn't a thought as to where she was or why she was there. "I don't know what happened, Ashton. I've never been down that road before. I've never experienced anything that caused me to behave less than circumspectly. You see what you did?" she said, trying to smile.

As if he understood that her comment was an attempt at levity, his arms went around her in a brief gesture of reassurance.

"It was completely out of my hands, baby. So help me God. You were all I saw, felt or heard. Are you still frustrated and annoyed about it?"

"What I'm feeling now is… I don't know. I'm just… out of sorts. Are we still having dinner together tomorrow night?" she asked him.

"Yes. There's a nice little restaurant over near the United Nations. Diplomats won't be interested in you and me. I'll be at your place a seven. Okay?"

"I'll be ready. How do you dress?"

"Business suit. Come on and let's see the remainder of this place. We have to get the five o'clock shuttle."

They walked out of the smokehouse arm in arm. In the few minutes she spent in his arms, her life changed, and she knew she would never be the same. Maybe he would become important to her, and maybe he wouldn't, but he'd taught her how she could feel in a man's arms, and for that, she would never forget him. She had thought she knew but, in fact, she hadn't had a clue.

He appeared engrossed in their surroundings, pointing out the birds and the foliage, things that he evidently hadn't observed earlier. "Wonder what kind of plant that is," he said, pointing to an evergreen.

She stopped walking, put her hands on her hips and looked up at him. "How can you act as if nothing happened back there. I don't care how many strange plants George Washington had or how many pigs he slaughtered every week. How can you—"

He interrupted her, seemingly unperturbed by her outburst as his eyes sparkled. "Is that the way it appears to you? You're neither as tough nor as combative as you want me to believe. You're in untried, virgin territory, and it's making you uneasy. I don't have a long face right now, because I'm not worried. You're one hundred percent woman, and all that other stuff you show is no more than a fire cracker shooting at stealth bombers."

She didn't mind if he saw through her veneer; no other man had bothered to look. Still, she refused to make it easy for him. "Don't be so self-satisfied," she said.

He brought her back into the curve of his arm. "I'm not self-satisfied. I'm satisfied with the signals you're sending me. What's bothering you, Felicia? Is it your job, your personal life? What?"

She didn't answer his question, because she didn't know the answer. She heard herself telling him something that took shape in her mind as she spoke the words. "I'd like to be somewhere in the midst of a peaceful, quiet oasis, where birds chirped, a brook rushed along and flowers bloomed everywhere. Maybe I'd find out what's going on between us."

"You're a genuine romantic. I'll see what I can do to accommodate you."

They strolled through the storage house and around the grounds holding hands, and neither seemed aware that they hardly spoke to each other. Felicia remained deep in thought as they went from room to room in the mansion and until she stepped out on the front porch. A vast segment of the Potomac River decorated with shadows created by the late-afternoon sun captured her vision, and a gasp escaped her.

"It's so beautiful," she whispered.

"Yes," he said, "but not nearly as beautiful as you."

At the tip of her tongue were the words, "Don't make jokes," but she looked at him, saw the seriousness of his mien and let the words die unspoken. "Maybe he thinks so," she said to herself. To him, she said, "Thank you, Ashton. If you think so, I won't argue about it."

"Why should you? There used to be a little café down the road a piece. Would you like some coffee, tea or a cold drink?"

"Thanks. I'd like some ginger ale."

He took her hand and started toward the café. *Here I am all lovey-dovey with the most eligible man I've ever gone anywhere with, a man who says I'm beautiful, who kissed me silly, and I haven't fainted. What am I going to tell my editor as to why two days have passed since I handed in my daily column? He is not going to be happy doing reruns on consecutive days.*

"You've become pensive," Ashton said. "What's the matter?"

She told him and added, "You're muddling my brain."

He opened the café's door and walked in behind her. "I hope you don't think Dream or anything like it has been on my mind since you kissed me as if there was no chance of doing it again. This is new, and so far, it's…well, it's wonderful…at least for me. So expect to think about it a lot. If you don't, it hasn't made much of an impression." He found seats, and they sat beside a window, holding hands.

"I haven't spent a leisurely weekday afternoon since I was in college," he told her, "and the strange thing is that I don't feel guilty right now, that I'm not horsewhipping myself for wasting time. Maybe it's because I need this as much as I need the solace of success."

"You're your own boss, Ashton. I'm not. At contract time, I tell my editor that my column sells papers, so I have to produce. Besides, I feel a responsibility to my readers and to myself."

"All of which is commendable, but I don't think that's the problem right now. Level with me, Felicia. Aren't you afraid this is getting away from you, that you can't control your feelings? Well, I wasn't looking for it, but I certainly am not going to run from it. Give us a chance."

It didn't make sense to feel as she did about a stranger, a man of whom she knew almost nothing other than his ability to fire her up with his touch. She risked looking him in the eye and shuddered at the softness she saw there. "Let's start slowly, Ashton. I'm thirty-eight, and I'm feeling the way I should have felt when I was twenty."

His hand tightened on hers. "You've never been in love?"

"I thought I was, and maybe at that age and that time it was real, but I don't think so now, because it never took control of me the way…" She stopped talking. She wasn't so besotted that she'd confess it to him. Some things were best left unsaid. His arm eased around her shoulder, and he didn't have to tell her that he understood all that she hadn't said.

"What we feel in our youth is fresh and new," he said, "but I have a feeling that it's nothing compared to a mature relationship. My love for my son is so all-encompassing that I can't conceive of life without him. Just being with him gives me so much joy."

This man loves deeply, and I want him to love me like that. If only I can make myself believe that it's possible. If I can forget that Herman Lamont ever lived.

"Is Teddy enough for you?" she heard herself ask Ashton. "I mean, do you want any more children? Can you…is there room for…for more?"

"I'd love to have the experience of planning a family with my wife…with the woman I love. As of now, I have no idea what that's like. I told you how I happen to have Teddy. Maybe that's why he's so precious to me. But I don't want to raise him as an only child."

"He may not want to share you with siblings."

"I would teach him to love them. I am not worried about that. I've prepared myself to be a single father. I can't be a mother to Teddy. Eartha falls apart if it thunders loudly, but with her at least he has the benefit of a feminine presence. Every child needs that. Do you want a family?"

He'd touched a sore spot. She could get pregnant at any time, or at least she hoped so, but she needed a husband first, and so far, the only one who she had considered a good prospect had also been a good liar, a polygamist working on wife number three. Fortunately for her, he'd slipped up and made a casual reference to "my wife." It was an occasion in which her reporter's nose had served her well. She'd checked on Herman, and as a result, he currently resided in jail.

"Yes, I want a family, and I've decided that if I don't have a child by the time I'm forty, I'm going to adopt two children, preferably two who are siblings."

He signaled for the waitress who arrived immediately and stood as close to him as the chair would permit. The woman took their order of cheese cake and cappuccino, smiled at Ashton and left.

"I thought for a minute that she planned to take the order while sitting in your lap," Felicia told him.

"I noticed that your bottom lip dropped. I started to tell her that my wife was an Olympic boxer, but since I don't know what kind of sense of humor you have, I restrained myself."

"That tells me about *your* sense of humor, though," she said. The woman returned with their order and while putting the food on the table did her best to give Ashton an eyeful of her ample bosom.

Felicia leaned back in her chair and smiled. "Miss," she said, getting the waitress's attention, "your bosom won't impress my husband. As you can see, what he's got at home is more than ample." The woman's face reddened, Ashton's eyes increased to twice their size, and Felicia examined her nails before buffing them on her sleeve.

"Well," Felicia said to Ashton, "from what you said earlier, I figured you've got a sense of humor, and I don't care what that brazen chick thinks."

The grin started around his lips, then his eyes sparkled, and suddenly his entire face lit up, his head went back and laughter poured out of him. She stared at him, poleaxed. If only she could hold him and love him until she was drunk on him. She realized that he had stopped laughing, and when the silence brought her back to the moment, the expression on his face told her that he had read her thoughts and that he wanted what she wanted. He dropped a bill on the table, stood, held out his hand and said, "Let's go. If I walk up those stairs with you, we'll be here all night."

As they walked to his rented car, she said, "I didn't know that was an inn."

"It boasts that Thomas Jefferson once slept there. Of course, it's been renovated and modernized since then. We'll have to come back when we have more time. There's so much more to see in this area."

At the airport, they got through security and arrived at the gate a few minutes before time to board the shuttle. He

didn't ask where she'd like to sit, but took the seat next to
the window as he'd done previously.

"Are you comfortable?" he asked her. She nodded, and
with her hand clasped in his, he leaned back, closed his eyes
and remained that way until the plane landed in New York.

"Have you been asleep?" she asked him as they made
their way through the terminal.

"Not a wink. I've learned that silence can speak louder
than words."

"Yes," she said. "So have I, and the last fifty minutes
added credence to that idea."

He didn't ask what she meant, but winked and smiled.
He gave the taxi driver her address, took her hand and, as
far as she could tell, was as comfortable as if he'd known
her for years. She wished she could say the same. She
didn't think she had ever been so emotionally out of sorts.
Not that she was confused; she wasn't. She just wished she
knew where she was headed.

It didn't surprise her that he paid the taxi driver, got out
of the cab and walked with her into the apartment building
in which she lived. And she told herself to calm down
when he got on the elevator and continued to her apartment with her. She fumbled around in her bag for her door
key, embarrassed that it took her so long to find it. When
she located the key, her fingers trembled so much that she
could not insert it into the key hold. He covered her hand
with his own and steadied it while she turned the key. She
looked up at him, but couldn't read his facial expression.

"I want to come in with you." His voice reminded her of
a sensuous saxophone enticing dancers to move to its rhythm.

She opened the door, walked in and turned to him. "I
didn't want you to kiss me in the hallway."

"Do you want me to kiss you?" he asked her.

"Yes. If you want to."

"If I want to? On that plane and in that taxi, you saw an example of self-control. I wanted you in my arms so badly. Hell, it's damned near unreal, how I felt and what I'm feeling." His hands seemed bigger as they clasped her to his body and he began stroking her back. She longed to feel the man's power, but she didn't dare provoke it. Still, she could hardly bear the tension as he stared down at her, his eyes hot with desire and his bottom lip quivering. She couldn't stand the wait.

"Kiss me," she whispered. "Stop doing this to me. "Kiss—"

He swallowed the rest of her words. With her hand at the back of his head increasing the pressure of his kiss, she let him know how much she needed his embrace. Then, realizing that he might not stop if she didn't call a halt, she broke the kiss, kissed his cheek and stepped back.

"I think we should leave some for another time. Don't you?" she said in an attempt to bring levity to a situation fraught with tension. "When we're together tomorrow, let's try to keep the heavy stuff in abeyance, Ashton. I wouldn't be comfortable with a deeper level of intimacy at this point in our relationship. Can you handle that?"

"I can handle it, and I agree with you. Between now and tomorrow, think of a way for us to avoid it."

"I'll do my best." She tweaked his nose. "Suppose you spend a little time on that, too."

She liked his grin, although she wasn't quite sure what it meant. "Go now. Teddy is waiting for you to read to him."

"Right. That isn't a thing I'm in a habit of forgetting." The heat of his lips singed her mouth. "I'll be here for you tomorrow evening at seven. Good night."

Chapter 3

One block from Felicia's apartment, Ashton hailed a taxi, gave the driver his address and sank into the back seat. In the forty years of his life, he wouldn't have dreamed of living such a day. He released a long, deep breath. All he'd wanted from Felicia Parker was the promise that she wouldn't publish in her column an account of his evening as her paid escort. He had that promise now, but that wasn't all he got in the course of his day with her. Somehow or other, one or both of them had fanned the flames of their initial attraction to the point of combustion. Knowing himself, he accepted that unless she sent him some negative and unattractive signal—and he doubted that possibility—she couldn't count on his walking away from the prospect of the loving he suspected she would give him.

Life without a warm, loving woman hadn't been in his plans for himself, but neither had single parenthood, and unless he found a woman who loved Teddy as much as he did, he didn't plan to change his marital status or even to involve himself deeply in an affair. He rubbed his forehead. "That woman gets to me. In that smokehouse this afternoon, I'd have tasted her if it had meant getting a blow from a sledgehammer." He wouldn't let himself think what could have happened in her apartment a few minutes earlier if she hadn't called a halt to it.

"She's right," he said to himself. "I'd better work on slowing this thing down, too. Something tells me that if I ever make love with her feeling as I do now, she'll own me. No woman has been able to claim that."

He paid the driver and had his door key in his hand when he stepped out of the taxi. As soon as he put the key in the door, he heard Teddy scream, "Daddy. Daddy." He stepped inside his house, opened his arms and Teddy bounded into them.

"What did you do in Zandria today, Daddy? Did you see Uncle Damon? Miss Eartha said you went to see Uncle Damon."

"Alexandria. Yes, I saw Uncle Damon, and he sent you a big hug."

"Did you see Uncle Cade and Granddaddy, too?"

"I'll tell you all about my trip, but first let me wash my face and hands."

"Okay, but don't take too long, Daddy. We have to read my book tonight."

After changing his clothes, he carried Teddy to his room and sat in the overstuffed chair he'd put there for the purpose of reading to his son while the child sat in his lap. With chamber music playing softly, he began the most precious time of his day.

Teddy loved the stories of *Pinocchio, Jack and the Beanstalk, Puss 'n Boots* and, especially *Isra the Butterfly,* but he seemed to enjoy anything that his father read to him. Ashton recalled writing Young-Robinson a note thanking her for his son's delight in her story of the little butterfly.

Teddy got down to say his prayers but, as usual, he knelt at his father's knee rather than at the edge of his bed. He repeated the prayer correctly and added, "I was very good today, Lord." He got up and leaned against Ashton. "When is Sunday, Daddy? You promised me to play the piano Sunday."

He put Teddy in bed and covered him. "Sunday is five days away. If I get home early enough and have time, I'll play for you before Sunday."

"Okay," Teddy said, "but I can count on Sunday. Right?"

"Right. You can count on Sunday. Do you have anything to tell me?"

"No, sir. I didn't do anything bad today. I was good, Daddy. I tried hard. Real hard, and Miss Eartha gave me ice cream for supper."

"Hmm. Did you tell her you'd be good if she gave you ice cream?"

"No, sir. Honest."

"Did she tell you she'd give you ice cream if you behaved?"

"No, sir. She told me we couldn't bribe anymore, and I would just have to be good. So I tried. But, Daddy, why is it bad to jump down the stairs?"

"Because you can hurt yourself, break your arm or your leg, even your neck, and maybe never be able to walk again."

Teddy's eyes rounded. "Gee. I won't do that again."

"Of course you won't, because I told you not to. Now, close your eyes, count to twenty and go to sleep. Good night, son."

"Good night, Daddy. Daddy, do I look just like you? Miss Eartha said I look so much like you she thinks you spit me out. What does that mean, Daddy?"

"It means you look like me, and you're supposed to look like me, because I'm your father."

"Okay, Daddy. I'll tell Miss Eartha that. Good night."

He turned out the light, closed the door and ran down the stairs to get his supper. He didn't require much care, and he especially didn't want Eartha to pamper him. He went directly to the kitchen where he expected to see covered pots on the stove or a covered plate in the warmer, since it was after eight and an hour past their dinnertime.

"You're still in here?" he asked Eartha. "You know you don't have to wait up just to serve my supper."

"I cooked a real good supper tonight. Even Teddy asked for seconds. I wanted you to taste it just like I fixed it, so you go on in there and sit down."

She brought in a bowl of mushroom soup, placed it in front of him, sat down and said the grace. He had a feeling that she didn't trust his relationship with the Lord, because she insisted on saying grace herself. "Mr. Ash—" she never used his name properly "—Teddy's teacher says he's bored in class. She doesn't have time to teach him like he wants to be taught."

Now what? He finished the soup and looked at the woman who made his life easier with the loving care she gave his son. "Is he having a problem?"

"She said he learns fast and gets restless while she tries to teach the other children what he's learned. She said you need to put him in a different kind of school, and she gave me two suggestions. He's too young for first grade and too advanced for kindergarten."

"Thanks, I'll look into it tomorrow. What else am I eating?"

She put a feast in front of him and sat down to watch as he enjoyed filet mignon with red wine sauce, lemon-roasted tiny potatoes, green asparagus, breaded cauliflower with sour cream and a mesclun salad.

"I can't eat dessert, Eartha. This was wonderful." Just what he needed to remind him that bachelor life wasn't so bad.

"I know you're not going to pass up my sour-lime pie, don't matter how full you are. Teddy sure loves this pie."

He ate the pie, partly because it was his favorite dessert and partly because she stood over him waiting to see happiness on his face. "Thanks for a great meal, Eartha. I won't be home for dinner tomorrow night," he told her, "so you can treat Teddy to his beloved hamburger."

"Yes, sir. He'll love that."

A minute earlier, basking in Eartha's caring, his thoughts had dwelled on the virtues of bachelorhood. But as he walked up the stairs to his room, his steps slowed and he became suddenly pensive. After such a meal as that one, a man should relax with a fine cognac, music and a beautiful woman. With that thought, a sense of loneliness pervaded him. He went into his room, kicked off his shoes, lifted the telephone receiver and immediately put it back in its cradle. He got up, walked over to the window and looked out at his garden, still bleak at the end of an usually cold

March. He had to do something about Dream, and he ought to increase his shares of the Skate newspaper chain, because the value would shoot up when he bought that company. Why couldn't he put his mind to work on his business interests? When had he ever spent an evening at home doing nothing? After Teddy went to bed, he usually worked. But on this night, he couldn't summon the will. He went back to the phone and dialed his grandfather's number.

"This is Jake Underwood. What can I do for you?"

"How are you, Granddad? This is Ashton. Everything all right?"

"Everything's fine. When you coming down here? Damon's studying for his finals, Cade's solving the world's problems somewhere, and I need to do something about this riding school."

"What do you mean?"

"Either we expand it or close it. I have about two dozen requests that I can't fill right now, because I need at least three more grooms and three mares. We have enough stallions. You know that most of our students are women and girls."

"You shouldn't have responsibility for this, Granddad, but with Damon busy till June or whenever he passes the bar, I don't see an alternative."

"I didn't suggest that it's too much for me, and it isn't. I'm saying we need to make a business decision." Ashton didn't like the idea of his eighty-three-year-old grandfather holding down a full-time job, but Jacob—or Jake as he was known—Underwood had always worked and claimed he was happiest when his mind and hands were fully engaged.

"All right. Teddy and I will be down this weekend, and

maybe Damon can get away for one day. I'll speak with him. Cade probably won't be home for another week."

"We know where Cade stands. He always thinks big, so he's going to say we should expand, but we need to study it."

After hanging up, Ashton reviewed his accountant's report on Dream's finances, decided how much additional stock he would purchase, closed his computer and flipped on the television. He didn't want to watch television. He wanted Felicia. After pacing from one end of his room to the other, staring out of the window and retracing his steps, he went to the telephone and his fingers did the work for him.

"Hello?"

He sat down on the edge of his bed and let peace flow over him. "This is Ashton. I did not intend to call you tonight, but since you won't leave my mind, I had no choice."

"Hi, Ashton. If that's true, I've merely been repaying you."

"Are you suggesting that you've been thinking about me?"

"No, I am not suggesting that, Ashton. I am stating it as a fact. Was Teddy awake when you got home?"

"You bet. He wouldn't have considered going near the bed. He and I have a pact. He keeps his promises and I keep mine. And his memory is infallible." He didn't care what they said to each other as long as he could talk with her. "Teddy is currently counting the days until Sunday."

"What happens Sunday?"

"I've promised to play the piano for him, and that means playing it until he gets tired or sleepy."

"Do you play well?"

"I chose between an M.B.A. and a graduate degree in music. I went for the M.B.A., because I love to eat, but I'm a pretty good musician. I just promised my granddad that Teddy and I would see him this weekend, and I don't know whether that piano at home is tuned properly, but it will have to suffice. A promise is a promise."

"Where's home?"

"My granddad lives in Rose Hill, Maryland, and that's still home for my brothers and me."

"Did you call to cancel our dinner date for tomorrow, Ashton?"

"Is that a polite way of asking me why I called you? I don't mind telling you that I'm still dealing with what went on between you and me today. I called you because I needed contact with you, because any contact was better than none. Does that answer your question?" The sound he heard could only have been that of Felicia sucking in her breath. He believed in honesty; she asked for it and he gave it to her. But he didn't expect her to back down easily.

"Are you still going to be circumspect when we meet tomorrow?"

He couldn't help laughing. "When we meet, yes. But if you have the effect on me that you've had the other times I've been in your company, I can't promise about the re- mainder of the evening."

"Hmm. In that case I'd better wear my Oxford-gray suit and brown turtleneck sweater, which I think of as my man-tamer."

"Your what?"

"You heard me correctly. Did you grow up where your grandfather lives?"

"Yes, it's a tiny hamlet in what we call horse country. My brothers and I still consider that our home, although

Damon and I also have residences elsewhere. It's a beautiful region with bridal paths through wooded areas and along the brooks and little rivers. You can isolate yourself from the world. It's so peaceful. But it's a big responsibility for my eighty-three-year-old grandfather, although he has a manager and expert grooms and riding instructors."

In his mind's eye, he saw her in a dark gray suit and brown high-neck sweater and cringed. "Felicia, if I promise to be circumspect, as you put it, all evening, will you wear something red tomorrow?"

"I don't know. Red makes me, uh, want to be kissed. You know…frisky. Do you think you can handle that?"

"Listen, woman, you don't live that far from me, and I'm still dressed."

"Tish. Tish. You should be getting ready for bed. You're setting a bad example for Teddy."

He stretched out on his back. "Teddy is four. I'm forty, and that is one hell of a difference. Try not to get too frisky tomorrow, not that I wouldn't enjoy seeing the sophisticated Ms. Parker shake it up. You're as refreshing as a crisp spring breeze. See you tomorrow evening at seven."

"Good night, Ashton. Sweet dreams."

He hung up, wondering what would come next. He'd always thought he was up to any task, but he hadn't met a woman like Felicia Parker. Sharp, intelligent and quick-witted. Fine. That didn't impress him too much; he was used to that. But she had that other side of her, the warm, soft sweetness, the sexy femininity that was like hot quicksand. He blew a sharp whistle. He'd be a fool if he didn't find out what she was really like. If he got sucked in, he'd probably enjoy himself.

* * *

Felicia hung up the phone and leaned forward with her elbows on her knees and her palms cupping her chin and cheeks. If she had any sense, she'd stay out of Ashton Underwood's way. There was nothing ordinary about him. Any woman in her right mind would avoid a man with Ashton's looks, but there was that other side of him that attracted her the way honey drew Winnie the Pooh. Perfectly postured and tailored, as well as good-looking described the circle of men which she worked with and traveled among. But Ashton's bearing, charismatic personality, manners and apparent values set him apart. Lord, that man was sweet. He surprised her with his seriousness, sweetness and tenderness. And men who came near Ashton Underwood's looks didn't usually impress her as being gentlemen. Good looks notwithstanding, he was the man she had dreamed of finding. She wanted to meet Cade. If he was like his brothers, she'd have to ask their grandfather for his recipe for raising boys to become men.

"He won't do a thing I don't let him do," she said to herself, jumped up from her perch on the edge of her bed and ran to her closet. He wanted red; she'd give him red. Her gaze landed on a red-velveteen sleeveless dress with a matching jacket that covered just enough of her hip to make the effect tantalizing.

"If he can't stand the heat," she rationalized, "he should stay away from the kitchen."

The following evening she combed her hair down, put silver hoops in her ears and slipped on the most frivolous spike-heeled shoes she owned. He may as well learn that he was getting two women in one, she told herself and let the laughter pour out of her. She dabbed Givenchy's

Organza perfume in strategic places, glanced in the hall mirror at the total effect and, satisfied that she'd done her best, headed for the door as the bell rang. Seven o'clock. She'd known he would be punctual.

His eyes widened when she opened the door, and when she reached up and kissed his cheek, his bottom lip dropped. "Hmm," she said. "Come in. You look… Gosh, and just think, I don't even own a gun."

As if he were confused, a frown covered his face. "A gun? Why would you need a gun?"

She sent one of her eyebrows up. "Are you serious? I don't have the strength to spend the evening fending off women."

"Hold on here," he said. "I can get fresh, too." He leaned forward and brushed his lips across hers. "You look wonderful. I'll be careful about suggesting that you wear red. You're fresh enough without it." He shook his head as if bewildered. "I hope you're not planning to give me a hard time, because if you do, I swear I'll get even. Truce?"

She wanted to wrap her arms around him and hug him, but she restrained herself. "Truce. Remember, Ashton, that I surprise myself every time I surprise you. I honestly don't know this woman you've created, but I definitely like her."

His grin softened his lips, lit his eyes and then covered his face with a smile that weakened her. She gazed at him. "Sometimes, like right now, I could…" She nearly bit her tongue at that lapse in judgment.

"You could what?" He stepped closer to her.

"Let's go, Ashton. That slipped out, and you know it."

He dropped his hands to his sides, and she didn't think she had ever seen an adult with such an innocent facial expression as when he said, "I won't touch. Do with me as you like. I'm yours for the evening."

"Sure you are. And what will you exact in exchange?"

His smile, so sweet and beguiling, almost made her believe him when he said, "I only want your happiness and well-being, and whenever you're with me, I'll try to see that that's what you get."

She walked right into that. He meant it, and because she knew he did, she couldn't play and tease. He kept his hands at his sides, and she walked to him, put her arms around him, hugged him and heard herself whisper, "You're so…so sweet. I can't believe you're real."

"I'm real, all right, Felicia, and I'm not acting. Neither, I see, are you. We'd better go before we light up this place."

She hadn't noticed that he carried a red rose, and when he handed it to her, she had to fight back the tears. He'd given her the first red rose she had ever received. "I'm going to dry this," she said, hating the tremor of her voice. "And I'll wrap it in tissue paper and keep it." She got a vase, filled it with water and put the rose in it.

"I'm ready," she said.

"Where's your purse?"

She handed him her door key. "I don't need one, unless you want to split the bill."

His lips curved into a grin and she said to herself, "Turn your head, girl, before he makes mush out of you again."

"Sure you trust me?"

"As sure as I am of my name," she told him. "Thanks for the beautiful rose. I'm glad I didn't wear my gray suit."

His right hand rubbed the back of his neck, and he shook his head from side to side as if disbelieving something, she didn't know what. "Woman, you get to me. Let's go."

"You look so great," he said after dinner, "and the evening's been so short. I wish we could find a place to dance. It's too early to take you home."

"Let's just walk," she said. " Maybe sometime we can go to a supper club. Then we can dance." She grasped his hand. "It's such a wonderful evening. Let's just enjoy it. We don't really need to dance, do we?"

His fingers tightened on hers. "No, we don't. Let's go over to Lincoln Center, watch the fountains shoot up, and drink an aperitif. Or would you rather we took a taxi over there?"

"Taxi? It's only seven blocks. We can walk…unless you don't feel like it."

He dropped her hand and put his arm around her waist. "I hope and pray that you're real, Felicia."

What an odd thing for him to say at the moment. She wouldn't pry, though. He seemed content, even happy, and that was what mattered. From Columbus Circle they strolled along Broadway, and even in the night, she saw the great boulevard as she'd never seen it before, bustling with energy and alive with secrets. "Where have I been living?" she asked herself.

"You're so quiet," he said.

"I—I'm taking it all in. The streets are alive with people, cars and buses. The screeching of tires seems so controlled, as if wary. The subway rumbles along noisily beneath us. One radio spews rap and another delivers a drummer's para-diddle. The odd and, somehow endearing, sounds of the city. It's a strange, modern kind of music, atonal but with its own special rhythm. I've lived here all of my life and I never heard it before." When he didn't respond, she said, "Do you…does it sound that way to you?"

They entered the Lincoln Center Plaza just as the center
fountain sprang to life. After it dazzled its audience, he
walked with her to a table. "I'm having Cointreau," he
said. "What would you like?"

"Tia Maria, please. Thank you."

He placed their orders, leaned back in the chair and
gazed at her. "You asked me if I heard that music. I may
not have heard the same music that you heard, but I heard
some." He reached for her hands and held both of them.
"The way you talked to me as we walked along Broadway,
with every word, you made love to me, Felicia. I wished
I'd had something on which to write, and I could have kept
those thoughts forever. Don't tell me you always think like
that. Your columns are written by a realist, but your de-
scriptions of this night were the thoughts of a romantic,
and one capable of deep feelings. Where do you think this
budding relationship is headed?"

She felt exposed, naked, and she was tempted to tell
him that he was way off, that he had misinterpreted her
words, but she had promised herself to be honest with
him, so she said, "I don't know where this is headed, Ashton. I hadn't thought at first that it would go anywhere."
She looked away, for his eyes seemed to drag her into him.

"But now you know better," he said. "Where do you
want it to go?"

"That question is consuming too much of my time
lately," she told him. "I'm not even sure I want to answer
it."

"I'll tell you what I want," he said. "I want a chance to
know you, to find out whether what I feel for you has
staying power. That means spending a lot of time with you,
getting to know the most personal things about you. What

makes you cry, laugh. What hurts you, makes you happy. I want to know everything about you."

She wanted to know that and more about him, but he wouldn't learn it from her mouth. If he proved to be the man she thought he was, in time, he'd know her well enough. "Can't we…take it as it comes?" she asked.

He winked, and a grin formed around his lips that nearly unglued her. "Isn't that what we've been doing? I'll be in Rose Hill with my granddad this weekend, and I usually leave Friday. Can we see each other Thursday evening? What would you like us to do?"

"I don't know what you like, Ashton. If it were summer, we could have a picnic or go bicycling in the park, maybe even take in an outdoor concert, but it's still too cool for all that. Anyway, I don't do much other than work, so you'll have to decide. We can't stay out too late, though. I get up early on weekdays."

"So do I, and if that's a hint, I'd better take you home."

At her apartment door, he handed her the key that she had entrusted to him earlier and she opened the door. "Would you like to come in for a minute?"

He stared down at her. "You sure?"

She nodded. "I don't think you should kiss me in the hallway. Do you?"

"As long as you think I should kiss you…" He left the rest unsaid, stepped into her apartment, and his arms, strong and warm, locked her to his body. She waited while he gazed into her eyes. The pressure of his fingers on her body excited her. What if he…

"Open your mouth for me," he said, and when she parted her lips, he went into her, loving her and possessing her, searing her with his heat until desire plowed through her. She held the back of his head, telling him that she wanted all he would give her. He backed away.

"Don't you…know that isn't circumspect?" he asked her, panting for breath. "Honey, you make it hard as hell for me to keep my word."

"You're… Maybe you'll have to keep your hands off me. I mean, if you don't touch me, we can't start these fires. Right?"

"I'm definitely not promising that," he said. "We'll work something out. I'll call you tomorrow morning. All right?"

"I'll look forward to that," she said. "Thanks for a wonderful evening. Good night."

She couldn't believe the grin that flashed over his face. What a devil he must have been as a child! "You don't really believe I'm leaving here without a kiss good-night, do you?"

"But I thought—"

His kiss, hard and possessive, stunned her. "Good night." He opened the door and left.

Felicia slumped against the wall, took a deep breath and told herself to back up. "No point in losing your head, girl, just because the man has bedroom eyes and a smile you can't resist." She vowed to spend more time on her career and less time thinking about Ashton Underwood.

Intent upon taking the advice she'd given herself the previous night, Felicia hired a speakers' bureau to set up engagements on topics that would showcase her skill as a political analyst. She meant to put the business of writing a society column behind her and become a political columnist. However, Felicia couldn't know it would be as a society columnist that she sealed her future happiness.

She stepped up to the podium for her first talk in a series scheduled to take place at Brooklyn College, looked down at the first row of attendees and into the face of her arch rival, Reese Hall. After forcing herself to smile at the woman who occasionally addled her, she spoke about domestic abuse, its forms, prevalence and consequences, as well as the reasons why women continued to endure it. Reese appeared awestruck, and Felicia didn't doubt that the woman had considered her a lightweight when, in fact, she was a journalist trained at an Ivy League school. At the end of the question-and-answer period, Felicia thanked her audience and walked over to Reese.

"What a pleasant surprise, Reese. Thank you for coming." She knew that by being gracious, she'd taken the wind out of Reese Hall's sails, and she let herself enjoy the little victory, for she knew it would be short-lived. Felicia had not expected that her talk would be reported in the media, or that it would generate invitations to speak on social issues concerning women.

"You got four or five hundred letters here," her editor told her two days after her first lecture. "Maybe you want to start putting some of this in your column."

That was what she wanted to hear. "Thanks, Ray. I'll do my best, but if it's all right with you, I'll continue reporting society news…for now."

She thought he half frowned, but he said, "Okay." And as far as she was concerned, he had committed himself. She wondered what Ashton would think of her ambition to write a column covering political and other serious topics.

At the moment Ashton's concern focused on Dream and the possibility that he might lose it. Conversations with his brothers gave him very little comfort. "Julian Smith is almost three times Kate Smallens' age," Cade said. "He wants to give her our company, does he? We'll see about that. Hang tight for a few days, Ashton. Smith may no longer have a reason for trying to purchase Dream." Cade Underwood's ethics were much the same as his brother's, but he was not above playing by his adversary's rules.

Cade telephoned **Kate. "Hi. This is Cade** Underwood. Did I see you at Plaza Athenée last night?"

"Why, no," she said. "Gee, Cade, it's been ages."

"You're right," he **said,** "which is why I've been wondering about the tales going around about us. Can't you put a stop to this gossip?" He knew there hadn't been any gossip about them, but he also knew she would hope that there had been.

"Really. Oh, come on, Cade. It does a girl's reputation good to be linked to a man who looks like you."

Never mind what he had accomplished. To Kate, what mattered was a man's looks and the way he moved in bed. He hadn't been foolish enough to let her get her talons in him. "Knock it off, baby. I'm serious. It won't do you any good with your old man, either."

"Oh, he doesn't read the gossip sheets. The only thing he ever reads is the *Wall Street Journal,* and that, only on Tuesdays. He hires people to do his reading."

"You can't be too careful, babe. One little seed of doubt can finish it."

"You may be right, Cade. I don't know how to thank you."

Cade hung up, satisfied that the threat of losing Dream would soon be history, at least for a while. He bought half a dozen daily papers and leafed through them until he saw a columnist who might complete the job. He chose Felicia Parker and Reese Hall, and called Felicia first.

"Ms. Parker, this is Cade Underwood. I don't know whether you use such information, but I'd appreciate it if you would let your readers know that there's nothing between Kate Smallens and me, and you can verify it by calling her." He gave Felicia the woman's phone number.

Felicia's antenna shot up. "Are you associated with Underwood Enterprises?"

"I am, indeed, but this is strictly personal."

He wondered at her hesitation, but finally she said, "All right. I'll call Ms. Smallens and confirm this. Thank you, Mr. Underwood."

Several days later Ashton opened the newspaper and, as usual turned to the second section and Felicia's column. "'Beautiful and sexy Kate Smallens wants everybody to know that she isn't having an affair with Cade Underwood, and she handed me another little tidbit. She thinks Cade's to die for, but she's tied up with a certain bottling company mogul whose wife doesn't understand him.'"

"What the hell!" he exclaimed. Since when had Cade been involved with Kate Smallens? He read the remainder of the paragraph and wondered if he was about to faint. The woman hadn't missed the opportunity for a bit of coquettishness by adding, "'Not that any woman in her right mind wouldn't love to hang out with a guy like Cade Underwood. People are always linking me with somebody.'"

He put the paper down and telephoned Felicia. "This is Ashton," he said without the pretense of friendliness. "I just read your column. I didn't know you'd been in contact with my brother."

Here it comes, she thought. "I wasn't certain until now that he's your brother. He called me, introduced himself and suggested that I'd be interested in that information. He's a very impressive man. I related precisely what he said. He told me she would confirm it and gave me her number. I figured you knew all about it, and that you would eventually give me the background."

"I haven't mentioned you to Cade, and I doubt Damon has because he doesn't gossip about my personal life."

"All right, but what's it all about?"

"I haven't seen you in four days. Can we meet for dinner?"

"I'd rather go to a movie," she said.

"So would I, but we can't talk in the movies."

"I'd rather we didn't talk at my place, Ashton, because…well, we need to cool off."

"You need to cool off, perhaps, but I'm not in the habit of leaving anything half done, and this thing between us is far from finished. Meet me somewhere. Anywhere. Today's Wednesday. I'll even go to a prayer meeting with you. Felicia, don't do this to us. Look, the public library's open till nine. We can meet there."

"Ashton, we can't talk in the library."

"No, but we can hold hands. You want us to be circumspect? Well, no place is more likely to ensure that than the library."

"In that case, we can meet at Barnes & Nobel across from Lincoln Center. It's a lot closer."

"Meet you there in an hour," he said. He wished he knew what she feared so much that she refused to be alone with him. A woman her age should trust herself not to do anything she didn't want to do. If she didn't trust him, he may as well forget about her.

When he walked into the bookstore, he saw her at once, sitting alone with a magazine in front of her. Since it was upside down, she couldn't have been reading it. He kissed the side of her mouth and sat down. "Here's the story," he said, and told her what the man who proposed to take over Dream planned to do with the company.

"You mean he plans to give it to that lemon head? She's a vacant lot, if I ever saw one. If I were you, I'd stop worrying. Even if he doesn't drop her voluntarily after what she said, his wife will be after her like a hawk after a rabbit."

"Maybe that's what Cade had in mind, but you didn't mention the man's name."

"That's because I didn't know it, but if I had, I probably wouldn't have used it. What are his initials?"

He told her and asked, "Are you doing this for me or for your readers?"

"My readers don't need to know everything, Ashton. Let's go."

He took her hand. "May I see you to your door?"

"Yes, if you want to."

"I'm afraid to ask if you want me to."

"I do." She wiped her eye.

He stopped walking and asked her, "Is there something wrong with your eye?"

She shook her head. "I think an awful lot of you, and it happened too soon, Ashton. So soon that I don't trust it. It frightens me, because I don't trust me."

"And you think that if you let a lot of time elapse while you treat me as you would your kid brother that we'll arrive at a point where, as mature individuals, we can pursue this relationship?"

"Something like that."

"Don't count on it, Felicia. The physical attraction between you and me is as strong as a bull, and unless one of us loses respect for the other, nothing will destroy that chemistry. By forcing us to go slow, you are merely guaranteeing that when we finally give ourselves to each other, we'll produce an explosion, and we'll probably never be sated."

"How can you say that?"

He put his right arm around her and relaxed when she seemed to enjoy having it there. "I can say it because I know how we respond to each other. You know it, too. That's why you're scared."

She didn't disagree, and they walked silently until they reached a traffic light and stopped. He hugged her as close as he dared, and his heartbeat accelerated when she leaned into him.

"I miss you when I don't see you," he told her.

"I know," she whispered. "Me, too, but we were headed for a quick affair, and that's not what I want for myself. I could have had that a dozen times, Ashton. I need someone to love and cherish me, and I need desperately to love in return. I need to love friends, my brother, children and a man. What I've got is not even half a life. Yet, I can't complain. I have a good life, even if it isn't perfect."

He stood at her door gazing down at her. Could she love Teddy as he did? "Give us a chance, Felicia." She opened the door, walked in and looked up at him. Trusting. Waiting. He thought the next move was his, but he couldn't be sure, so he whispered to her, "Come to me, Felicia. Come here. I need to hold you."

"Oh, Ashton."

He lifted her into his arms and held her as fiercely as

he dared. "If I kiss you the way I want to, the way I need to, I won't leave here until I've buried myself in you, and you aren't ready for that."

She pressed her face into the curve of his neck. "No. When I am, you'll know it. Aren't you going to kiss me before you leave?" She parted her lips, and he plunged into her, savoring every crevice of her sweet mouth, caressing and stroking her as her moans threatened to destroy his self-control.

"Hold on, sweetheart," he said. "If you're not ready for us to make love, remember that I'm not seeing other women, and I'm as starved for you as you are for me. Possibly more so." He tried to think of something they could do that wouldn't end in unrequited desire. "Suppose we take a ride around Manhattan, Saturday. I haven't done that since I had high school dates."

"Yes, but not this Saturday. Don't you remember you promised your granddad you'd take Teddy to see him?"

"Good Lord, I'd forgotten, and I don't break promises to my granddad. He wouldn't stand for it. Besides, Cade will be home, and I haven't seen him for a while."

She reached up and kissed his cheek. "I'll see what I can come up with." He hugged her and left. With that one short kiss, she'd heated him up so thoroughly that he doubted he would sleep. Instead of hailing a taxi, he walked home, grateful for the exercise. One thing was certain: he had to do something about Felicia Parker. She didn't know it, but every time they spoke and each time he was in her presence, she gained ground with him. It became harder and harder to leave her.

Chapter 4

Felicia walked into her office the next morning and found a note from her boss. "Come see me as soon as you get in. R." She dropped her briefcase on the floor beside her desk and went to Ray Gilder's office.

"Seems the Underwoods are in for it," he said. "You had a line on this a couple of days ago. Barber-Smith, Incorporated is trying a hostile takeover of Dreams. Something peculiar about it. I'd like to know how Kate Smallens got into the picture. That woman seems to make a living by being popular. See what you can get."

"I'll do what I can," she said.

He narrowed his left eye. "You'll do…what kind of response is that? If you don't want to write it, I've got reporters who'd love to. Come to think of it, I don't want that in your column. Give me a straight story on it."

"I'll get to work on it, and that means I have to get that story and write my column, too."

"Yep. That's what it means, but it shouldn't make you sweat, you love challenges."

Maybe, but she certainly didn't welcome this one. She went back to her office and telephoned Ashton. "My boss has learned about Barber-Smith's hostile takeover attempt of Dream," she told him. "And he has instructed me to write the story. Not in my column, mind you, but on the business page. I don't mind telling you that he became suspicious when I showed no enthusiasm for the job."

His silence didn't disturb her, for she knew he had to consider his answer. "All right. Do what you have to do, but be certain you include the fact that I'm fighting this attempted theft tooth and nail, and if you want a quote, I'll give you one."

"I will certainly want a quote, and I'd like to report what you just said. However, I think I'll call Cade, too. He's a bit less gentle about this than you are."

"By all means do that. He'll give you a quote that will be long remembered."

"I wouldn't want to cause him a problem by including something slanderous."

"Don't worry, Felicia, my brother's clever. He won't say anything that he can't prove."

She frowned at that, for she remembered how he'd tricked Kate Smallens into boasting about her relationship with the bottling company mogul who proved to be Julian Smith. "He's clever, all right, and he may have some other angles on this, Ashton. If you're sure you don't mind, I'll call him. I'll be in touch."

"You bet you will. We have a date for Thursday," he said. "How about a kiss?"

She made the sound of a kiss and said, "That's not for the office, but I'll make an exception of you."

"What?"

"'Bye." She hung up and phoned Cade Underwood.

"Underwood speaking." The similarity of their voices shocked her. It was as if she were still speaking with Ashton.

"Mr. Underwood, this is Felicia Parker. I have an assignment to write the story of Barber-Smith's attempted take-over of Dream, and I'd like as much information as you can give me. But first, I want to know whether, when you phoned me last week, you knew that Ashton and I are friends."

"I didn't know it for a fact, Ms. Parker, but I figured that unless something was wrong with him, you should have been friends by then."

She was certain that he heard her gasp. "Would you mind explaining that?" she asked him in a voice that was neither friendly nor pleasant, her annoyance making her risk his refusal to let her interview him.

"Don't mind at all. I saw the two of you dancing together at the Sterling gala, and you all but burned up my TV set. He'd have to be pretty slow not to capitalize on that."

She nearly swallowed her tongue. "Do you always say what you think?"

"Pretty much. Let's put it this way. If you don't want to know, never ask *me*. I don't pussyfoot with the truth."

"Hold on there. There hadn't been a rumor about you and Kate Smallens until you had me insert your denial of it in my column, and you knew she'd grab at any publicity."

"I told the absolute truth. There was not and never had been anything between us, hard as she tried to get something going. I try not to develop relationships with vacuous people."

So far, all she'd gained in that call was the information that Cade Underwood wasn't to be toyed with, and that he didn't believe in politeness for its own sake. By asking whether he'd called with information for her society column because she knew his brother, she had meant to put Cade at a disadvantage, obligating him to reveal what he knew about the takeover. But that move had netted her nothing. Might as well get down to business.

"Does Kate Smallens figure in Barber-Smith's move to take over Dream? If you permit me, I will quote your answer." She'd put him on the spot, but she figured that with this man you had to be direct.

"I don't know about Barber, but Smith's planning to give Dream to Kate, provided he succeeds in taking it over."

Her pen fell to the floor, and she was certain that her eyes rounded. Surely a businessman of Julian Smith's reputation wouldn't do anything that stupid. With the Kate Smallens she'd talked with a few days earlier in control, the company would all but evaporate.

"That's so incredulous that I'm reluctant to print it."

"The old fellow must be getting either senile or desperate. Surely he knows by now that Kate loves only two things—Kate and money."

"You haven't given me anything that I can quote."

His long sigh told her that he was becoming either bored or exasperated. "Ms. Parker, haven't you been listening? I dislike repeating myself. Didn't you write it down?"

"I did, but I'd planned to paraphrase it. I didn't think—"

He interrupted her. "I prefer not to be paraphrased, Ms. Parker. I tell it like it is, and you do the same."

"All right, Mr. Underwood. I'll… Look, is there any reason why you and I can't use first names? This formality isn't necessary."

"You're right it isn't, but it was your call."

"Uh…I expect you know I'm going to run this past Ashton before I send it to my editor."

"Oh, yeah? Why don't you send him the part in which you quote him and send me the part in which you quote me?"

So he wasn't above a little sibling rivalry. "I'll send each of you the complete text, but I don't promise to accept any editing."

His laughter surprised her. He'd been so serious that she hadn't associated mirth with him. "You stand your ground, eh? Well, it's hard to respect a person who doesn't."

"Thanks for your help, Cade. Ashton would probably never have told me this."

"Definitely not in those words. Ashton believes in fighting as cleanly as possible, though make no mistake, he's a tough adversary."

"I imagine he is, but probably not more so than you. Thanks again."

She had enough information to begin her story, but she needed more, something to give it a punch. She phoned Ashton. "I had a good talk with Cade, and I know what Smith plans to do with Dream if he acquires it, but what I need to know are your plans for warding off this takeover," she said, not bothering to coat it with a personal overture.

"Hello, Felicia." She thought she detected a little testiness in his voice, but since she didn't see a reason for it, she discounted the possibility until he said, "I hope you're not serious. You want to print my plan to foil a takeover of my flagship company and guarantee a win for Smith? Hell, he'd hardly have to stretch himself if you laid it all out for him."

"How can I write a one-sided story? I have to be fair and present all the facts."

"I agree that you should present all of the facts *that you have.* I wouldn't be where I am today if I tipped my hand in business deals. I also don't see how you can treat this so impersonally. Is writing this story the most important thing in your life? I'll be in touch. Goodbye, Felicia."

He hung up, and she stared at the receiver in her hand, mouth open and eyes wide. If he didn't support her efforts to do the best she could in her work, why should she need him? Irritated and hurt, she called her brother Miles and poured out her thoughts and feelings about her conversation with Ashton.

"Do you know what happens in a takeover?" he asked her. "How would you like to work your tail off building a business, it hobbles along, you allow others to invest in it so you can get the money to develop it, the business flourishes and then some Joe comes along and decides to outsmart you, buy up a lot of shares when you're not looking, get the support of other investors and ease you out of your job? You're no longer the boss, he is, and he can run your company as he pleases. And he can do that easily, if you advertise your plan to thwart him, but if you surprise him, he's more likely to lose the fight.

"As smart as you are, Felicia, I'm surprised that you asked him, and I'd have been stunned if he'd told you and you printed what he said. I thought you had a personal interest in the man."

"I have, but I still have to do my job."

"Really? Then I assume it's all right with you if Ashton Underwood loses Dream, one of the largest cosmetic companies in the country. You can bet that's what he's thinking right now. If you want that guy, you'd better straighten it out, and soon."

Just what I need: a choice between upsetting the man I want and who means more to me than he realizes and getting ahead in my job. I have a chance to write a lead story for the business section of the *New York Evening Journal,* and I don't have enough material for two good paragraphs.

"You do care, don't you?" her brother asked.

"Of course I care, Miles. I care a lot, but shouldn't he see my position?"

"Look, Felicia, I've never thought of you as a selfish person, but you're thinking only of yourself now. You don't need Underwood's plans in order to write a good story. You can write something about the history of Dream, how he started the business, why and how it grew to where it is—"

She interrupted Miles. "Go no further. You're absolutely right, and I don't know why I didn't consider that. I can give my editor a good story, and at the same time condition Dream's investors to sympathize with the man who struggled to build the company into what it is. You're not a lawyer for nothing. I'm going to call Ashton back as soon as I work out a list of questions."

"You may find it very productive just to let him talk. Ask how he started it and let him take it from there. And, sis…When you're talking to him, lock the journalist in a closet. You got my drift?"

"You wouldn't say that to a man."

"Not unless he was trying to get it on with the person he was about to interview. There's a time and there's a season for all things, Felicia, and that's not original with me. The idea dates all the way back to Christ."

She didn't get out of line with her older brother, and not because he was six years older than she, but because she loved, admired and respected him. From childhood, she had almost idolized him, trailing behind him, basking in his approval, happy whenever she was with him. For Miles treated her as if she were a precious gift from their parents to him.

"All right," she said. "Please, no lectures. I'd better telephone Ashton."

"Hello, Felicia. What can I do for you?" was the way in which Ashton answered the telephone, taking advantage of Caller ID. From his tone of voice, one would think he had never met her. She steeled herself for another splash of cold water, well aware that the next move was hers, and that her brother had judged the situation correctly.

"Ashton, I've thought over our conversation and particularly your concern, and I—I want to try a different angle. Rather than exposing your defensive strategy, which I realize now could be fatal and therefore foolish, I'd like to write about Dream's history, how you started it, developed it and made it what it is today. Would you be willing to talk to me about that?"

"Well. This is an about-face. I'll talk with you if I'm satisfied after you explain to me why you changed your mind."

She'd made a mistake with Ashton, but that didn't mean she had to tuck her little tail between her legs and beg for mercy. "You hung up on me, and I realized you did that not because you were angry, but because you were hurt. I could tolerate your anger, but I do not want to hurt you, and I apologize sincerely for doing it. I've had time to think over the implications of what I was asking of you and to appreciate the damage that reporting your plan could cause, and I would be deeply sorry if you lost Dream for any reason.

"As I turned it over in my mind, I realized that I had a chance to tell your investors why they owe you loyalty, not in those words but by making them know that Dream is the product of years of your hard work during long hours, of your disappointments, pain and tears. I want to let them conclude that this is a human issue, not commercial volleyball generated by a foolish man's whim. That's…it." She stopped talking and waited. If that didn't satisfy him, she'd throw in the towel with regard both to him and the story. The silence screamed at her, but she refused to plead.

Finally he spoke and her heartbeat returned to normal. "I don't have time right now to do justice to the story you want, and besides, I need to look up a few facts. I'd offer to go to your office, but your editor would know at once that we have a personal relationship. Would you be willing to come to my office Thursday morning?"

"Yes. Of, course. What time?"

"Is nine-thirty too early for you?" he asked her.

"Nine-thirty will be fine. I'll be there."

"Thank you, Felicia. You can't imagine what a help this will be. I'll call you later."

"Thanks for the interview, Ashton. I hope you didn't eat nails after you hung up earlier. You didn't need the stress."

"Eat nails? That's putting it mildly. Talk with you later. 'Bye for now."

He'd been as genial as he could, but the strain was there; he hadn't been jovial, and he hadn't asked for a kiss. It wouldn't be the last mistake she made, but it could be the most meaningful. She made a few notes, hoping that they would help her guide the interview, but she was going to take Miles's advice and let Ashton lead the interview. She got up from her desk and walked over to the gray-metal file cabinet that stood in a corner—every office at the *New York Evening Journal* had one—opened the bottom drawer and removed a copy of her first published newspaper story.

She looked at the date beside her byline. Had it really been ten years? Three thousand, six hundred and fifty days since she'd jumped, shouted and laughed until she cried for joy. She had succeeded; she was now a journalist, and on her way to wider acclaim. And that very night, overcome with the joy of her "success," she had relaxed whatever it was that had always made her think and act sensibly, and she'd lulled herself into believing what Herman Lamont told her and let him lure her into his bed. For months thereafter, she thought only of him, until the day he let it slip that he had a wife and children. She woke up then to the knowledge that her "success" had slipped away while she dawdled with a man who, in the end, offered only heartbreak.

I don't ever want to forget that. I got over Herman, but I still have the scars that he etched into my heart. If I allow myself to become callous, to do anything in order to get a story, I'll be no better than Herman. I hurt Ashton, because somewhere in the archives of my mind resides the notion that men don't have deep feelings—Herman's gift to me.

She put the old newspaper back in its place, locked the

drawer, went to her desk and started writing her daily column. After she interviewed Ashton, she was going to produce a story worthy of her abilities, and Ashton Underwood would relish every word of it. She looked at the notes she'd made for her daily column. Heather Skylock wanted it known that she'd switched designers. Now sixteen pounds lighter, Jacobs's styles suited her better. And Amber Jenkins's publicist wanted it known that Amber was dropping the Jenkins from her name. In the future, she would be known only as Amber. Felicia pulled air through her front teeth and rolled her eyes toward the ceiling. She pulled out another card. Anyo Adedee—where on earth did those names come from?—had called to report that her client, LaTenja Jones, had been mistaken for Beyoncé.

Felicia leaned back in her chair, grimacing. "I'm a good writer, and I'm tired of spending my time puffing up the egos of frivolous women and self-satisfied men. What happened to the people who spend their leisure time doing charity work? Damned if I'll write another note about a rap 'artist' or a celebrity who makes a living being by being a personality and nothing else." She locked her desk and decided to go out and look for something newsworthy.

She got on the elevator at the twelfth floor and settled against the back rail. When she smiled at the handsome man who got on at the next floor, he smiled back, pulled a gun and said, "Give me your pocketbook."

Her eyebrows shot up as she faced her worse nightmare, stood straighter and said, "I worked for what's in this pocketbook. Why should I give it to you?"

The man was not smiling when he said in tones so soft that she believed him, "Because you don't want me to pull this trigger. That's why." She knew that the high-speed elevator was close to the street floor, so she slid the bag off her shoulder and handed it to him just as the door opened. He grabbed it and tried to bolt from the elevator, but she stuck out her foot and sent him sprawling into the people who were waiting in front of the elevator.

"He pulled a gun on me, and he has my pocketbook," she yelled as the man scrambled up in an effort to get away, but a delivery man knocked the thief down, put his foot in the man's belly, took out his cell phone and called the police. Noticing the thief's attempt to retrieve his gun, which fell out of his hand when Felicia tripped him, the delivery man put a halt to the thief's effort with the weight of his left foot.

"Well, I wanted a story," Felicia said to herself as she rode to the police station to give an account of the attempted theft. "And it looks as if I'm the story." At home that night, Felicia wrote the story for her column, ending with the would-be thief's assurance, when he was booked at the police station, that she would see him again. She had wanted to interview the man so as to include in her column something of his background that would explain how he'd become a criminal, but the police advised against it. She faxed her column to the paper at a quarter of nine, went to the kitchen and put a frozen quiche in the microwave oven and prepared to eat her supper, which in addition to the quiche Lorraine included a salad of lettuce and tomato, and half a glass of Pilsner beer.

She was in no mood for wine. After what she had experienced that day, beginning with her gargantuan mistake with Ashton, she'd had a taste of the nitty-gritty of life and, with drinks, beer was as close to that as you could get. Still hungry after finishing her meal and her last swill of beer, she opened the freezer, took out a bar of Snickers and enjoyed what she regarded as her favorite vice.

The telephone rang and she hesitated to answer it, fearing that the man who'd tried to rob her may have been released. But her caller could also be Ashton. She lifted the receiver. "Hello?"

"Hello. You sound as if you're scared. This is Ashton. What's the matter?"

"My day started down during our first call this morning, and except for that little upward spiral when we agreed on the interview, it has gone downhill ever since. But as the song goes, I will survive."

"Do you feel like talking about it?" he asked her.

It usually didn't pay to speak candidly; whenever she did that, she regretted it. But if she didn't tell him, he'd find out when he read her column the next day, and that would be one more strike against her.

"I'll sketch it out and when we see each other I'll fill in the details. First, I realized that I no longer enjoy writing my daily column. It's such as waste of time. So I left my office in search of news for a lively column and would you believe a man held a gun on me in the elevator and asked for my pocketbook?"

"What? What elevator? When?"

"I work on the twelfth floor, the man got on at the eleventh—"

"I don't care about that. Did he hurt you? Are you all right?"

"He didn't hurt me, Ashton, and he's in custody, but I realize I'm a wreck, so I'm going to have another beer, and

I'm going to bed." When he didn't respond for a full minute, she wondered if he'd hung up. But he hadn't, and she knew he'd been musing over her remark.

"I take it then that you don't want any company tonight," he said at last, in effect taking an exception to her saying she was going to bed.

"Considering how reserved you were when we last spoke, I hadn't thought you cared to see me," she said, getting some of her own.

"Felicia, I am forty years old, and my thoughts, feelings and emotions are not the ephemeral agitations of a pimply teenager. If you care for a man, you should want to share with him what you experienced in that elevator and what you're feeling right now. If I'm not that man, forgive me for intruding."

How could she tell him that she resented being put on the spot without exacerbating their already strained relationship? "I wanted to call you," she said. "I had beer with my supper, and I only drink beer when I'm in the dumps. But you haven't given me the right to call you and dump stuff on you, and I haven't learned how to do that. I'm used to taking the lumps, shaking them off and moving on."

"You don't want to rely on me or any man, is that it?"

"You're wrong, Ashton. I have a loving relationship with my older brother, who's been my idol since I knew myself. Do you want to come over here?"

"Will you be happy to see me if I go there?"

"Yes."

"Should I bring beer or wine?"

She couldn't help laughing. "With you here, why would I need beer?"

"I'll be right there."

Less than thirty minutes later, Felicia opened the door and looked up at Ashton. Neither spoke as he walked in, closed the door and stared down at her. She wanted to thank him for coming, to tell him how glad she was to see him, to welcome him in some way, but words wouldn't come. As if he had known she would need prompting, he handed her a red rose that was wrapped in cellophane and tied with a red ribbon.

She took the flower, sent her gaze from it to his face and worked at holding back her emotions. His eyes glimmered with warmth and, she thought, uncertainty, vulnerability, robbing her of her defenses. She didn't decide to do it, but as if directed by her heart, her arms moved up to his shoulders and, at last, she knew the joy of being held tight to his body. His lips captured her mouth, then her eyes, cheeks and her mouth once more. He hadn't kissed her that way before. He had replaced the hot urgency of his passion with a sweetness that stirred her to the depths of her being. And although she knew he was intent upon preventing the usual escalation of their passion, she hugged him fiercely, for in her nestled a feeling she had never known before.

"It isn't all right between us yet, is it?" she said. "I can feel you holding back."

"No, it isn't all right, but it's a helluva lot better than it was."

"Can you forgive me?" she asked him, though she was well aware that forgiveness wasn't the problem, that his apparent coolness stemmed from his doubt as to her loyalty.

"I've already forgiven you, Felicia." He looked around. "Let's sit down somewhere." It did not escape her that he glanced at the sofa, but looked farther, chose a chair and sat there.

"I care a lot for you," he told her, "more than I thought or wanted to. You threw me a hard punch, and forgetting it may take a while. But I'm here for you, even if at a little distance."

She blanched at that, but he could see that in spite of the pain reflected in her face, she didn't rattle easily. "And you think you can't trust me?" she asked him.

It was a logical conclusion, but she was way off, because he knew from their abortive conversation that morning that she prided herself in her integrity.

"Oddly enough, I don't think that at all," he said. "But I do think we ought to step back until we know what we mean to each other and you know what I mean to you. I know what you mean to me. This thing between us is too wild. It's going headlong like a runaway train. If I'm wrong, tell me right now."

She had no answer for him, because she knew he hadn't overstated it. She'd known him a month, and she spent most of her waking hours thinking of the way he made her feel and wanting to be with him so she could feel that way again. She prayed that he would have enough faith in them to allow what they felt for each other to mature.

Ashton knew Felicia would live inside of him for a long time; the pain he felt when she argued against his best interest assured him of that. But he meant to walk softly with great care and to leave very few tracks. So far, what he liked about her outweighed her one action that hurt him, but that one thing was enough to alert him. He'd been traveling too fast.

"Do you think you'll be able to sleep?" he asked her. "As soon as you close your eyes, that scene may replay itself."

"I hope not. I wasn't really scared when he pulled that gun. I started shaking in the patrol car when the policemen were taking me to the station."

"I've glad you kept a cool head. Steady nerves can save your life."

"What I feel is that I'm vulnerable, that…that I'm not safe. I… No, I don't mean that."

Whether or not she knew it, she did mean it. "Did you feel safe when you got inside your apartment?" he asked her.

"I don't know. For the first time, I looked in every room and closet, even under my bed, and I—I had to resist turning on every light in this place."

"But you weren't afraid. That's great." He didn't believe it, but he didn't think it good psychology to lead her to the conclusion that she was afraid of being alone. "I don't think you were seriously threatened, because the man ran as soon as the door opened. Was the gun loaded?"

"The police didn't say, so I suppose it was. You know, I feel a little as I did five or six years ago when my car was stolen with a lot of my personal things in the trunk and the glove compartment. I feel…I guess you'd say, violated."

"Oh, no. You don't want to feel that way. Anger is much healthier."

He watched her swinging her long, shapely legs, unconsciously but rhythmically and seductively, and told himself to get his mind on something else. Intimacy was not on his agenda. Yet, in his heart, he wanted everything with her that he had ever desired. And why not? Her lovely brown face was as beautiful as ever, her dark eyes as luminous, and her breasts jutted at him as high and inviting as ever. His mouth began to water as he wondered how her nipples would taste. He dragged himself away from that thought when he realized that she discerned the direction in which his mind traveled.

"If I leave you now, will you be all right?" He noticed that she still held the rose in her right hand. "Will you?" he reiterated.

"I'll be okay," she said. "You can't know how much your coming here tonight means to me. I have a great deal to learn about relationships, Ashton, and you've taught me a lot tonight. My previous experience conditioned me to look out for myself."

"Are you telling me that you had a man who mistreated you?"

"If you call pledging eternal love and, after several months of a blissful relationship, suddenly announcing that he had to get on with his life, that he'd spent too much time away from his wife and children— If you'd call that mistreatment, I'd say yes. And especially since up to that time, he'd represented himself as a bachelor. Yes, I'd say I was mistreated."

His whistle split the air. "And I'd say that man should be horsewhipped. It explains a lot. How long ago was that?"

"Ten years, and you're the only man who's gotten close to me since then."

Hmm. So her finesse and toughness covered a tenderness that he'd spotted a few times. Her warm femininity was almost always evident, but she cloaked that other part of her, the gentle sweetness and the tenderness that he needed. Yes, he'd go slowly, but he would cultivate in her what he most needed from her.

"I'd better go. Are we still on for Thursday morning at nine in my office?"

"Yes, of course," she said, and he steeled himself against the sadness he heard in her voice. He didn't pause when he reached the door, but reached for the doorknob. She stopped him with a hand on his shoulder, reached up and kissed his mouth, quickly and as if in theft. The fire of it shot through him with such speed that he let the wall take his weight. She gazed up at him, letting him know that she didn't plan to cooperate in his plan to put some distance between them.

"Oh, hell, Felicia," he said, locked her in his arms and gave himself to her. "See you Thursday morning," he said, shaken and unable to hide it. He opened the door and walked out into the hallway, certain of one thing: Felicia Parker was in his blood. As he walked toward Riverside Drive, he didn't promise himself anything. Deep down in his gut, he wanted more of what she gave him minutes earlier, that and much more. But he had to think of Teddy as well as of himself, and he meant to take it slow even if it killed him.

Ashton was not alone in resolving to put a lock on his life. For at least ten minutes after Ashton walked out of her door, Felicia remained where he left her. Finally, her equilibrium restored, she folded her arms across her middle and wound her way to her bedroom. He wanted space, and she'd give it to him, but she'd bet her mink coat that he'd make the first call. She had to interview him Thursday morning, but she intended to make it as businesslike as possible. He cared more deeply for her than he wanted to, but he'd come around. He hadn't been able to leave her without holding her and kissing her as if he couldn't get enough of her, and he'd be back for that...and more.

"I'm going to let him take the lead," she told herself. "That is, unless he has too much success in staying away from me."

She wore a tailored gray suit and a lighter gray felt hat to her interview with him—she had to buy the hat, for she hadn't previously owned one. She ignored his raised eyebrow, conducted the most businesslike interview she'd ever pulled off, shook hands with him at the end of it, thanked him and left. From the corner of her eye, she saw him scratch his head as if perplexed when she walked out of his office. They hadn't made plans to see each other again, but she knew that eventually they would be together.

"The longer he stays away from me, the more he'll need me when we're finally together."

Several nights later she walked into the Exhibition Hall of the New York Public Library at a benefit for Off Broadway theaters, hoping to get material for her column and, while speaking with a famous author about whom she had decided to write—for want of a more interesting subject—her gaze landed on Ashton leaning against a wall, arms folded and looking directly at her. She nodded to him and smiled as brightly as she could, but if he didn't come to her, they wouldn't meet. For now, she planned to let him call the shots. The emptiness in the region of her heart served notice that she could expect plenty of pain, but she had resolved not to chase him, and she meant to stick to it.

She took satisfaction in the fact that no woman hung on to his arm. After wondering for a moment why Ashton Underwood, a businessman, would attend a fund-raiser for

Off Broadway theaters, it occurred to her that he might be a philanthropist. She tried to focus on the author, but his obvious self-absorption made that difficult.

"Does the play have a message other than that urban life is hazardous to one's well-being?" she asked him, hoping to get a perspective on his views about the obligations of playwrights and authors to the theater-going public.

"It's the best job I've done in years," the man replied. "Of course, I have to adlib in the key places, because the writers didn't give me much to work with."

Dear Lord, and I'm stuck with this for a column. A glance at Ashton told her that he sensed her frustration and refused to extend his sympathy. If she had the nerve, she'd turn her back to him, but she imagined the immense pleasure he'd get from that. "I'm not spending the rest of the evening with this loser," she told herself.

"I've enjoyed our conversation, Mr. Orlan," she said, and started away from him, but he detained her with a hand on her arm.

"Be sure and quote me correctly, Ms. Parker. I noticed that you didn't take notes while I talked. Here's my card in case you want to check anything with me."

She managed not to gasp, but took the card, smiled and stepped out of his way. She hadn't realized that he knew who she was, and it vexed her that she'd even considered reporting the nonsense he'd fed her. A ballet dancer who she admired waved at her as he passed, then came back and greeted her with a kiss on each cheek as theater people are wont to do. She wished Ashton hadn't seen that, because she didn't want him to think she was caught up in that world of make-believe and pretense.

The dancer went his way, and she wondered if she'd

have to write one of the gossip columns that she hated: who was seen where with whom and when. Just as she decided to find one of the fund-raiser's promoters and write about the event and its importance, she saw Ashton walking toward her.

"Hello, Felicia. Were you planning to ignore me all evening?"

"Hi, Ashton. I was surprised to see you here. You indicated that you'd like us to slow down, sit back and take stock, as it were, so I figured it was your call."

"Really! And that tells you we can't greet each other? Woman, I've been almost as close to you as a man can get, so don't tell me you can act as if I never existed."

"I didn't say I could do that, Ashton. You're the one with the misgivings, so I have to take my cue from you. For now, that is."

He stood with both hands in the pockets of his trousers, relaxed and more handsome than a man had a right to be. She ran her tongue across her lips and, realizing what she'd done, focused her gaze on the glossy polish that covered his shoes.

"What do you mean by that?" he asked her.

"I mean a butterfly doesn't wait for a flower to bloom, it dips into one that's already open."

Both of his eyes narrowed, an indication—she'd come to realize—of his displeasure. "And that's what you've been doing tonight?"

She couldn't help laughing, for she hadn't realized he would consider those men of interest to her. "Ashton, I'm working. If I'm fortunate, I'll get material for an interesting column. So far, I'm batting zero."

"In that case, I'd better let you get on with your work.

It's good seeing you." He leaned down and kissed the side of her mouth. Her surprise must have been mirrored on her face, for he grinned and said, "In this kissing crowd, nobody would take exception to that. See you."

She gazed at his back, wondering if he noticed how the women stared at him. *If, by that kiss, he meant to knock me off balance, he succeeded,* she admitted to herself. After a few minutes she saw from across the room a black woman with red, wooly hair, and headed for Dorothea Epps, copromoter of the event.

"Looks as if it's a success, Dorothea. You must be gratified. What can you give me for my column?"

"Felicia, darling. I'm so glad you're here. Come with me, and we can talk." An hour later, with enough material for two columns, she went home and got busy writing.

This man is serious, she thought when Ashton didn't call her the next day or the next. That Sunday night, two days after she'd last seen Ashton, it stunned her as she walked into the Lincoln Center jazz festival in Columbus Circle, that Ashton Underwood followed her by no less than three feet.

"Hi," she said. "Imagine running into you here. Of course, I recall that you like jazz."

"I love jazz," he said, his deep and lilting voice rolling over her like the waves of an incoming tide. "Who're you hoping to interview?"

"At these events, I catch as catch can, so I never know who I'll get. Not everyone is newsworthy. See you later." She'd like to know why Ashton arrived at the concert more than half an hour early since he would certainly have a ticket that guaranteed him a seat. Using her cell phone, she called the music director and two of the performers and asked for interviews. She got the interviews, but it meant remaining there for an hour and a half after the program ended. What a way to make a living.

When she got home, the red light on her answering machine sent her heartbeat into a gallop for she hoped her caller was Ashton. She checked her voice mail, lifted the receiver and heard, "This is Ashton. Please call me when you get home." She couldn't call him at two o'clock in the morning, although it would serve him right if she did. It was his fault that they didn't get together.

She phoned his office the next morning but was told that he was out of town for the weekend. She remembered then that he'd planned to visit his grandfather. What would he think about her not having returned his call last night? He'd probably jumped to the wrong conclusion.

He couldn't believe that Felicia ignored his request that she call him. All right, so she didn't plan to telephone him, but she could at least return his call. He started to say, "To hell with it," but remembered that it was he who had set the terms; she accepted his wishes and evidently meant to abide by them. Maybe she means to show me that she doesn't need me, he thought, but didn't believe it.

He went into Teddy's room and gazed down at the face of his precious son, peacefully asleep. "Wake up, Teddy. Don't you remember that we're going to see Granddad today?" The boy opened his eyes slowly, and as his father moved into his line of vision, he raised both arms for a hug. He gathered the child in his arms, lifted him from the bed and hugged him as he carried him to the bathroom.

"Now hurry. We leave in an hour. I'll be back in five minutes for your shower."

"I can take a shower by myself, Daddy."

"Not yet you can't. I at least have to be there to prevent you from drowning."

"That's what Miss Eartha says. Okay. I'll count to five and—"

"Teddy, you don't bargain with me. Do you understand?"

"Yes, sir. But I love to count, Daddy."

Ashton went to his own room to finish dressing. Had he been that conniving when he was four? Admittedly, Teddy would soon be five, but how could his little mind work as it did? He went back to find Teddy brushing his teeth and humming an unfamiliar tune. After breakfast, he told his housekeeper, "We'll be back Sunday evening, so have a good rest."

"Why do I have to sit behind you, Daddy?" Teddy asked as he strapped the child into his car seat.

"How many times have I answered that question, son?"

"A lot. I want to sit up front with you."

"You can't, and you know it. I want you to relax and enjoy the ride."

"Okay, Daddy. Let me know when we stop for ice cream."

Ashton laughed at the boy's attempt to manipulate him. He couldn't help it, and the laughter continued to roll out of him.

"What's funny, Daddy?"

"I'm happy," he said, and put on a CD of Mozart chamber music and headed for the New Jersey turnpike.

He had considered flying, but decided that, considering the crowding, confusion and time wasted at airports, traveling by car with Teddy would be easier. With very little traffic and one stop, he arrived in Rose Hill a few minutes after twelve noon.

Eighty-three-year-old Jake Underwood opened the screen door of the front porch and walked down the steps to meet his grandson and great-grandson. "I know it's still early, but it seemed like you'd never get here." The big man opened his arms and embraced Ashton, who held Teddy in his arms.

He took Teddy from Ashton and walked into the house with him. "Gee, Granddad, are we going to swim in that pool and ride on those horses? Can't I stay down here with you sometime? Daddy won't let me bribe Miss Eartha, but he didn't say I couldn't bargain with you."

"Son, your father's rules apply here and everywhere."

Teddy stared up at him. "What does that mean, Granddad?"

"If you want something, ask for it. If you can't have it, you can't have it. Your father has a rule against bribery, so you don't bribe anybody anywhere."

"I know. If I do, he'll punish me." Teddy suddenly smiled. "But I can have ice cream, can't I?"

Jake Underwood wiped his brow and looked at Ashton. "Is his mind always this active?"

"It sure is. When you get tired of it, play Mozart chamber music, or Haydn. He listens to chamber music, and he listens quietly."

"Thanks for telling me. This child can exhaust a man my age," Jake said.

"Trust me, he does the same for a man my age. What time is Cade coming?"

"Cade's over at the school checking out the equipment."

"Really? I think I'll head down there. I haven't seen him for a while. Teddy, you stay here with Granddad."

Feeling the warmth of spring in Maryland, he tossed his denim jacket in the backseat of the Town Car and headed for the riding school about three miles from his grandfather's house. He parked the car practically at the building's steps, jumped out and ran into the building.

"Ashton! Son of a gun, I wasn't expecting you till around four." They hugged each other. "Let me look at you, man," Cade said. "Yep, same old Ashton—not a flabby muscle in sight." They both laughed at the reference to Ashton's preoccupation with his physique during his college days.

"Seems like years since I've seen you, Cade. You're really a sight for sore eyes. How's your project going?"

"Couldn't be better. I have a written report in case we don't have time to go into the details. It was easier when we all lived together."

"Yeah, but the best we can do now is meet often."

"Right," Cade said, "and we can have conference calls, say, once a week. By the way, did you bring Teddy and Felicia Parker?"

Ashton didn't beat around the bush. "Teddy's at the house with Granddad, and Felicia's in New York. Things between us have stalled, you might say."

Cade braced his fists on his hips and looked at his older brother. "I see. So you got to thinking and decided that you were going to die a bachelor, as the West Indian song goes. Right?"

"Not quite. I decided that it was moving too fast, so I put on the brakes."

"Hmm. So how'd she take that? Surely you don't think that she'll sit on her thumbs till you decide you know enough of her past, present, future, why she wears her hair as she does, why she eats crab and hates shrimp and a host of other silly things. Ashton, you should cultivate that woman's feelings for you. You're a rich man, and it obviously doesn't mean a thing to her, because she fell for you before she knew it."

"She doesn't act as if she knows it now. When I asked her what she'd like us to do one Sunday when it gets warm, all she could think of was picnicking and similar outdoor activities, nothing over fifty bucks. I couldn't believe my ears."

"How's she behaving while you straighten out your head?"

"While I…" He caught himself scratching his head and stopped. "She's letting me do it without making one move in my direction."

Cade's eyes lit up. "Hallelujah! His honor has met his match. You go, Felicia."

"What time did Granddad say Damon would be here?" Ashton asked Cade, changing the subject.

Cade leaned against the staircase, relaxed and at peace with himself. "When I asked him two or three hours ago, he said 'any minute,' and you know how Granddad treats time."

"Indeed, I do, and I've long suspected that ignoring it is what keeps him so healthy and mentally fit," Ashton said.

"You're probably right, and it wouldn't hurt us to take heed. Ashton, we have to replace some of this tack, especially reins, blankets and some of these girdles that are badly worn. It seems to me one of the grooms should have mentioned this. What the hell are we paying 'em for?"

Ashton didn't want Cade to get on the warpath and start firing the grooms. "We can straighten this out as soon as Damon gets here," he said

"And I'll still be mad when he gets here," Cade said.

"Look at this. Somebody could break their neck holding on to this rein. Granddad is worried about our being able to provide the service, he should have been worrying about this equipment."

"It isn't he, but the grooms who're responsible, Cade."

"I know. When the devil is Damon going to show up?"

"Right here, brother. Who pricked your balloon, Cade?"

Cade and Ashton whirled around at the sound of Damon's voice, got up and headed toward their younger brother. With their arms around each other, they laughed and joked.

"Am I looking at my brother the lawyer?" Cade asked, gripping Damon's shoulder.

"You are, indeed," Damon said, his voice filled with pride. "I'm taking my national bar exams next week, and if I pass…scratch that. *When* I pass, I'm throwing a party." He looked at Ashton. "And I expect you to bring Felicia. By the way, how is she?"

"Brother dear is in the process of self-destructing," Cade said. "He hasn't even hooked the woman yet, but he thinks she should give him some space."

Damon's eyebrows went up as if programmed to do so. "What on earth for? Man, that gal is choice," he said to Ashton. "Don't tell me you're coming down with a case of dementia."

"I have to consider Teddy."

"Yeah, sure," Cade said. "And I suppose you're teaching him to call Eartha 'mother.' Right?"

"Oh, come off it, you two. Let's go back to the house. Granddad said he hadn't seen all of us together in ages. It's been about four months, but considering his attitude toward time, that must seem like years." They got into Damon's BMW and rode back to the house.

"This is a glorious sight," Jake said. "You're all here, all four of you." He picked Teddy up and held him. "You're growing fast as weeds, Teddy. I know your daddy can't get along without you, but it sure is good to have you here. So you tell him you want to come see me."

"Can you tell him to let me ride in the front seat, Granddad?"

Remembering that he was in his grandfather's house, Ashton restrained a whistle. "Teddy, one more slip like that and you're going to your room for the rest of the day. I am not joking with you."

"What did I do, Daddy?' the boy asked with all the innocence of a vestal virgin.

"You were trying to bargain with your grandfather, and you know I do not allow that."

"Sorry, Daddy, but it's so hard not to. I forget."

"Forgetting is not an excuse, son." Ashton didn't look at his grandfather, because he knew what was coming. A few minutes later while Cade and Damon enjoyed Teddy's antics, Jake said to Ashton, "I don't envy you raising that boy. I went through pretty close to the same thing with you, and I'll tell you it was exhausting. When you think it's getting the better of you, remember that you turned out just fine, and take heart."

"You mean, I was like that?"

"Absolutely. You were just as clever and just as manipulative, but don't worry, he'll grow out of it if you stick to your guns. He's a great little kid," Jake said. "I wish he was with me all the time. Now that we have a minute to ourselves, son, what about that lovely woman I saw you with on TV a few weeks back? She was enchanted with you. What happened?"

He wouldn't mislead his granddad, so he told him the

truth and added, "She means a lot to me, but the relationship just steamrolled to the point that I didn't know whether I was doing the right thing or letting my emotions do my thinking. I backed off."

"How does she feel about your taking a leave of absence from the relationship? Most women wouldn't care for that."

"So far, she's leaving it up to me. I'm learning that she knows the value of self-discipline."

"The two of you should make an interesting pair. Another word for self-discipline is stubbornness, and you have your share of that. I wish you well, but I don't mind telling you I'm disappointed that you didn't bring her with you this weekend. How do she and Teddy get along?"

Ashton cleared his throat. "Uh, they haven't met."

"You haven't… Would you mind telling me why?"

"I've never taken a woman to my home because I don't want Teddy to think it's all right for a man to have a stream of women flowing in and out of his life. Most of all, I don't want him to become attached to a woman only to lose her if she and I break up. If I'm ever certain, I'll take that woman home to meet my son."

Jake nodded his head very slowly, obviously contemplating his grandson's words. "I can't argue with that, son. A child needs stability. But from what I saw on that TV show and what you've told me about her, that woman is exceptional. She likes you a lot, and she likes you for yourself."

"I know that, Granddad. But I have to move according to my vision."

"And you're right. Do you want us to keep the riding school?"

"Yes, sir, but if we repair and replace the tack as needed, we may not need to expand. With so much stable gear unusable, that may be the root of our problem."

The four men spent the evening and the following day examining the equipment, placing orders and repairing tack. "This is why you couldn't register all the people who wanted to attend," Cade said. "I want the pleasure of firing a couple of the grooms."

"No. No," Jake said. "They just need closer supervision. Never expect anybody to take care of your business the way you would. I've told you that from the time you were knee high to a duck."

"I'll be back in a couple of weeks, at least for about a month, Granddad," Damon said, "and we'll get it straightened out. The new tack we're ordering should be here by then, and maybe we need to hire a man just to take care of all that equipment. It's hot, and I need a swim. Want to swim with Uncle Damon, Teddy?"

"Yes, sir, Uncle Damon. Can I have some ice cream first? Or maybe some lemonade. Daddy said it's hot outside. And can Granddad swim with us?"

"Of course he can, if he wants to. Suppose you wait till after you swim before you drink lemonade."

How good it would be if they all lived closer together, Ashton thought. Teddy would thrive among his uncles and with his great-grandfather. But he knew it wouldn't come to pass soon. When Teddy started school, Ashton wanted him to attend a private school in New York.

He went to his old room and fell across the bed. The contentment that he always experienced in his grandfather's home and in his presence eluded him. Why hadn't she called? He reached across the bed for the cell phone that lay on the nightstand and dialed Felicia's home phone number.

"This is Ashton, and I'm at my granddad's home in Maryland. Why didn't you return my call?"

"Because I didn't get home until two-thirty, and I didn't think you wanted me to wake you up just to say hello."

"I see. You must have been having a great time."

"I got an interview with Dorothea Epps, the promoter, and with the director, and that meant staying until after the end of the program. What did you want to say to me?"

He couldn't answer that question truthfully. "I wanted to remind you that I'd be down here this weekend and… and to tell you that you looked…well wonderful that night."

"Thank you. I… How nice of you! Is your grandfather well?"

"He is, and he asked me why I didn't bring you with me. He saw the TV's broadcast of the Sterling gala."

"I'm curious as to what you told him."

"I always tell my grandfather the truth. Always. Will you have dinner with me one day next week? Name a day that's convenient for you."

"Ashton, you seem to be assuming that I'm always busy in the evenings. I am not. If you want us to have dinner together, invite me for a specific day and time, and I'll be happy to join you unless I have a previous engagement scheduled. Okay?"

It wasn't okay at all. He'd put it that way so that she couldn't refuse, giving a previous engagement as an excuse. However, she had skillfully backed him into a corner, and wasn't that his fault? His decision to put some distance between them had made their relationship more formal and much less intimate. He didn't like it.

"Will you have dinner with me Monday evening?" It surprised him when he realized that he held his breath.

"I'd love to, Ashton, but I'm lecturing at the University of Connecticut Monday, and I'll get home late."

Precisely what he sought to avoid. "Let's leave it this way. I'll call you early in the week, and we'll work something out." If she wanted to see him, it would happen; if she didn't, then what?

Chapter 5

The last person Felicia expected to see at a political rally in a Harlem church was Ashton Underwood. She'd worked as a reporter for over ten years and had never seen Ashton until he came to the Willard Hotel to escort her to the Sterling gala. But suddenly, he had a reason to attend every function that she covered. Dressed in a manner befitting his status and position, he held a cup of coffee in his left hand and gestured with his right one as he spoke animatedly with the pastor of the church and an older woman who seemed captivated by Ashton's charisma. This time, she didn't wait for his move, but walked up to the group and spoke directly to Ashton.

"Hello, Ashton. I hope I'm not intruding, but I'd like to speak with you when you're free. Good evening, Reverend, Mrs. Holt." She smiled at the three of them, turned and looked around for someone who might be of interest to her readers, someone who wasn't always in the news. She didn't get far before she felt his touch lightly on her arm.

"You wanted to talk with me?" he asked her.

The man looked good enough to eat, and he stood there asking her in so many words what she wanted. She laid her head to one side and looked him in the eye. "What I want, Ashton, is for you to stop toying with me. If you don't, we're not going to see much of each other. Every place I go, you're there. I've been on this circuit for the past ten years, and I never saw you. Not once. And believe me, if I had seen you once, I definitely would not have forgotten it. So what's this all about?"

· She didn't think Ashton would answer candidly, for he had told her that he disliked showing his hand when he wasn't ready, and she figured he wasn't ready. "I consider it my good fortune whenever I see you, Felicia. You were busy last night, tonight and tomorrow night. Surely you don't begrudge me the pleasure of seeing you for a few minutes, even at a distance." His lips curved into a half smile, and she could see that he was laughing at himself. At such times, she could hardly resist holding him and spreading kisses all over him.

"Ashton, your devilish streak will get you into trouble one of these days."

His grin broadened, and his eyes sparkled with delight. "I don't doubt it for a minute," he said, "but when I get into trouble, I make sure I enjoy it."

She thought she might wilt beneath the heat of his gaze. "You're offering an invitation to pure madness," she said, hating the quiver in her voice, "and I knew it the first time I looked at you."

"Madness? I wouldn't say that. Ecstasy is more like it. What time do you think you'll finish work tonight?" he asked her.

"Can we meet at the front door in about an hour? I should have what I need by then."

An hour later with a tape of her conversation with three political candidates in her handbag, she rushed upstairs, raced through the vestibule and sailed into Ashton on his way to keeping their rendezvous.

In a flash, his arms brought her body close to his, and once more her heart beat with his. With a forefinger, he tipped up her chin and stared into her eyes. "You could never guess how much I want you this minute." Then, as if he'd gone too far and knew it, he released her, took her hand and they left the building. "Starvation isn't good for a man. It can make him do or say things he regrets."

"What did you do or say that you regret?" she asked him. "I haven't noticed that you did or said anything offensive. Did you break one of your rules? Or were you more candid than you thought wise? Ashton, I know you want me. I take my cues from your behavior, from what I see, not merely from your words. Where are we going?"

"Have you eaten dinner?"

"I had a piece of cheese and some coffee at the rally, and I could use some real food. We could go to the Brasserie or some place like that. Service is fast."

"All right, if that suits you."

"You sound as if it's ordinary," she said. "The food's pretty good."

"It's okay, Felicia, but it isn't the place I'd take a date."

"You can take me to one of those places some other time, but right now, I'm too hungry to wait while a maître d' shows off, then a sommelier gives his ego a workout and all the while the waiter hasn't showed up with a menu. Then, of course, the chef and his assistants have to impress you with their cleverness by making you wait an hour for what you ordered. It's fun when I'm prepared for it, but tonight, my tummy would be happy with a hot dog if it arrived quickly."

He opened the front passenger door of his Town Car for her and waited while she seated herself. "Did I remember to tell you that you're precious? An earthy woman with your other attributes is a delight."

"No, you didn't," she said, with not a little satisfaction. "You haven't said anything nice to me lately. How was your weekend with your family?"

"Great. We hadn't been together for a while, and I realized how much I missed being with them. Teddy revels in the attention he gets from Granddad and his uncles."

"Of course he does. Children can't get enough love. They need it, but it should be tough love."

"Believe me, it is. He gets enough pampering from my housekeeper. He's not yet five, but he knows how to wind her around his finger."

The chance to ask Ashton a question that plagued her may not come again soon, so she seized the opportunity. "How has he responded to your lady friends?" She made it past tense, because she didn't want him to think she was trying to find out whether he had a woman friend to whom he was closer than he was to her.

He aligned the Town Car with the curb about a block from the Brasserie, cut the motor and turned to her. "Felicia, in response to your question, my son hasn't met any lady friend of mine, as you put it. Furthermore, since my divorce, you've been in my house as often as any woman other than my housekeeper. Does that answer your question?" Relief flooded her, and she knew why. The contours of her face betrayed her, and a smile lit up her features.

"I see that that pleases you," he said.

Remembering her pledge to herself that she would always level with him, she said, "I'm human. Of course it pleases me."

"Do you want to be more important to me than any other woman?"

"I'll answer that when you give me more encouragement than I've had from you during the past fortnight. And, Ashton, you don't encourage me by being noncommittal or by staying away from me. An independent, competent woman needs warm loving as much as any other woman needs it." She reached over and stroked his cheek. "Don't forget that."

He hadn't expected either her remark or her gesture, and with eyebrows raised, he stroked his chin, obviously taken aback. "You shoot for the bull's-eye. I won't forget that." He walked around the car to open the door for her. She stepped out and stood facing him, almost touching his body.

"Don't deal me an ace and think I won't play it," she told him, easing aside the lapel of his jacket and letting her fingers trace the stripe in his dress shirt. "This isn't a game for me, so please don't treat it as one, loving me one week, and the next showing me how easy it is to ignore me. If you do, I'll be as gone as gone can get."

"You pick a fine time to talk to me this way," he told her, took her hand and headed for the restaurant. They sat in a corner at a small table on which sat one lighted candle and a few sprigs of tiny purple orchids. He stroked the back of her hand. "I take it you aren't challenging me. Are you?"

"No, I'm not. I want you to know what this relationship is like from my point of view. I'm not afraid of pain, Ashton, so I know I can walk away from what I want if I believe it's not good for me. And I see that you can and will do the same. So if that's the case… I mean, if you want me, but think I'm not good for you, tell me now. I promise not to shed a tear." *At least not where you can see me do it,* she thought.

"Do you feel so little for me?" he asked.

"Think over what I said, Ashton. I didn't even hint as to the quality or depth of my feelings for you."

After that remark, they ate in silence. Both refused dessert, and as they left the restaurant, he asked her, "Do you think our coming here tonight was a good idea?"

She took his hand. "Any opportunity that you and I have to understand each other better is a good and useful thing."

"Do you understand me better?"

She shook her head. "Not really, but you understand me better."

He parked in front of the building where she lived, walked around to open the door for her and this time she let him do it.

"May I see you to your apartment?" he asked her.

"Yes," was all she said.

Ashton figured that by backing away from Felicia in order to view their relationship from a distance and to gain some perspective on it, he'd loss some ground with her. But he was damned if he'd be dragged headlong into marriage by his emotions and the demands of his penis.

He'd taken a breather, but it had merited him nothing; he wanted her more than ever.

How could he tell her that meeting her at fund-raisers and social functions had not been accidental—that he would phone her paper, ask her editor's secretary whether the paper would cover the event and take it from there. He needed to see her even as he let her think otherwise. Her fingers shook as she tried to unlock the door of her apartment, but he pretended not to notice and waited until she managed to open the door. Then, he closed it with his right elbow and brought her into his arms so suddenly that the contact with her nearly took his breath away.

"I've missed you every second since the last time I had you in my arms. It was no accident that you saw me so often. I arranged it, because...oh, Felicia—"

Her mouth moved beneath his, warm, sweet and giving, and he thought he'd go insane with love and with the pangs of desire. She stepped back from him and gazed into his eyes with such innocence that he hugged her back into his embrace.

"I'm feeling so much for you right now," he said. "It's overwhelming. Tell me it isn't one-sided."

"You know it isn't. But I won't let you love me like this, promising me the world, and after thinking about it decide that we're moving too fast, so you'll pull back—sell some shares as it were, the way big shots manipulate the stock market—and lower the value. Don't do that to me, Ashton."

"Sweetheart, can't you feel what's inside of me?"

He had her tight in his arms, where she wanted to be, needed to be. She wrapped her arms around him and let herself relax. Somewhere in the inner chambers of her heart, he lurked, and she knew at that moment that he would always be there.

She had to get something straight. "Have you accepted what you feel for me, or are you still worried about us? Why are you reticent?"

"You're known to half of the eight million New Yorkers and many people beyond, why should you settle for me?"

She moved out of his arms then, stepped back and looked into his eyes, eyes that weakened her knees. "Isn't the real question, why would *you* settle for *me?*"

"Are you out of your mind?" he asked, scowling. "Woman, I'm in love with you!"

She'd never expected to hear those words from him or from any man, and she cherished them. But in spite of the joy and excitement she felt, she had to stay focused on reality. "And you haven't been happy about it, either," she said. "I know you have to consider the interests of your son, and that is admirable, but be aware that your charm is like a magnet, and use it sparingly, especially if you don't want to get involved. What are you laughing at?"

"Us. Something tells me we could be at a standoff fifty years from now. There's a cure for it, sweetheart, and we both know what it is. This bantering is a substitute for a deeper, more intimate involvement. You're always candid. Am I right?"

"Even if you're right, we're too adult to settle things that way."

His tongue poked his right cheek. "Really? How old do you think I am, for Pete's sake? Let me tell you I can't imagine being *that* adult."

His eyes sparkled with mischief, and a grin sweetened the contours of his lips until she began to imagine what it would be like to have him locked inside of her body driving her mad with the power of his loins.

He swallowed so hard that she heard it. "Felicia! You're the one dealing aces now. Come here to me."

She sprang into his arms, and he plunged into her parted lips, tasting, testing, moving in and out of her in a semblance of the love act, stroking and squeezing her. She moaned her frustration as her blood raced hot and headlong to her loins. She had needed it so badly, needed him. She grabbed his wrist, placed his hand on her left breast and rubbed vigorously.

"Sweetheart. What do you want? Tell me. Tell me."

"Kiss me," she sighed. "Kiss me." His long fingers went into the neckline of her dress and waited. When she did nothing to stop him, he released her breast, pinched and rubbed her nipple.

"Oh, yes. Yes," she said.

He lifted her, and she thought she'd go crazy at the touch of his warm breath on her flesh while she waited for the feel of his lips and tongue. "Ashton, please!" she said. He sucked the nipple into his hot mouth, lifted her to fit him, and tortured her libido as only a lover can.

"Oh, Lord. Oh-hh." She moaned, and he suckled her vigorously until she could feel him hard and heavy against her. "I can't stand it, Ashton."

He put her away from him, though with care. "Do you want me?"

"Yes," she whispered.

"I don't want you to regret it tomorrow, Felicia."

"Will you regret it?" she asked him.

"Never!"

"Then neither will I."

* * *

He'd never been nervous about making love with a woman, but he hadn't ever loved one as he loved Felicia, and he wanted desperately to make her happy. "Where's your bedroom?"

"Down the hall on the left." He lifted her and, as he knew she would, she advised him that she could walk there.

"Not now, you won't. You are in my care, and if you do as I ask, neither of us will ever forget this night. Do you trust me?"

She rested her head on his shoulder. "I trusted you even when I thought you were a professional escort. There's something about you."

He placed her on the bed and pulled off her shoes. Then he undressed her down to her bra and panties. Gazing down at her body, he whispered, "My God, you're beautiful." Within seconds, he stripped down to his shorts.

"Let me," she said, rolled his shorts down to his knees, leaned forward and kissed him.

"Hold it, baby. I've been celibate since the day we met, and anything will tick me off."

She lay back, raised her arms to him and sent frissons of heat racing through his body. He calmed himself and leaned over her, intent upon kissing every inch of her. He sucked her right nipple into his mouth, paying homage to his ally and, within minutes she began thrashing for relief. He twirled his tongue around the diamond in her belly button while his fingers tortured her breasts. She swung her hips up to him, but he ignored the offering. She was a feast, and he meant to dine on her.

* * *

Ashton didn't know her well enough to expect that she'd go after what she wanted if she didn't get it soon enough. As his tongue caressed her belly and the inside of her thigh, she had the feeling of a mountain climber reaching for the summit without a pickax to help her. "Aren't you going to get into me?" she asked him. "I'm on fire for you."

"I am. That's just the way I want you, hot and eager."

"Now," she said, and reached for him.

"Not until I get what I want."

He spread her legs, plunged his tongue into her and licked, nipped and sucked until she howled for relief. She'd never felt anything like it. He brought her to the edge time and again, but wouldn't let her explode.

"Honey, please. I need to burst."

He raised his head. "But is it good to you? Do you like it?"

"I love it, but you won't let me… Oh, I think I'll die if I don't burst wide open."

"You will. Tell me you love me."

"I do. You know I do. Get into me. I want to feel you inside of me."

"All right, sweetheart. I'll give you what we both want." He moved up her body. Slowly. Tantalizingly. "Look at me, love. This can't happen to us but once." He kissed her nose and nearly drowned her in the sweetness of his smile. "Take me."

She held him in her hands. Hard, big and velvety-smooth, and raised her body to meet his thrust. Slowly he moved, but she couldn't wait, so she forced his entry.

"Ow!"

He stopped. "Easy, sweetheart. Did I hurt you?"

"I don't care. I'm just a little surprised. Please don't stop."

It wasn't her first time, but he was a big man. She swung her body up to him, closed her eyes, pressed his buttocks and took him into her. He kissed the tears that flowed from her eyes.

"Is it all right? Have I hurt you? How do you feel?"

"Wonderful. I'm…I'm happy, Ashton. I'm so happy."

"I'm happy, too," he said, and she knew his kiss sealed a new beginning as he started to move within her. She could hardly bear the pleasure he gave her, the massaging of her live-wire nerve ends, the merciless pumping and squeezing of her vagina, enslaving her until she erupted around him.

"You're mine. Do you hear me? You're mine, Felicia," he said as he spent himself and collapsed in her arms.

His lips adored her with soft kisses on her eyes, neck, cheeks, nose and chin. Then he suddenly gathered her up in his arms and hugged her. "You said you loved me. I know passion can overwhelm a person and cause you to say things that you regret. But we're calm now. I love you. Did you mean it when you said you loved me?"

"I love you, Ashton. I don't know what triggered it or when it happened."

A half smile floated over his face and he pressed his lips together as if he were suspended between amusement and incredulity. "You got to me the minute I saw you. You don't know how happy I was when you told me there was nothing else I could do for you that night. It may have seemed crass of me to ask you if you wanted anything else—considering what that implied in the circumstances—but I had to know what kind of woman you were."

"That didn't tell you much."

"But what I learned was important. Where do we go from here? I want to see you on a regular basis. Is there another man in your life who matters?"

"Only my brother. Listen, Ashton, I've finished that story and tomorrow I'll fax it to you, but I don't promise to take your suggestions. We may have our first fight."

He looked down at her and grinned. Did this man know how drop-dead gorgeous he was? "Whatever it is, we'll work it out. You're not slipping away from me."

"But what if you don't like what I wrote?"

He cradled her to his body. "You already know whether I'll like it. If I don't, I can't promise to be sweet about it. I have a Republican acquaintance who's been married to an active Democrat for about twenty years. If they can get along, so can you and I."

Actually, she saw nothing in her report that would rile him, but the day might come when words under her byline infuriated him. She couldn't resist testing the water. To his credit, she thought, he didn't ask her about the content of her story while they were intimately locked together.

"I don't want to leave you," Ashton told Felicia. "I could stay right where I am indefinitely, but I didn't tell Teddy that I wouldn't be home tonight. Furthermore, I don't know what kind of neighbors you have, and I don't want to embarrass you. Perhaps we can spend a weekend together someplace. Would you like that?"

He had begun to understand that she didn't varnish the truth in order to make it palatable, and she didn't do that when she said, "I'd love to wake up in your arms, but before we plan a tryst, let's see how we get along."

He separated them and fell over on his back, but he held her hand. "All right. Now you're the one who wants to go slow. Will you at least agree not to see other men?"

"I agree, but that means you don't see other women."

"I won't. I'm not seeing anyone now other than you, and I haven't since we met. I'm straight, Felicia. I don't like games, and don't have time for them. As far as I'm concerned, you and I are a couple. I'm your man, and you are my woman." He turned on his side, facing her, and rubbed down the bridge of her nose with his right index finger. "I'll trample any other bear that tries to dip into my honey."

Her mouth became one large O, and her eyes got bigger. "You what?"

He leaned over, flicked his tongue over the seam of her lips and worked his way into her mouth where she welcomed him. "You heard me. I was only half joking."

"I said I wouldn't see other men, so don't worry about the honey."

It surprised him that she didn't smile when she said it, and he realized that she took his comment seriously. "I'm known for a weird sense of humor, sweetheart. I surprise myself sometimes. Lord, I hate to leave you. It's been years since I had such a feeling of contentment. But I have to go. Kiss me?"

With her arms around him, she pulled him onto her and took him into her body. He thought his insides would come out, and that his mind was deserting him, for she loved him wildly, wantonly and sweetly, however it suited her, loved him until skill and reason left him and instinct alone powered him. He gave her all that he could, and then she stripped him of his essence, and he cried out, "Love me. Love me," and came apart in her arms.

Later, sitting in his car, too poleaxed to drive, he wondered why he'd bother to try slowing down the momentum of their relationship. *What a woman she was!* She had sheared him of his reserve and he'd bared his soul to her. Had he thought he could end it? He'd been so enamored of her that, like a teenager, he found ways to see her and to be with her surreptitiously, as if she weren't intelligent enough to know that running into him three or four evenings a week at various affairs couldn't be accidental.

He hadn't meant to fall in love with her or with any other woman, and he didn't know where he was headed with Felicia. He did know that he wasn't calling the shots, a strange feeling for a man who, for years, had set the time and the program for practically everything that involved him. Yet, he was not upset; she said she loved him and, if he was impressed with anything about her, it was her honesty. He turned on the ignition, moved away from the curb and headed home. For the first time in years, he didn't feel as if going home was his only choice.

Felicia pulled the sheet tight around her body, fell over on her belly and buried her face in the pillow. Who was this woman who went wild beneath Ashton Underwood, exploding in orgasm time and again, telling him what to do to her and how to do it? What in the name of kings came over her? She didn't think she could face him again. She wrapped her arms around her middle and hugged herself.

"Thank God I never knew loving could be like that, because it would probably have gone to my head, and I'd be a street woman." She rolled over on her back, giggling almost uncontrollably as she envisioned herself in that role, the sound of her laughter adding to her joy. She dragged herself out of bed, showered, slipped on a lavender-colored lace teddy and crawled back into bed. In a fit of loneliness, she rubbed her nose in the pillow on which his head had lain, kissed it and hugged it. The smell of their sex lingered, arousing her libido, and she got out of bed.

"He's gone, so I can't feast on him, but I ought to find a tuna sandwich in here," she said, exasperated at herself as she headed for the kitchen. She ate half a sandwich, drank a glass of warm milk and went back to bed.

The next morning at work she faxed copies of her story on Dream to Ashton and Cade, and got to work on her column, the first completely political column she'd ever written. Fortunately the local Democrats and Republicans eased her problem with the brickbats they had started slinging at each other. By lunchtime, she had a first draft.

"Hello?" she said when her phone rang minutes before she would have left for lunch.

"This Ashton Underwood. May I please speak with Ms. Parker?"

"Hello, Ashton. This is Felicia. How are you?"

"Pretty good. I've always said you're a fine writer, and I definitely like what you did with this. I think Cade was too caustic, but I know you didn't misquote him because it sounds like him. Your history of Dream is accurate and appealing. If Cade hadn't done his thing in your interview with him, I'd probably be dancing. This is a fine job."

"Thanks. Did you speak with Cade about his quote?"

"For what? He meant it, which means he wrote it in stone. That's the way he is. I hate the thought of Mrs. Smith learning about her husband's infidelity at the same time that her friends read about it."

"Is that your main concern?"

"Actually, it's my only concern. She'll be devastated."

"Probably, but not because she doesn't know it. Any woman would know if her husband had a mistress, especially one forty years her junior. I'm sorry about it, but my editor will get it as soon as I hear from Cade."

Minutes after they said goodbye, she answered the phone and heard Cade's voice. "Great job, Felicia. It's perfect."

"Cade, Ashton has some misgivings about your quote. He said it's too caustic and that Mrs. Smith will be devastated."

"That sounds just like my big brother. He's a sweet boy, and I love him, but my quote stays."

She thought she heard laughter in his voice. "Are you meddling with Ashton?"

"Ah, Felicia. Ashton's a gentleman, and he insists on thinking and behaving as one. That can get in the way of real life."

"Are you saying you aren't a gentleman?"

"No, I'm not saying that, but if you're in a nudist colony, for Pete's sake, pull off your damned clothes. Get my drift?"

Laughter poured out of her. "I get it, all right. Something tells me you're odd man out in your family."

"Not quite, but I don't dance to anybody's tune but my own."

"Really? Wait till you fall in love. I'll mail you a copy of tomorrow's paper."

"That won't be necessary. I subscribe to it. Thanks for everything. By the way, how *is* my brother?"

Fishing, was he? Well, she'd give him something to fry. She crossed her knee and leaned back in her chair, prepared to enjoy the effect of her sally. "When he left me last night, he was in a great mood."

His whistle reached her through the wire. "Way to go. Be seeing you."

Felicia gave the report to her secretary. "Take that to Ray, please." If the report satisfied her editor, maybe she'd get a raise, but the least she expected was a chance to write more columns that had nothing to do with who was who, when and where. She'd begun to suffocate beneath the weight of bloated egos. She would have left the office early if she hadn't been waiting for Ray's views on her column. She wanted to write reports in which she took pride, stories that made a difference in the community if not in the country.

"Mr. Gilder on line two, Ms. Parker," her secretary said through the intercom. "Pick up, please."

"It's a good piece, Felicia. How'd you like to go to the conventions?"

She controlled her enthusiasm, because from Ray Gilder's perspective, appearing happy about an assignment was tantamount to saying you didn't mind not getting paid for it. "That would be nice," she said. "I've always wondered what the mood behind the scenes is like. That's one thing the camera can't capture, because politicians show their teeth the minute a cameraman approaches."

She thanked her boss, packed up and drove to the supermarket. "I want something good to eat," she told herself. "And I deserve it." As she strolled through the produce department trying to decide what she wanted for dinner, her cell phone rang.

"Felicia Parker speaking."

"Hello, sweetheart." Perspiration dampened her neck, back and arms, and she thought, How can he do this to me with just two words? "Hi, Ashton."

"I suppose you know what it cost me to put on that business face while we spoke this morning. Thank you for not saying 'Ashton, have you lost your mind?' There's a wonderful little restaurant in Riverdale. Would you like to eat there with me this evening?"

She thought for a minute. As much as she wanted to be with him, she didn't think she'd be happy if she saw him every evening…at least not yet. And didn't he need to spend some evenings with Teddy? But she knew it wouldn't be wise to get ahead of him. He hadn't said he wanted them to be together every evening.

"I'd like that, but it's warm tonight, and we could stroll around, people watch. You don't have to take me to swanky places. I'll be happy as long as we're together. Besides, I can't hold your hand while you're driving. Or at least, I shouldn't." A man passed her and the odor of his cologne lingered in his wake, the cologne that Ashton always wore.

"All right," she said quickly. "If you want to eat in Riverdale, why not?"

"I'd like to know what happened to change your mind," he said. "Just as I was preparing to warn my taste buds that they wouldn't have the pleasure of greeting fancy quenelles in lobster sauce, you give them a reprieve."

"Does that mean I have to wear something red?"

"Any color you wear will suit me. I'll wear a jacket and tie. Is seven good for you?"

"Yes. See you then." She hadn't had a chance to put the phone away before it rang again.

"Felicia, this is Miles. Has Ashton Underwood told you that he's planning a takeover of the chain that owns the *New York Evening Journal?* That's the paper you work for, isn't it?"

She gaped at the phone. "Who told you that?"

"I just heard it on the radio. Doesn't that mean he'd be your boss?"

"I—I don't know. This is the first I'm hearing about it. He wouldn't necessarily run it just because he owned it, would he?"

She imagined Miles making a pyramid of his fingers to prop up his chin as he often did when musing over an idea. "Depends on his management style. In any case, an intimate relationship with your boss is bad policy."

"Who says we're intimate?"

"I do. You've had just about enough time to cross over that bridge. The two of you were headed for it the night you met, and he didn't get where he is today by dragging his feet. If he succeeds, having him as a boss could become a problem for both of you. My last word on the subject—for now."

"I'm not answering this phone again," she said. But she remembered that Ashton had her cell phone number, dug into her handbag for the phone and answered. "Felicia Parker speaking."

"This is Ray. I just got news that John Underwood is making a bid for Skate newspapers. Get some details, and put a paragraph on it in your column for tomorrow."

"Ray, I've already written my column, and that news doesn't fit it. Give the story to another reporter."

"Underwood is news right now because you made him and his company news, so you should be the one to keep the public's interest going."

"That's worth three lines, Ray. Tomorrow's column is on political issues, as you know, because you've read it. Where does this fit in?"

"Okay. I got the message. Make it a first paragraph, three italicized lines. How's that?"

"You're the boss."

She phoned Ashton and told him about the rumor. "I'm bringing it up now, because I don't want to talk business during our dinner."

"Perhaps we can talk about it after dinner. We can sit on the Lincoln Center Plaza, have an aperitif or some coffee and we'll talk then."

He hadn't denied it, and it seemed that he wanted her to hear his views on the matter before she wrote a story about it. She felt like a kitten tripping over hot coals.

Felicia dressed in an avocado-green dress and jacket of silk crepe. Ashton liked her in red, but she had a feeling that red would send the wrong message that night.

He rang her doorbell at precisely seven o'clock, and she relaxed at his boyish smile and eager kiss. Maybe the evening would be all that she hoped for.

She gasped as they entered Palms Restaurant, a haven for lovers. Candles provided its only light, palms gave it a garden atmosphere and bouquets of roses adorned each table.

"Oh, Ashton," she said. "If I had imagined you were bringing me to such a place, I really would have worn something red. It's beautiful."

"I've wanted to come here for a long while, ever since my secretary gave me a picture of the place. I hope the food matches the décor."

A red dress wouldn't have matched the pale yellow tablecloth, napkins, candles and roses, so her choice of avocado-green had been a good one. They placed their order, and almost immediately a man at nearby table got up and walked over to them. Ashton rose, stuffed his hands into his trouser pockets and stared at the man, who pointedly ignored him.

"Miss Parker, I never dreamed I'd see you here tonight. I don't know whether you've heard, but I'm reading at the 92nd Street Y Sunday afternoon."

"I've heard," she said, doing her best to smile. "If you'll excuse me…"

"Yes, of course," the man said, and dropped a business card on the table. She didn't look at Ashton, for she knew he couldn't help but be displeased.

Ashton sat down, and when he remained quiet for a minute, she knew that he was waiting for his irritation to dissipate. "What does your editor want you to say about my attempt to purchase Skate?"

"I thought we were going to discuss this *after* dinner. I'm not working now," she said, smiling to make light of her remark.

"No? You couldn't prove it by me."

She was about to answer when a woman whose popularity had long ebbed rushed to the table. "I wasn't sure it was you, Ms. Parker, but the maître d' assured me it was. Could you please sign this, and would you mention that you saw me here with Bill Schubert, producer of *Fly Away Baby?*"

"Miss Pickett," she said, not bothering to hide her anger, "you're disrupting my dinner engagement."

"But you're powerful, and I need the publicity." Realizing that the woman was about to create a scene, she signed the card. "Please excuse me."

Shock reverberated through her when Ashton stood and said, "Would you please leave here before I have you removed?" The woman gasped and rolled her eyes, but she hustled away.

"I'm sorry, Ashton. I didn't think this could happen way up here."

Ashton made no attempt to hide his annoyance. "I suppose you'd have had a line if we'd been in Manhattan."

"I couldn't help it, Ashton."

"I know that, and that's the problem." With those words, the joy she'd felt when she'd enter the restaurant drained out of her, and she wanted to leave. But to suggest it would have put an even heavier damper on their evening together. He signaled for the maître d'. "Ms. Parker does not wish to be disturbed by any patrons, so please do not identify her to anyone."

"Yes, of course, sir. I'm extremely sorry, sir," the man said, genuflecting as he spoke.

She barely tasted what was probably a delicious meal, for her thoughts dwelled on the emotional distance between them. No one would have imagined that on the previous night they confessed to love each other and made love for the first time, spine-tingling love. Both declined dessert, a signal that the evening had disappointed them. She had already judged Ashton to be a private person, conservative for a man of his age, stature and wealth, and she knew that the evening's events had impaired their future relations. *I can't help it. It's who I am.*

"Are we going have that aperitif in the Lincoln Center Plaza?" she asked him as he drove toward Manhattan.

He flexed his shoulder in a careless shrug. "Print whatever you think is fair."

From the route he took, she could see that Lincoln Center was not in his plans. "You'd better tell me something," she said, annoyed that he should blame her for the bad manners of two publicity-seekers. "If you don't, I'll tell my editor that you wouldn't discuss it with me, so he should assign the story to another reporter. If Blaine Phillips gets it, you'll be sorry. Forgive me, I should watch my tongue. If you do acquire Skate, you'll be my boss."

"You're angry, and I can imagine why, Felicia, but I can't help the way I feel right now. I know it wasn't your fault, but it's a fact of your life, and I don't know whether I can handle it."

"I'm a journalist, Ashton, a public person, and you knew that from the beginning, but if it's too much for you, let's break it off right now. I only wish to hell you'd come to this conclusion before you rocked me out of my senses last night. That's the cruel part of it."

He parked in front of her address and cut the motor. "Do you think I'm happy? I haven't said I wanted to break it off, but I know myself. That guy behaved as if I wasn't there, and by the time I cooled off, that foolish woman showed up and began to create a scene. If there had been a third one, I know I would have been ready to knock him down."

"But I thought you smiled at that man."

"When I'm angry, that smile is a reflex. It doesn't have a damned thing to do with the way I feel at the moment."

"Is it always a reflex?" she asked him, trying to soften the moment.

"No, it isn't, and you already know the difference."

"Where does this leave us? I'm in limbo, and if you force me to dig my way out of this without your help, we probably won't see each other again. I'm not good at crawling, Ashton. My knees don't even know how to bend. I love you, but I'm damned if I'll suck up. It isn't in me."

He leaned back and stretched his right arm across the

back of the seat, though he didn't touch her. "My grand-dad said he'd like to be around if the two of us came to loggerheads. He's a wise man."

"How did that come up?"

"I told him that I was putting some distance between us and you were letting me do it. He knows that two plus two equals four." A half smile crossed his face, and he turned to look at her. "I was so happy with you last night. The whole day today was a blast of sunshine after years of frost."

Without warning, he gathered her to him and held her. "I don't like to think that I'm self-centered, but I work hard at creating a normal life for myself and for Teddy. I avoid bars, nightclubs and high-society things. I've avoided the hostesses who are always looking for an unattached, eligible man for their dinner parties. That's not the kind of life I want. Some good music and the smell of hamburgers or hot dogs roasting in my backyard and Teddy enjoying it with me have been the joys of my life since I left Rose Hill, Maryland. I could enjoy that even more with you, but I'm not convinced that it suits you at all."

She thought for a long time before answering him. In spite of his success as an entrepreneur, Ashton Underwood had not become enamored with his importance. Wrapped in his arms, she knew she belonged with him, just as she'd known it the night before when he was buried deep inside of her. "I can't give up my work, Ashton. If I did, I would be unbearable. Oh, I could change the way I do it…at least for a while, but—"

He interrupted her. "You mean, if you were starting a family?"

"Yes. I'd work at home, but at the appropriate time I'd be back on the beat."

"If you had a family, would you still regard yourself as a journalist first?"

He was fishing for answers without asking a direct question, but she wouldn't be clever about it. She wanted him to know precisely where she stood, because after tonight, they would either go forward or split permanently.

"If I had a family, I would see myself first as a child of God, as I do now, and then as a wife, mother, journalist, sister, friend and colleague, in that order."

"Did you enjoy the attention of those publicity-seekers tonight?"

She attempted to move out of his arms, but he wouldn't release her. "That couldn't be a serious question. If I did, I'd be guilty of extremely bad manners. I was annoyed, because I knew what your reaction would be. I would have been displeased if I'd been alone."

"All right. It wasn't a fair question." He got out of the car, walked around and opened the door for her with his key.

"You left the lock on so I couldn't get out," she said. As they waited for the elevator, she told him, "Be careful how you leave me tonight."

His left eyebrow shot up. "I don't know how to take that. If I could suit myself, I wouldn't leave you."

If she could suit herself, she wouldn't let him leave her. But she didn't intend to allow them to solve their problems by making love. Give that man an inch, and he'd send her right out of her mind.

He held her hand as they walked down the long corridor to her apartment. "I think we should say good-night here," she told him.

"For the way I want to kiss you, I need some privacy."

She had no shame about handing him her key and

letting him know that she welcomed the feeling that being in his arms would give her. He opened the door, walked into the apartment with her in his arms and flicked his tongue across her lips, demanding entry. She clung to him while he possessed her.

"I know it won't be easy for us," he said after catching his breath, "but I can't let you go."

She leaned against the opposite wall, away from him. "If you're going to be halfhearted about us, Ashton, let's agree to drop it. I couldn't stand the torture. And remember that no matter what you decide, I'll know the truth by the way in which you behave."

"Was I halfhearted a minute ago?"

"Lord, no! Honey, what about Skate?"

"It's true, but I'm not publicizing it. In a couple of days, it should be a done deal."

"In that case, there's no problem. It will be a couple of days before another of our reporters will have time to file a story. I'll tell Ray that I can't do it, but unless he pushes me, I won't tell him until late tomorrow. Good luck with it."

He stood there looking down at her, not speaking, and she wondered at his thoughts. Finally he closed the space between them and, with his arms tight around her, he spread kisses over her face and seared her lips with his own. "Good night, sweetheart."

She closed the door. Yes, he loved her, but he had misgivings, and for the first time, so did she.

Chapter 6

Ashton didn't rest well that night. After he left Felicia, it hit him forcibly that he hadn't merely fallen in love with her, but that he'd fallen deeply and had, subconsciously, considered his relationship with her to have the possibility of permanence. Making love with her had sealed it, for he had never before known the total completeness that he experienced with her. Previously, what mattered most in lovemaking was the sexual relief, but with her, it was the loving, the giving and receiving, the revelation of who and what he was as a man. In the disregard of himself, he had found heaven in her. And after the way she held him and kissed him a few hours earlier, he knew that she'd be the same woman every time they made love. Oh, she would own his heart, but he had some power over hers. If only she didn't come with that self-seeking entourage!

Sleeping fitfully enabled him easily to arise early the

next morning, and eight o'clock found him in his office. He phoned Cade. "How's it going, brother?" he asked when Cade answered. "Don't you think that quote you gave Felicia could cause problems?"

"Nah," Cade said breezily and self-assured. "My spies never mislead me. Smith is in for trouble. Still, I think we'd better increase our shares of Dream. Granddad said he's going to do that, and we ought to urge Damon to do the same."

"I've already done it, and I think I'll have my secretary check on Smith's shares and any recent activity."

Ashton flexed his knee and eased his right trouser leg to prevent his trousers from creasing. He could be as casual in dress as the next man, but when he faced business associates, he looked his role. "It's the way to go, Cade, but if we're going to buy large blocks, we ought to do it now. When it comes to money, Smith's a savvy man."

"I'll tell Damon what we're doing," Cade said. "By the way, how are things with you and that long-stemmed beauty?"

"Felicia and I are fine. Stop pestering me about her."

Cade's laugh had the ring of triumph. "When I spoke with her this morning, she indicated that you left her last night feeling good, man. Way to go."

"You imagined that."

"Whatever you say. Incidentally, the tack arrived this morning, and the grooms are sorting it out and putting it in order. Granddad hired another instructor, and man, she's *da bomb*."

"That doesn't surprise me," Ashton said. "Granddad knows a leg when he sees one."

"Tell me about it. As soon as we modernize this riding school, I want us to get to work on Underwood Systems."

"Anything wrong?"

"On the contrary. It's beginning to explode, and I'm wondering if we should move the operation from Frederick to Baltimore."

"It's a thought, but you're right. We modernize one company at a time. Excuse me a minute." He pushed the intercom button.

"Attorney Hayes on line three, Mr. Underwood."

He opened the line. "Underwood. What do you have for me?"

"We've done it. Underwood Enterprises now owns Skate newspapers, and we got the deal on our terms. You're the CEO, and you call all the shots. It seems old man Skate is not well. His only child, a daughter, is an addict, and his wife isn't up to being the chief operating officer, so the deal excludes them. You own it lock, stock, and barrel."

"You've done a great job. I'm extremely pleased. Did you hear any of that?" he asked Cade, who had remained on the line.

"Some of it. We own Skate?"

"Right. We and we alone. Hayes will send a note on it to you, Damon and Granddad. Now, if we can just hold back Barber-Smith, we can concentrate on building our businesses."

"Ashton, relax. I am not worried about Barber-Smith. Smith is an old fool, and Barber has no business acumen and leaves business matters to Smith, who's his brother-in-law. Let's increase our shares of Dream by the end of tomorrow. And you work on your girl. She's choice, man."

He didn't need anybody to remind him of that. If only some way could be found to remove the problems attending her celebrity. He couldn't and wouldn't even consider asking her to choose another writing genre. That was her profession, and she had worked hard to earn the recognition that she received. But, by damn, he had to provide a stable environment for his son. If the three of them went to a restaurant…he didn't want to think of what would happen.

"But I love her, and I have to deal with it."

Felicia faced another, and equally compelling, dilemma, and in that connection, she phoned a colleague, Duke Jackson, financial columnist and editor of the paper's business section. "Duke, this is Felicia. Would you clear something up for me, please?" She gave him the information available to her on the proposed takeover of Dream. "You know I'm following that story. Underwood wouldn't tell me what he's doing to ward off the takeover, so I'm left with skimpy coverage."

"My Lord, Felicia. The man would be stupid to give you that information. Smith would clobber him less than twenty-four hours after the paper came out. In that game, surprise is what matters."

"Thanks, Duke. I'll stop pressing. I definitely do not want to be a nuisance, because I have a feeling that this story has barely begun. Thanks."

"My pleasure."

She'd heard rumors that the Underwoods were buying stock in Dream, the perfect opener for her column, but if that was Ashton's weapon against Barber-Smith, she couldn't wreck his plan by publishing it. For the first time in her career as a journalist, she deliberately sat on a piece of news.

"I can't help it," she said to herself. "I'm not going to write anything that will adversely affect his business. Besides," she rationalized, "only the rich care about the buying and selling of stocks, and my refusal to use this information definitely won't hurt them."

She telephoned Miles, her brother, for his opinion on her decision. "If you do that," he said, "it's because you feel a lot for him. I'm not asking you how far this thing has developed, but I do know that the two of you don't have an understanding. If you did, you would discuss the rumor with him and ask him how he'd feel about your printing it. I want you to get an understanding with this man, Felicia. Please don't drift into an affair with him and find yourself with a broken heart five years down the road."

"I don't intend to do that, Miles, even though I…I'm nuts about him."

"If that's the case, you don't hold the cards, sis."

"Maybe not, but I've got the music that makes him dance."

She loved hearing Miles laugh. It always started in the pit of his belly and rolled up slowly like water beginning to boil. "Maybe *now*. But you be careful. A man with sense doesn't rush out to buy what he can get for nothing. And another thing. I want to meet his man."

"I'll bring him to see you, provided he ever gives me a reason."

"That's precisely my point. When is he going to give you a reason? End of discussion. I got a note from Aunt Lou. She said Papa's not well, but I'm not exercising my behind to go to California to see him."

"He definitely wasn't there when we needed him, but—"

"It's up to you, sis. I don't want to embarrass him or to lay a guilt trip on him by showing up in order to help him breathe his last breath. Besides, I'd botch it. I don't feel a thing for him, and why should I? I haven't seen or heard from him directly in thirty-three years, and I'm forty years old. To hell with him! I cried enough about him when I was seven."

"I don't even remember what he looks like," Felicia said. "Anyway, he made the choice, I didn't. And he's one reason why I can't stand philanderers. He remarried the same day that his divorce from our mother was final. I wish him well. Thank God for Uncle Adam, God rest his soul."

"Amen to that. See if you can get some tickets to a good show. I think I'll take a trip to the Big Apple. Make it a Friday or Saturday."

"Okay. I'm so glad you're coming up. See you soon."

"Right, and don't forget anything I told you."

Felicia took pride in her brother. Miles Parker was a Distinguished Professor of Law at GW and a frequent media consultant. "I won't. 'Bye for now."

"By the way," Miles said. "Is Damon Underwood related to Ashton Underwood?"

"Why, yes. Damon is Ashton's youngest brother. Why?"

"He just passed the national bar exams with high marks, and it's his first attempt. That's a good show. As I recall, he took a class under me and got the top grade. Be seeing you."

She hung up and dialed Ashton's office number. "Hi," she began when he answered. "I was talking with my brother a minute ago, and he told me that Damon just passed his national bar exams. I'm not sure Damon knows it, yet. He made a high score, too."

"Thanks for telling me. Mind if I hang up, call Damon and then call you back?"

"Of course I don't mind. Congratulate him for me."

Minutes later, she answered her phone and heard Ashton's voice. "My brother is delighted. He hadn't heard the news, and probably wouldn't have known he passed until he received a notice in the mail. He's a happy man. I had intended to ask if you'd like to go with me to the Village Vanguard tonight. Horton's there. I hope you don't have another engagement."

"I'd love to go," she told him. "What time?"

"What if I'm at your place at a quarter of eight, and we make the nine o'clock show? I want to have dinner at home with Teddy tonight."

"Fine. See you then."

"Is there a reason why I can't have a kiss?"

She made the sound of a kiss. "'Bye."

On the way home after work, she bought a pair of horn-rimmed glasses and a reddish-brown curly wig that, she had to admit, looked great on her.

"This disguise should give us some privacy," she told herself. The idea of disguising herself for any reason gave her an odd feeling, however, for she didn't regard herself as a celebrity or even as a famous person. If she were a political columnist, nobody would approach her, she figured, because frivolous people rarely became attached to a serious writer: they neither read nor appreciated literary work.

At home, she made a shrimp salad and garnished it with slices of tomato and avocado, toasted one slice of whole wheat bread, made a cup of tea and sat down to eat her dinner and to read over what she'd written for the next day's column.

She had to keep her mind off Ashton; thinking of him interfered with her work. When the pages that she turned reflected his face, she closed her notebook, went into her living room and sat down.

She rarely allowed herself the luxury of enjoying her apartment. Now, she gazed around her, seeing the brown-velvet sofa, the beige overstuffed velvet chairs and the brown-and-gold Tabriz carpet as Ashton must have seen them. She'd chosen each item carefully, but she was most pleased with the walnut unit that housed her television, books, curios, valuable crystal vases and other important things. She kicked off her shoes, rested her feet on the brass-framed glass coffee table and crossed her ankles. The entire apartment bespoke elegance and not a small amount of money, but it wasn't a home. To her mind, a home sheltered a family.

Oh, why had she allowed Ashton Underwood into her life? If he'd wanted to settle down, he would already have done it. That man only had to whistle and he'd have more choices that he could sample in a month. And she should stop fooling herself; she wanted to spend the rest of her life with him. She showered, dressed in a yellow seer-sucker suit and white sandals and flipped on the television set while waiting for Ashton.

A few minutes before seven, the telephone rang and shivers crawled down her spine as she went to the tele-phone. A strange feeling told her that something was amiss. "Hello? This is Felicia."

"Miss Parker, Mr. Ashton asked me to let you know that he has to cancel your date. He's very sorry."

Her heart began to race. "Is anything wrong, miss?"

"Yes, ma'am. It's Teddy. Mr. Ash took him to the emergency room."

She sat down. "The hospital? Which hospital?"

"Columbia Presbyterian."

"Are you Mr. Underwood's housekeeper?"

"Yes, ma'am."

"Thank you for calling me. Good night." Felicia got the telephone book, found the hospital's address, grabbed her pocketbook and left. She hailed a taxi at the corner of Central Park West and Seventy-third Street and a few minutes later stood at the hospital's information desk.

"Did you register Theodore or Teddy Underwood in emergency within the last couple of hours?"

The woman eyed her dispassionately. "Yes, he's here, but you can't visit this time of night unless you're a close relative, a parent or sibling. Are you his mother?"

Felicia presented her *New York Evening Journal* ID. "I'm his mother."

The woman recognized the name Felicia Parker and didn't question the absence of the name Underwood. "This way, Miss Parker." She called a guard. "Jack would you please take Miss Parker to room E-7L?"

Felicia thanked the woman and hurried along behind the guard who seemed determined to give her a good workout. At the E section, the guard spoke with a nurse who escorted Felicia to Teddy's room. Ashton sat on the side of Teddy's bed holding the child's hands.

"Ashton, how is he? Tell me what happened? Is he all right?"

Ashton appeared startled at first as his head came up suddenly, and he blinked several times, as if to assure himself that she was not a mirage. "Felicia. I don't know how he is yet. He ate something that he's evidently allergic to. Eartha thinks it was endives. It's the first time he had those. They've pumped his stomach and given him medicine, but he's still not himself. He's full of gas, has chest pains and stomach pains. And the worst part is that he can't stay awake."

She pulled a chair close to the bed and sat down. "The medicine may be making him sleepy. Excuse me. I want to speak with the nurse." She rushed to the nurse's station. "Miss, I saw a bubble in the intravenous feeder."

Without a word, the nurse bolted from her desk and ran down the hall to Teddy's room. When Felicia arrived there, she found the nurse adjusting the tube. After she finished, the nurse examined Teddy with her stethoscope, and Felicia could see the woman breathe a sigh of relief. "Thank goodness you were here," the nurse said as she left them.

"What was that about?" Ashton asked her.

She didn't want to alarm him, so she said, "That tube wasn't set up properly, and I told the nurse."

Ashton's eyes narrowed. "That nurse seemed frightened when she ran in here. Whatever it was, was serious, wasn't it?"

Felicia nodded. "Yes, but all's well that ends well. Right?"

He took her hand and held it. "Thank you for coming. I hope you don't like endives."

"Actually, I do," she said. "Anyway, you're not sure what caused it, are you? Perhaps it was a combination of things."

"That's what the doctor said. We gave them a list of everything he's eaten today and the time he ate it."

"Ashton, do you mind if I get a closer look at him. I want to see him."

"Of course I don't mind."

She leaned over and looked at the small replica of Ashton. "He's a beautiful child, Ashton, and he's so much like you." She continued to look at Teddy, and suddenly she leaned down and kissed his cheek.

"Why were you shaking your head?" Ashton asked her.

"I—I just can't figure how anybody wouldn't love him. He's… I'm sorry. I shouldn't have said that."

He squeezed her fingers. "That's all right. I often think that myself. He's a wonderful child. I'm…fortunate to have him. He's…" His voice broke, and when she put her arms around him, he relaxed in her embrace. "He's got to be all right. I don't know what I'd do without him."

She held Ashton close while she whispered a prayer for the child's healing. "He'll be fine. I'm going to the cafeteria and get you something to eat. Would you eat a ham sandwich and drink some coffee?"

"I don't want you to leave, but I'm hungry. I didn't get any lunch today, and I didn't have a chance to eat dinner."

"Would you like me to call the housekeeper? She seemed upset when we spoke."

"Good grief, I forgot that. You can't use a cell phone in here, so if you'd call her while you're in the cafeteria, I'd appreciate it. Her name is Eartha Clarke."

She stopped at the nurses' station. "Nurse, Teddy seems so…so pallid. Do you think he ingested something poisonous?"

"No. He's allergic to something, but don't worry, he'll come out of it. He's already much better than when he came." The woman's arms stroked her shoulder in a gesture of comfort. "We can be thankful that your husband noticed the changes in Teddy and got him here in a hurry."

"Thank you," Felicia said, and hurried to the elevator. She should have told the nurse that Ashton was not her husband, but if she did that, she wouldn't be able to stay with him. When the elevator reached the basement, she stepped out and dialed Ashton's home phone number.

"Miss Clarke, this is Felicia Parker," she said, when the woman answered. "I'm at the hospital, and Mr. Underwood wants you to know that the nurse thinks Teddy is out of danger. I don't know what time Mr. Underwood will be home or whether Teddy will be with him when he gets there."

"Thanks for calling me, Miss Parker. I've been out of my mind. Lord, if anything happened to Teddy, I'd die. The precious little thing is like my own child. I'm so glad he's going to be all right. Do you think I should keep Mr. Ash's dinner warm?"

"I doubt it. Get some rest. Goodbye."

She bought the sandwiches, coffee for each of them, and some grapes. When she got back to the room, the nurse was examining Teddy, and Ashton paced the floor with a frantic expression on his face.

Felicia rushed to Ashton. "What is it?"

"He began to perspire, so I called the nurse. I thought he was getting better, and this…this—"

She put the food on the table beside Teddy's bed and went back to Ashton. "I know you're worried, but have faith. He'll come out of it a well and happy little boy."

"I want to believe that." He walked over to the nurse. "Why doesn't he wake up?"

"The medicine makes him sleep. He should wake up in about half an hour, when the medicine wears off. Talk to him. He'll recognize your voice. Right now, all his vital signs are normal, but I'll ask the doctor to take a look at him so you'll be less stressed."

The nurse left them, and they sat on the side of the child's bed and ate their sandwiches. Ashton nearly spilled the coffee when Teddy said, "Where are we, Daddy?"

He put the coffee on the table and gathered Teddy into his arms. "We're in the hospital because you ate something that made you sick."

"As soon as I drank that juice, I started to hurt."

"What juice did you drink?"

"I don't know what it was. Can we go home?"

"I'll ask the doctor."

"Who's she, Daddy?"

"Her name is Felicia, but you have to call her Miss Parker."

"Do you have any little boys for me to play with, Miss Parker?"

"No, Teddy. I wish I did."

"Oh. Maybe my daddy can find you a little boy. Daddy, I'm hungry."

The muscles of Ashton's face worked furiously, but he didn't manage to hold back the grin that altered the contours of lips. "Out of the mouths of babes—"

"I know the rest," she said.

Immediately, Ashton's mood switched to serious. "You can't know what it has meant to me that you came here tonight," he told her. "I won't forget it. I'd never felt so alone."

"What else could I do? I know how much you love him, and I knew you were miserable. It didn't occur to me not to come."

"Excuse me a minute," Ashton said to Felicia. "I'll be right back." He placed his son in bed and pulled the sheet over him. "I'll be right back, son."

"I'm going to be sick," Teddy said.

She grabbed the towel at the foot of his bed, picked him up and held him while he gagged. "What on earth?" Ashton said when he came back. "What…Good Lord!"

"It's dangerous for a child to regurgitate while lying down," she said. "Anyway, he warned me."

"But your dress. It's—"

"It's hardly soiled at all. The towel caught most of it."

"I'm sorry, Miss Parker."

"Ashton, would you wet this washcloth in some cold water, please?" She laid Teddy on the bed. "It's all right. You were a smart little boy and you warned me." She took the wet cloth from Ashton and washed Teddy's face. "Don't you feel better?"

"Yes, ma'am."

She leaned over and kissed Teddy's cheek. "You'll be well and back home in no time."

"Gee," he said. "You smell so good. Can I have another kiss?"

She didn't look at Ashton, but cradled the child in her arms and kissed his cheek. She knew that Ashton hadn't been ready for her to meet his son, for he had avoided inviting her to his home. But she wouldn't refuse the child a kiss, and especially not since she enjoyed the exchange. When she straightened to a sitting position, he grabbed her shoulders with both hands and, standing behind her, said nothing, but communicated with a gentle touch an emotion that she knew possessed him. After a minute, she turned and he pressed her face to his belly.

He leaned down and kissed the top of her head. "Looks as if it's out of my hands." She didn't ask what he meant, because she knew.

* * *

A little after seven the next morning, the doctor told Ashton that Teddy could go home, but that he shouldn't eat anything exotic for the next two days. "He's in no danger, Mr. Underwood. You'll get a report on what we think caused this as soon as I get it from our laboratory. Fine boy you have here."

"Thank you, Doctor." He left the hospital with one arm holding Teddy and his other hand locked tightly with Felicia's hand. It had been one of the most stressful nights of his life, almost as bad as the hours in which he'd waited for Karla's decision as to whether she would marry him and deliver the child or have an abortion and go her way.

"I'll take a taxi home," Felicia said. "There's no point in your dragging Teddy by my place."

"You're right. I'll grab a couple hours of sleep and call you later. I won't thank you, because I can't." He leaned forward and brushed her lips with his own.

Teddy held out both arms to her. "Can I have a kiss, too, Miss Parker?" She kissed Teddy's cheek and, to Ashton's amazement, Teddy's face shone with the most beautiful smile he'd ever seen on his child. Teddy waved at her. "Goodbye, Miss Parker."

"Goodbye, Teddy."

"Why can't she come with us, Daddy?"

"She has to go to work." It was a lame answer, and he knew it wouldn't be Teddy's last question about Felicia. The child had the memory of an elephant, and he would nag until he either lost interest or got an answer that satisfied him. "She smells good, Daddy."

Didn't he know it! "She does, indeed, son."

In spite of his happiness in learning that Felicia was

there for him if he needed her, in knowing that she hadn't hesitated to hold Teddy at the risk of ruining her dress, and in seeing in her the maternal instincts that Eartha lacked and Teddy needed so badly in a woman, he felt that his life was suddenly being orchestrated for him.

That afternoon, less refreshed after a short nap than he would have preferred, he opened his copy of the *New York Evening Journal* and turned directly to Felicia's column. He read it and relaxed; the editor hadn't changed one word. He looked at his watch and saw that it was exactly one-thirty, an hour before the markets closed.

He phoned his broker. "Any action on Dream today?"

"Quite a bit in the last hour. It's up four dollars a share, and I expect it will really jump tomorrow, after people read the afternoon papers."

He thanked the man and contemplated his next move. Smith obviously hadn't increased his shares, because he would have bought a big block. So far, so good.

Felicia telephoned him one evening and told him that her brother would be in town to see a play, and that she would like them to meet. As he listened, the feeling resurfaced that he wasn't running his life.

Nonetheless, he told her, "I'll be delighted to meet your brother. Is he the one who's a law professor at GW?"

"Yes. I only have one brother, Ashton. How about dinner at my place Friday at seven?"

"I'll look forward to it. I presume you brother will be staying with you."

"Unless he has some connections that he hasn't told me about, yes. How's Teddy?"

"As good as new. He considers the trip to the hospital to have been a great adventure."

"He's a child who gets to you, a chip off the old block. Did you discover what made him sick?"

"Eartha makes a tea of aloe and rosemary for her arthritis, and he decided to taste it when she left the kitchen. Whether it was that drink or the fact that he drank it after eating ice cream, we don't know, but we're sure the aloe triggered it. He's used to food seasoned with fresh rosemary. I gave him a good talking to, and he convinced me that he won't drink anything unless either Eartha or I give it to him."

They spoke for a few minutes. "If your brother is leaving Sunday, can we have dinner together Sunday evening?"

"I'd like that," she said. "I'll wear my horn-rimmed glasses and reddish-brown wig."

"Your *what?*"

"That's what I had on when Eartha phoned me the night Teddy got sick. I figure no one will recognize me, and you won't have to get bent out of shape."

"Well, at least you'll look normal when I see you Friday night."

Now what? He wondered how much Felicia had told her brother of their relationship, and how modern an outlook her brother possessed. *Oh, hell, I have to trust her and my feelings for her, but I'll be damned if I'll be backed into marriage. When I'm ready for that, I'll shout it so loud that it'll echo from the mountains of Switzerland.*

He arrived at Felicia's apartment precisely at seven o'clock, wary, but sure of himself. He'd sent her a bunch of purple-and-white orchid sprigs and a basket containing three bottles of wine, one red bottle of Châteauneuf du

Pape, and two bottles of Pouilly-Fuissé, a white burgundy, earlier that afternoon. He rarely took advantage of his wealth to put special touches on little things, but he knew that Felicia's brother would watch his every move, and he wanted her to be proud of him.

When she opened the door wearing a shimmering red silk jumpsuit, and bunches of gold coins swinging from her ears, he thought his eyes would leave his head. Did she expect him to spend the evening looking at her in that getup without touching her? He kissed her on the mouth, deciding that he didn't care who stood behind her.

"Hi. You look good enough to eat. If the dinner is anything like you, beware!"

Hearing her warm and exciting laughter, he forgot about his misgivings. "Thanks for the flowers and the wine," she said, gave him a quick hug—he hadn't expected that, either—took his hand and walked with him to her living room.

"Miles, this is Ashton Underwood. Ashton, this is my brother, Miles Parker."

He didn't know what he had expected, but he experienced surprise at seeing the man. About an inch taller than his own six feet, three inches, Miles Underwood appeared as fit as a track champion, unlike the kind of man who sits bent over law books and students' papers. A handsome, smartly dressed man, he bore a strong resemblance to his sister.

"I'm delighted to meet you, Ashton," Miles Underwood said, and gripped his hand in a warm and sincere handshake.

"And I'm pleased to meet you," he said, and meant it. "Felicia has met some of my family, my younger brother, in fact."

"Yes," Miles said, his eyes twinkling. "I think I've met him, too. He took one of my courses on corporate law. I hope he's not planning to be a criminal lawyer. He excelled in that class."

"I think he's planning to be a corporate lawyer. He'll open an office in Frederick, but I suspect he'll move to Baltimore within a year."

"What would you like to drink, Ashton?" Felicia asked him. "Did you drive or take a taxi?"

"Taxi. Do you have any bourbon?" Her eyebrows shot up, and he knew that was because he never drank hard liquor.

"I do indeed." She served hot hors d'oeuvres, broiled bacon-wrapped liver, thumbnail-size quiches and grilled shrimp.

"Keep bringing this good stuff," Miles said, "and I won't need any dinner."

"Me, neither," Ashton said, enjoying the male support.

"I watched that great show you two put on for cable television," Miles said. "I'm sure that by now you're sick of hearing about it, but indulge me, that was a great show."

He leaned back and decided to enjoy himself. "It was the red dress, man. Drape Felicia in red, and she could stop an army. Look at her in that red thing she's got on now."

Miles's lower lip dropped, but only for a split second. He crossed his knee, sipped his scotch and said, "Man after my own heart. I was wondering about that."

"Keep it up, you two, and I'll be the only one who gets any dinner here," Felicia said.

She had annoyance plastered all over her demeanor, but he didn't care. She wanted to blow his mind with that outfit, and she'd better be glad her brother was here or, by now, he'd have had it off her, that and everything else she had on.

"Dinner is served, gentlemen."

She really laid it on. A seven-course meal fit for the most discriminating palate. "You're a terrific cook. I wouldn't have dreamed that a professional woman would be so domestically efficient."

"Thanks," she said. "It's simple. I put my whole heart, mind and energy into everything that I do." Felicia returned to the kitchen out of earshot.

He made the mistake of glancing at Miles and saw that the man looked at him for a reaction. Her insinuation wasn't lost on her brother. "You and Felicia are very close," Miles said, "at least, so I've gleaned this evening, casual though the two you have attempted to behave. So, what are your intentions?"

If the man had shot him, he wouldn't have been more surprised. After nearly three hours of good food, wine and conversation, Miles Parker got down to business and, Ashton suspected, his reason for coming to New York in the first place.

"Don't you think Felicia's old enough to look after her own personal affairs?" he asked Miles, serving notice that he could spar with the best of them.

Miles's lips parted in a grin. "Did she ever ask you that question?"

"No."

"Then she doesn't look after her affairs properly. We're talking about my baby sister, man."

He calmed his temper. The man had a right to ask. He sat forward and looked Miles in the eye. "Does Felicia know we're discussing this?"

"If she did, she'd raise hell."

"There's nothing casual about my relationship with

Felicia. I'm deeply in love with her, and she loves me. But I haven't made up my mind that I can handle her popularity. Go out to dinner with her, and you'll see what I mean. I came damned near socking a man who interrupted my date when he came to our table to make sure she saw him and would mention him in her column. Minutes later, a has-been actress walked over and demanded that Felicia autograph a card and mention her in her column. I have a four-year-old son, and I'm doing all I can to give him a stable environment. The three of us would never be able to have a meal undisturbed in any good restaurant."

"Didn't you expect this?"

"How would I? Man, I don't associate with celebrities and affluent people who're looking for the limelight. I eat dinner at home, go to the neighborhood movie, and I don't have a box at the Metropolitan Opera or Avery Fisher Hall."

"I see. How does she get on with your son? I don't really need to ask because Felicia's nuts about small children."

"They've only been together once, and I got the impression that they would get along very well."

"You say you love her, and I believe you. I suppose you know she's impatient. If she decides you're not going her way, she may love you, but she'll still walk."

"I definitely believe that, but I'm going to do everything I can to prevent her from walking out on me."

"The guaranteed way is to ask her to marry you. If she says no, and she might, she's responsible for the effect of her decision."

"You're right, of course, but—"

"I know. You are the master of your fate."

"Evidently not when it comes to women. I—"

Felicia walked in, carrying a flaming baked Alaska. "Sorry this took so long, but it can't be done in advance." She sat down, began to slice the dessert. "What happened to the conversation? Say, were you two talking about me?"

When neither he nor Miles answered, she narrowed her eyes. "To which one of you should I direct my ire?"

Ashton looked at Miles and quickly raised both hands, palms out. "Not me. Why would you be angry with me?"

"Don't look at me," Miles said. "I haven't done anything except have a pleasant and gratifying conversation with your guest. Incidentally, is that baked Alaska?" She nodded and continued to slice the dessert. "It's my favorite," Miles said to Ashton, "and she makes it every time I come, but this is the first time she's flamed it."

"I know you're getting me off the topic," she said to Miles, "but if you did what I suspected, I'll settle with you later."

At eleven, he figured he couldn't stay longer, but the more he looked at Felicia in that red jumpsuit, the hotter he got, and that gourmet dinner accompanied by good wine and followed by fine aperitifs did nothing to appease his libido. He could get used to sharing that kind of life with the beautiful woman facing him. *Fancy thoughts.*

He stood and shook hands with Miles. "It's been a genuine pleasure meeting you. I must be going." He turned to Felicia. "Thanks for a most wonderful meal and a precious evening."

She took his hand and walked with him to the door. "You're a fantastic hostess," he told her, "and what a cook! This was a wonderful evening."

"Thanks. Did my brother ask you what your intentions were?"

He couldn't help laughing. "He'll tell you all about our conversation as soon as I'm out of this door. I'm certain of it." At last he had her in his arms and his tongue in her mouth. "Easy, sweetheart. The minute I looked at you when you opened the door, I wanted to take you to bed. It got worse by the minute, and I've been looking at you for four hours." He kissed her lips, squeezed her close, and enjoyed the feel of her nipples against his chest. *Get it together, man. Her brother's sitting in there.* "I'll call you tomorrow," he said in guttural tones that betrayed his emotions. "By the way, I like your brother."

As soon as he stepped out of the building, he stopped, faced the rising wind and inhaled deeply a few times. A taxi slowed down, but he ignored it and began walking. He needed the exercise, and if he'd been wearing sneakers, he would have jogged home. At Broadway, two blocks from his house on Riverside Drive, a panhandler stopped him.

"I'm a foolish man, mister. I allowed myself to be scammed out of everything I owned, and now I'm flat broke. I need a job, and I need money for some food. Can you help me?"

From the corner of his eye, he saw a squad car parked not far away and decided that he could take a chance. He'd just had a satisfying meal and didn't feel like sending the man away hungry, that is if he was telling the truth.

"How about going with me over there to McDonald's, friend? I'll see that you get a decent meal."

"You serious? I'm not dressed up like you, man, but I sure will go with you. I haven't sat down to a decent meal in I don't know when. You wouldn't have one of those towelettes, would you? I'd like to wash my hands."

"I'm sure McDonald's has a restroom."

He sat at the little table waiting for the man to get back from the restroom so that he could order and pay for the food and go on home. "I may not get the chance again soon," the man said when he returned, "so I washed up and shaved as best I could. I never liked hair on my face."

Ashton's attention was suddenly riveted on the man. This guy was not a bum. "My name's Ashton Underwood," he said, motioning for the man to sit down.

"Ron Peters. You're an exceptional person, Mr. Underwood."

"Not really. Order whatever you want, and then we'll talk." He waited until the man finished eating before he asked him, "What kind of scam cleaned you out?"

"Two outstanding citizens inveigled me into investing in a sure thing. It was such a sure thing, that I borrowed the money to invest and put my house up for collateral. They took the money and made off with it, but thank God, their asses are behind bars. Unfortunately, I'm left with nothing."

"Why didn't you declare bankruptcy? That would have given you some relief."

"Because I believe in paying my debts."

Point in the man's favor. "What kind of work did you do?"

"I had a business that distributed prepared gourmet meals, bottled milk to subscribers, bread to restaurants, and other things. I've even had a kids livery service. But I lost all my trucks when I lost my house."

Ashton thought for a minute. If his instincts served him well, Ron Peters was a decent man. He wrote his office number on a piece of paper. "Call me at this number Monday around nine." He handed the man a fifty dollar bill. "This should keep you going until then."

Ron stared at the money, then focused his gaze on Ashton. "Is this real money? I'm going to buy myself a cup of good coffee first thing tomorrow morning. And you look to hear from me Monday morning. I won't try to thank you, but you know how I feel right now."

"I can well imagine. We'll speak Monday." He bade the man goodbye and left McDonald's thinking of his own good fortune. It had taken less than a minute in Ron Peters's presence for him to forget about his raving libido. "That was a jolt that I needed," he said to himself as he inserted his key into the lock on his front door. "I need to shift my focus for a while. If I still feel this way about her two months from now…no, six weeks, I'll ask her to go home with me to meet Granddad and Cade. I have to be certain, and right now, although I'm leaning that way, I am still not positive."

He raced up the stairs and tiptoed into Teddy's room. As he leaned over the sleeping child, his heart seemed to swell with love. And then the picture of Felicia walking into Teddy's room at the hospital, concerned and uncertain of her welcome, flashed through his mind's eye. If he gave them the chance, they would love each other. So what was he waiting for? He was an intelligent man, and he knew he couldn't expect certainty in a relationship. Why couldn't he be like Teddy…ready to open his arms and accept love? He reminded himself that he hadn't loved Karla, and that she hadn't professed to love him. So why couldn't he trust his relationship with Felicia?

"I've got to get a grip on this. If I don't, and soon, I'll lose her."

Chapter 7

At the moment, Felicia wasn't of the same mind, but by the time Miles returned home to Washington, D.C., she would be. She took a minute to compose herself after Ashton left her, then strolled nonchalantly back into the living room to face her brother's judgment.

"Ashton Underwood is not your average man," Miles began. "He's in love with you. He said so, though I had already guessed it. But being in love with you is not the only fuel driving his engine, sis. That man's head rules him. Yes, I asked him about his intentions, and he told me. He loves you, but in so many words he's not certain you're for him. He's very much concerned about your celebrity."

She flopped down in the overstuffed chair facing Miles, unmindful of the air of elegance that she had made a part of her being. "He told you that?"

"He's honest, as straight as the crow flies. I don't know

when I've met a man I liked as much as I like him after so short a time with him. I'd like to see you marry him, but the two of you are so much alike that I'm not sure it would work."

She slowed down her breathing in the hope of making her heart beat slower. "You think I'm like Ashton?"

"Absolutely. His main concern is his child. He doesn't want the boy exposed to the fame-seekers who hang around you. You know, I've never heard of a rich man living as simply and as privately as he says he lives. His idea of a wonderful evening is to barbecue hot dogs or hamburgers with Teddy in his backyard."

"I know how he loves that child, Miles, and Teddy looks exactly like him. He's so sweet."

"Underwood said that you love him, and he's right. But don't expect your relationship to gel easily. Do you know anything about his marriage and why he's divorced with custody of his son?"

"Yes. They married because she was pregnant. He begged her not to have an abortion, and she finally consented to carry it to term, with the understanding that the child was his to raise and care for. He married her and took care of her during her pregnancy. At the divorce, she didn't even want alimony, only her freedom, a ticket to Italy and one thousand dollars for hard times."

He sat forward and a frown settled on his face. "I never heard of such a thing. Were they dating casually?"

"So he said. They weren't in love."

"Is he bitter about it?"

"I don't think so, although I sense that he tries to be both mother and father to his son."

"Be careful, sis. I'd hate to see you brokenhearted about this guy, but there's a good possibility that you will be."

She leaned back, closed her eyes and let the truth flow out of her. "A little over ten years ago, I thought I was in love, and I left myself open to a horrible disappointment. In ten years, I didn't give a man a serious second look. Then, I saw Ashton Underwood leaning against that registration desk in the Willard Hotel. By the time he walked over to me, introduced himself and said, 'I'm your escort for the evening,' I was already a goner. That was then. The difference now is that I know *why* he poleaxed me and why he sometimes still does. He's as deep inside of me as anybody will ever get. If he wants to walk, I'll be miserable for the rest of my life, but I definitely won't die over it."

Miles looked toward the ceiling, frowned and an expression of pain drifted over his face. "You're in love with the man, so instead of telling yourself how stoic you can be if he walks out on you, do what's necessary to guarantee that he never leaves you no matter what happens."

"How do I do that?"

"If a man gets what he needs from a woman, and I'm not talking about sex alone, he goes nowhere. Understanding, loyalty, camaraderie and genuine friendship keep a relationship going. If that isn't working, sex will be the last thing on his mind. Be there when he needs you, and no matter how much you want a raise at that paper, never print anything that's against his interest."

"But it's my duty as a reporter to report the news, and to do it honestly."

"You may one day have a chance to decide what means most to you, your job or Ashton Underwood. I think I'll turn in. What are we seeing tomorrow night?"

"'Sound of the Trumpet.' It got rave reviews."

Miles yawned. "Great. This has been a delightful evening. See you in the morning." He kissed her forehead, headed for the guest room and left her to contemplate what he'd said about Ashton and Ashton's attitude toward her. It didn't take a mind reader to know why he had never invited her to his home: he didn't want his child to bond with her, because he didn't think their relationship had a chance of being permanent.

Miles looked at the relationship from a man's point of view; but from hers, she saw no reason why she should hang around waiting for Ashton Underwood to dump her. *The thing for me to do is to develop an interest in another man.*

The next morning, Saturday, after preparing breakfast for Miles and herself, Felicia got the papers at her front door and then sat down to eat. She gave Miles the paper for which she wrote, opened the *Brooklyn Press* as she did every morning, and turned to the column by Reese Hall, her principal competitor.

"What's the matter?" Miles asked, and she realized that her eyes had widened and her lower lip sagged.

"Would you believe this? That man spent four hours here last evening and didn't remember to tell me that he'd bought Skate newspapers. My paper is a Skate paper, and by damn, he knows it. This does it!"

Miles turned a page, picked up his coffee cup and took a long sip. "The man came to dinner. He wasn't here to discuss business."

She dropped the paper on the table and threw up her hands. "*Business?* The man's now my boss. He should've told me."

"And ruin his evening? Why would he do that? When did the deal go through?"

"Yesterday, according to this gossiping wench."

Miles threw back his head and let the laughter pour out of him. "I'll be damned. You pick up the paper, and the first thing you read is your rival's column. I'll never understand women."

"You'll understand them before I understand men, especially this one," Felicia shot back at him." She took the dishes to the kitchen, returned with the coffeepot and topped off their coffee. "And you can bet, brother dear, that I won't be holding the bag this time."

The following Monday morning, Ashton sat at his desk trying to figure out what he regarded as the cool reception he received from Felicia when he'd called to thank her for what he considered an unusually pleasant evening. Maybe she was reserved because her brother might have heard her end of the conversation. He hoped so. But shouldn't she have called him back and explained?

"No point in creating a problem where there isn't one," he said to himself. A call from Ron Peters took his mind off the matter.

"Underwood speaking," he said when Ron asked for him. "You're punctual. That recommends a man to me. I'm planning to change the way my newspapers are delivered locally. I don't promise anything, but I'd like to talk with you about it."

"I thank you, Mr. Underwood, but could you give me a chance to go by Goodwill and see if I can pick up something to wear? I could do that this morning and see you this afternoon."

He'd wanted to work out his plan that morning and discuss it with Damon in the afternoon, but the man didn't want to walk into an office looking like a bum. He appreciated that. He gave Ron the address. "Try to get here by three."

"I'll be there, sir."

He'd bought Skate newspapers at what he regarded as a bargain because management had allowed its sales and distribution systems to become outmoded. He intended to make changes right at the start.

Ron Peters arrived on time looking far better than expected considering his resources. After greeting the man, he told him about the distribution problem and that he intended to change it.

"The only way to distribute anything on a daily basis in a city like New York is to have your own trucks," Ron said. "Distribution is different from the kind of service that UPS, Fedex and those guys offer. You gotta get those papers out in a hurricane, a snow storm, sleet, every kind of weather, and on Sunday and every holiday. To do that, you gotta have men responsible directly to you. Now, I'm not trying to tell you how to run your business, but I built my delivery service on the fact that distributors often disappointed the small businessman. You know what I'm saying?"

He did indeed. "And, Mr. Underwood," Ron went on. "Those big trucks don't hack it anymore, 'cause they can't go everywhere. A good size minivan can go on any highway, over any bridge, or through any tunnel that takes a passenger car. So you save gas on two counts."

Ashton studied the man for a few minutes. "Do you have a family?"

Ron shook his head, and his personality appeared deflated. "All that went down the drain when I lost everything else. I guess that part was my fault. You can't be a man if you don't have the price of an egg. We didn't have children, so I told my wife to go back to her folks, and I guess she was glad to do it. She filed for divorce right away, and I didn't contest it. I cashed my one Series E Bond, lived at the Y and hunted for work till my money ran out. You know the rest."

"Then you can work in Philadelphia?"

He sat forward, his eyes lit up, and his entire body seemed primed for flight. "Mr. Underwood, I can work anywhere you got a job. I'm tired of living like an animal. I can do better if I just get a chance."

"I believe you. Can you plan route patterns for newspaper drop-offs in New York City?"

"Yes, sir, from the Bronx to Staten Island, I know this city like the back of my hand. I've driven a taxi here, delivered for stores, you name it. I know this town. You just give me the addresses. Yes, sir, this is right up my alley. Yes, sir."

Ashton called his secretary. "Find an office for Mr. Peters, please, and give him the list of the merchants that carry our papers." He looked at Peters. "You'll get eight-fifty a week to start, but you'll soon be working directly on the distribution, and your salary will increase. Does that suit you? I suspect you'll need a salary advance, too. I'll see to it."

Ron stared at Ashton. "Eight-fifty what?"

"Eight hundred and fifty dollars."

"Lord, yes to everything. I'm ready to work, provided I don't pass out from shock."

Ashton called Felicia. "Greetings, sweetheart," he said, hoping to inveigle her into a loving mood. "Honey, you kind of left me hanging when I called you this morning. How's Miles?"

"He's dressing. We're going downtown, and we won't be back until after the show. He wants to visit the Pierpont Morgan Library and Museum."

"I've been telling myself for years that I'm going there. Perhaps we can go together sometime."

"Miles is ready to go, and he's ready to bust out of his clothes if he has to wait. Talk with you later."

"Hey, wait a minute. Don't I get a kiss?" he said and, for once, it was a serious question.

She made the sound of a kiss. "'Bye."

"Something is not right. She came damned close to giving me a cold shoulder," he said out loud. "Just as I'm ready to commit fully to her, she let's me know how foolish I am." He sat there twirling a pencil and trying to figure out what had cooled off the hot woman who'd almost sent him into convulsions the night before in her slinky jumpsuit, spike-heeled sandals and teasing, unbound breasts, tidbits thrown at him in the presence of her big brother. "Look, and you can't touch" was the message.

He couldn't give up on that relationship easily, he knew, for he had invested too much of himself in her. He phoned Damon and got his brother's approval on the arrangements he'd made and planned to make with Ron Peters. Then he called his grandfather, talked for a while and turned his attention back to his work.

"Here're the morning papers, Mr. Underwood," the messenger said. He opened the *Brooklyn Press* and thumbed through it. His gaze caught Reese's column, a writer that he read only because she liked to take potshots at Felicia. But this time, he saw an announcement of his purchase of Skate newspapers. How had that leaked out so soon?

He snapped his fingers. So that was it. Felicia had also read the column, and she was angry because he hadn't told her of the purchase. He slapped his forehead with his right hand. *My Lord! I'm her boss. No wonder she's irritated.* He hadn't thought about the purchase in connection with her; certainly he'd given no thought to the fact that he owned the company for which she worked. *What a mess!* He considered calling her back and thought better of it. She should have voiced her concern; besides, she had already left home.

Ashton's failure to contact Felicia at that time proved to be a serious stumbling block in their relationship, for she had made up her mind to try and forget him by whatever means were available to her. A challenging means presented itself when she entered the Morgan mansion and Jeffrey Nash greeted Miles as only an old friend would.

After they threw high-fives and hugged each, Nash's gaze fell on Felicia. "Man, this lovely must be your sister," he said, "and thank God for that."

He didn't blot out the rest of the world as Ashton did, but the man was a number ten if she ever saw one. She extended her hand to accept his greeting, and wherever Jeffrey Nash had started now seemed unimportant in his scheme of things. He'd been on his way out of the building, but he now turned back and walked with them.

"You can't imagine how pleased I am to meet you," he

said. "Miles and I have been tight since we roomed together in undergraduate school. I knew he had a sister, but he was careful not to tell me how beautiful she is. What do you do?"

"I write a column for the *New York Evening Journal.*"

He released a subdued whistle. "You're *that* Felicia Parker? This *is* a pleasure." He took her hand and held it as if they had been lovers for years.

He amused her, but at the same time, she appreciated the attention. "Jeffrey. You move faster than a stud missile. May I please have my hand back?" But at that moment, she targeted Jeffrey Nash as the man who would ease Ashton Underwood out of her thoughts. She appealed to Jeffrey, and his every move broadcast his intention to go after her. She didn't consider how Miles would react to her plan.

As a first step, she didn't answer Ashton's telephone calls, believing that if she didn't hear his voice or see him, she wouldn't think of him. Instead, she allowed Jeffrey Nash to be her constant companion, taking her to dinner, meeting her at work, accompanying her on her reporting assignments, and taking her for long drives in Westchester and to whatever place she fancied. In spite of it, Ashton remained in her thoughts, although she smiled gaily as if her life had never been fuller or richer.

"I'm surprised at you," Miles told her one evening in late May when they talked by phone. "You know you're in love with Ashton Underwood, yet you're letting Jeffrey fall for you. Why are you doing this?"

"I'm not seeing Ashton, because I won't wait around until a man decides to dump me. Jeffrey cares a lot about me, and he's fun to be with."

"What? Underwood is in love with you...or was. If

he's got any sense, by now he's taught himself to get over you. I never would have believed you'd throw away that relationship."

"And I never would have believed he'd decide that I wasn't good enough for him."

"He didn't say that. I should have kept my mouth shut. I was trying to help you cement that affair, but you decided it was easier to run away than to mold your relationship with him into something permanent. Did you at least break it off graciously?"

"I, uh…stopped answering or returning his calls and…and we just drifted apart."

"He deserved better."

"Yes, I know, but if I talked to him or saw him…I—"

"You wouldn't have been able to go through with your stupid scheme, because you love Ashton Underwood, and he could change your mind at will. You're going to regret this. Look, I know Jeffrey has always been a ladies' man, and he probably deserves a couple of real hard knocks, considering how many he's dished out, but you don't have to be the woman to administer them."

After she hung up, a sense of loneliness pervaded her. She'd lost points with Miles, and…she checked the caller ID and answered the phone. "Hi, Jeffrey."

"Hi, sweetheart. It's nice out. How about going down to the Vivian Beaumont Theater at Lincoln Center? I'll get us some tickets. They're doing Jean Paul Sartre's 'No Exit.' I saw it once in Denmark years ago. It's fabulous."

"I'd love to, Jeffrey." At least she wouldn't be alone. "Are you wearing a jacket and tie?"

"Absolutely."

She liked the play well enough, but the subject matter

almost made her morose. Three people locked together for eternity—a lesbian, a nymphomaniac and a young but impotent man in a room that had no windows or doors. The lesbian wanted the nymphomaniac, and the nymphomaniac wanted the impotent man, who could do nothing for her. The play left Felicia badly in need of a pair of strong male arms.

"You're not talking much," Jeffrey said as they approached the building in which she lived.

"I guess that play made me sad."

"Unrequited love is a painful thing," he said. As usual he accompanied her to her apartment, and as she opened the door, he gazed down at her. "I want to come in with you." She pushed the door open and closed it behind him.

"I can offer you coffee or a glass of white wine," she said.

He shook his head, opened his arms and pulled her into his embrace. She put her hands on his shoulders to control the kiss, but he took charge of it, and within a few minutes fired her up as his hands roamed over her body, caressing and adoring her hips and breasts.

"Why not?" she said to herself. "If Ashton wanted me, he'd find a way to make things right." Jeffrey Nash picked her up and carried her to her bed. He wasted no time undressing her, and putting her between the satin sheets, but when he began to undress himself, she sat up, repelled at the thought of what she was about to do.

"Jeffrey, I can't. I'd give anything if I hadn't let it get this far, but I wanted to... I mean, I needed the affection. But I can't do this, Jeffrey. Please forgive me. I'm so ashamed."

He sat on the bed and looked at her. "For some reason, I'm not completely surprised. You've never opened yourself up to me. Something's always been lacking. Who is he, Felicia?"

"I won't cry. No matter how much this hurts, I am not going to cry," she told herself.

"Who is he?" Jeffrey repeated when she hesitated.

"John Ashton Underwood."

Jeffrey's eyebrows shot up. "And you're in love with him. You don't have to confirm it. I know you are." She nodded. He stood and began buttoning his shirt. "I'll let myself out." Halfway to her bedroom door, he turned. "I'm glad you didn't go through with it. My feelings run deep, and I'd have known if you faked it. I wish you luck."

She heard the front door close and fell over on her belly, mortified. How had she let herself think that she could let any man other that Ashton into her body? Yes, she needed love and affection, but not from Jeffrey, and she shouldn't have misled him.

"I'm not going to beat myself to death about it," she said out loud. "I learned a lesson that I won't forget." She showered, wrapped herself in a terry-cloth robe, went to the living room and watched late-night television until sleepiness sent her to bed. The next morning before leaving home, she telephoned the florist with whom she maintained an account and asked that she send Jeffrey a dozen white roses with a note that said "Thank you for understanding. Felicia." *It isn't atonement for what I did, but he will know that I know I was wrong.*

Little did Felicia know that her awkward behavior with Jeffrey would work in her favor. Ashton had known Jeffrey well since their days as undergraduates at Howard University, and receiving a phone call from Jeffrey did not surprise him. However, when Jeffrey asked to see him urgently and at his home, he hesitated.

"I gather this is important. Anything wrong, Jeff?"

"I'm not sure. You may think so, and that's why I want us to be together when we talk."

He didn't like the sound of it, but he regarded Jeffrey Nash as a friend and an honorable person, so he said, "I'll get Teddy to bed by seven-thirty, so come between then and eight. I'll ask Eartha to fix something that I can warm up, and we can have supper."

"Thanks, man, I'll be there shortly after seven-thirty."

Ashton left the office at four that afternoon, because he didn't want to rush Teddy to bed. He played the Barcarolle for the boy until he thought his fingers would cramp, but he enjoyed the child's expressions of joy whenever he played for him. Music fascinated Teddy, and he always sat quietly and listened to his favorite music.

"Thanks for the Barcarolle, Daddy. I'm going to learn how to play it."

"You have to practice more. That's what it takes." He put Teddy in bed and read Young-Robinson's *Chicken Wing,* the child's current favorite, until he thought Teddy was asleep.

"I'm going to start reading, Daddy, and then you won't have to read to me."

"I enjoy reading to you," he said, "but I want you to read."

"Okay. I'll see if I can learn to read and play the piano and do all the things Miss Eartha wants me to learn how to do. Why do I have to learn how to use the knife and fork, Daddy? I can eat with the spoon."

"Spoons have their uses, but not for everything. You're

trying to avoid going to sleep." He kissed Teddy's cheek.
"Good night, son." He wondered if Teddy had already
learned how to be sarcastic. He hoped not.

"'Night, Daddy."

He had just enough time to replace the button on Teddy's
shirt. The child loved that shirt and insisted on wearing it
every day. He also soiled it every day. Ashton sewed on the
button, went down to the basement and put the shirt in the
washing machine. With luck, he'd remember to put it in the
dryer before he went to bed. He put the casserole in the oven
to warm, looked in the refrigerator and found the salad. He
liked having his friends as guests, but not on Eartha's afternoon off. A note on the refrigerator door read "Apple pie on
the kitchen counter. Serve it with cheddar cheese, also on
the kitchen counter." The doorbell rang. He wiped his damp
hands on the back of his jeans and went to open the door.

"Hi. Come on in, man. It's great to see you. The food's
ready. I just had to warm it up."

"Thanks for having me on short notice."

Surprised at Jeffrey's formal manner, Ashton's head
jerked around. "You wanna talk now? I was thinking we'd
eat first."

"I don't know. I suppose it can wait."

Ashton put the chicken pot pie, green beans Southern-
style and the lettuce and tomato salad on the breakfast-
room table that Eartha had already set, sat down and said
grace. "Help yourself, Jeff. We have apple pie with cheddar cheese for dessert."

They spoke of the weather, the tennis championships
in Paris, their support of Habitat for Humanity and other
impersonal topics, as if they had never been college class-
mates and close friends.

"Do you mind if we eat the dessert later?" Jeffrey asked him. "I love apple pie, and I can enjoy it better if I get this business out of the way."

"Right. Let's go in here." In the den, Ashton poured two glasses of aged tawny port and sipped idly on his own while he waited.

"It's about Felicia Parker." Ashton bounced forward, spilling the wine on his jeans.

"What about her?"

"Not to worry, man. Her brother, Miles, and I are friends and occasional colleagues, and he introduced his sister to me when I ran into him recently. I don't mind telling you that I went for her, and we started seeing each other. Last night, I thought I was going to make it with her." He paused, and Ashton thought he'd never get his breath back.

"Don't get upset, now, Ashton, but she went so far as to let me put her in her bed, and then she told me she couldn't do it. She always kept some space between us, and I had sensed false gaiety in her. From the time I met her, she seemed hell-bent on being happy if it killed her.

"I'd never had a woman back out on me at that stage, and considering the type of woman Felicia is, I sat down and asked her who the man was. She said John Ashton Underwood, and admitted that she's in love with you. She said she was sorry she had encouraged me, but that she needed affection and thought she could do it. Anyway, this morning, I got a dozen, long-stemmed white roses and an apology from her. I thought over it after leaving her last night, and I realized that she had not encouraged me that much, but had accepted my company and my overtures of friendship. She has never telephoned me."

"I'm stunned. What the hell was she…" He gaped at the man before him who had just confessed to undressing and putting to bed the one woman he'd ever loved. He forced himself to remain sitting. Jeffrey didn't come to him to gloat. He was not that kind of man. Ashton rubbed his chin, deep in thought.

"All of a sudden, Felicia stopped returning my calls, and she didn't call me. I had a wonderful dinner—that she cooked—with her and Miles in her home, and when I left there, I was a reasonably happy man. Perhaps Miles advised her against our relationship."

"I don't know why he would," Jeffrey said. "I bumped into them at the Morgan Museum. Come to think of it, Miles didn't rush to make the introduction. Before you make a mistake here, buddy, get in touch with Felicia. I can't speak too highly of her, she's choice, man." Jeffrey leaned back in the chair, drained his glass of port and gave the appearance of one who'd just heaved a load from his shoulders. "I could use some of that pie."

"Yeah. Me, too. Thanks for telling me this, Jeff. You didn't have to do it, and I definitely will not forget it."

Several hours later, long after Jeffrey left him, Ashton sat on the deck overlooking his back garden, wondering what had caused Felicia to abandon their relationship. Somehow, he didn't think Miles spoke against him, for the two of them found common ground, and he enjoyed the man's company. Suddenly he remembered the question she asked him as he was about to leave that night. She'd wanted to know whether Miles asked what his intentions were toward her. He also remembered what he said to Miles, and if Miles repeated it to her, would she have become angry and thrown in the towel instead of helping him develop the relationship?

After musing over the matter for another hour, he slapped his thighs so hard that it hurt. "Damned right, she would," he said. It annoyed him that she focused on his concern for her celebrity rather than his telling her brother that he loved her. And as for his ownership of the paper she worked for, she didn't give him a chance to tell her. He intended to have some words with that lady. If she thought it was over between them, she couldn't be more mistaken. He had the proof that she loved him, and he meant to use it well, but knowing what he knew, he'd take his time. Didn't their confessions and promises to each other mean anything to her?

In spite of the loneliness that haunted her daily, Felicia worked long hours, writing and lecturing. Each day, she shifted her column closer to straight political coverage and commentary, and her editor offered no objections. She had some of her lectures at universities and conferences reprinted in the newspaper and posted some of them on the Internet in her newly created blog.

"I've got four TV interview requests for you," her editor told her one morning, "and three of them are from broadcast channels. Only one is a cable channel. The people must be asking for you. We've got a bunch of letters for you, too. You want to answer them yourself?"

"Thanks. I'd like to see 'em."

Why wasn't she dancing for joy? She was happy, yes, and she needed the recognition of her hard work, but she needed to share the joy...with Ashton.

After a challenging interview on one of the early morning TV shows, she realized that her prominence made her a target. She hadn't liked the interviewer, and she controlled her distaste with effort. However, her editor liked her performance.

"Senator Hoots has been lining his pockets," her editor told her, "and he's got a couple of allies. Where there are three, you'll find some more. Give me a column on it."

"Yes, *sir!*"

The following Monday, her story appeared with her name above the column's title. Pride suffused her. She'd made it at last. However, the paper's telephones rang constantly, and almost all of the calls had reference to Felicia's column, and many of the callers denounced and/or threatened her.

"John Underwood is on the phone, Felicia," her secretary said.

When she recovered her balance, she lifted the receiver. "Hello, Ashton."

"Hello, Felicia. I've been planning to make a personal call to you, but this isn't the one. I understand that the paper's phone is jammed with calls about your column, that the fax machine broke down because it became overheated with mail about your column, and that the e-mail box is full. More than half the mail is negative, and that's all right. People speak louder when they're against something than they do if they support a thing. But I'm told that most of those faxes and telegrams are threats against you." Chills streaked through her body, but she said nothing.

"Felicia, I don't want anything to happen to you. Nothing is worth it, not the news or the paper or anything. Please, Felicia, tone down the next column on this story. I—I couldn't…I can't let anything happen to you. These bigots are dangerous."

"I—I hear what you're saying, Ashton, but I have to do my job. Of course, if you say I can't do it, that you won't print it, I won't have a choice, will I? After all, you're the boss."

His long silence was evidence enough that she had either angered or hurt him, or both. "So that's the reason why you abandoned our relationship without so much as a go-to-hell. If you had returned my phone call, I would have told you. I hadn't signed the papers when the story got out, and I don't count my chicks before they hatch. At least your brother didn't speak against me."

She regretted her words and the bitterness with which she spoke them. "Don't blame Miles for anything. He's your best ally."

"Are you going to soften your stance?"

"If I did, I wouldn't recognize myself. I'm sorry, Ashton."

"Then you're going to have a bodyguard and bullet-proof transportation to and from work and on any professional trips. That's that, and I won't change my mind."

"You can't possibly be serious."

"The next time you start out of that building, even if it's an hour from now, you'll find out whether I'm joking. I need to talk with you, but I'll call you at home."

With chattering teeth and shaking fingers, she managed to place the phone on her desk, got up and walked across the room to the window. How dare he talk to her like that! She stood there for about a minute, taking deep breaths in the hope of calming herself, then she went back to her desk, sat down and said, "I suppose you hung up."

"I have better manners," he said.

"How dare you try to bully me, Ashton? Don't you know it won't work?"

She imagined his eyes narrowed when he said, "And don't you know that I am trying to protect you, to take care of you, since you haven't a clue as to what you've gotten yourself into? Woman, don't you know I care about you? Yes, dammit, you're going to have a bodyguard and an armored car. Period."

As if he'd punched the wind out of her, she slumped in her chair. "I didn't think it was that serious."

His voice softened to the mellifluous tone that always melted her heart. "Felicia, is your memory so short? I'm leaving tonight for Rose Hill, and when I get back, I want us to talk. Until then, search yourself to see if you can find any plausible reason for walking out on me, and while you're looking, remember that I can hurt as badly as you. I'll see you in a few days."

"'Bye," she said, thoroughly chastened.

Minutes later, her editor called. "You're to leave the building from the garage. Take the elevator down to the garage level and you'll see a gray Town Car in front of the elevator door with the license plate number 6WAJ50. The driver's name is Bob. Five minutes before you leave your office, call this number." She wrote down the number, thanked her editor and realized that, in exchange for success, she'd given up her freedom, for as badly as she wanted to, she knew she'd better not defy Ashton. He was not a frivolous man and he would not have ordered that level of protection for her unless he knew it was necessary.

Too concerned and too drained from her conversation with Ashton to concentrate on her work, she did what she'd always done when in trouble—she phoned Miles.

"I won't have any freedom," she told him after relating her conversation with Ashton. "Do you think all that's necessary? I'm tempted to ignore it."

"You really don't want this guy? Is that it? First, you

fool around with Jeffrey, although you know you're not interested in him as a lover. Ashton tries to protect you, not because he owns the paper you write for, but because he loves you and wants to take care of you. But you're so damned asinine, you want to prove you don't need him. Yet, you're in love with him. I don't get it. Go ahead and risk your life, so Ashton will realize how foolish he is."

"What do you mean?"

"After the way you treated him, I'm surprised that he cares at all. I wouldn't."

She hadn't wrung her hands since her mother died, but she balled and twisted them then. "Miles, I'm scared. I love that man so much that it frightens me. I know I didn't do the right thing, but he could have decided any day that…that he couldn't handle my lifestyle and just walk out, so—"

"So, expecting the worse, you walked out first? I can't think of anything more stupid. Talk with the guy. Not even in your next life will you find another man like that one, and a man that you'll love. My last word on the subject."

She had not encouraged Jeffrey to fall for her, but nonetheless she hoped she hadn't hurt him. No one knew better than she the pain of a lover's treachery. Besides, callousness was not in her nature. She couldn't work, so she decided to go home, access the Library of Congress through the Internet, and get some corroborating information on the senators for her column. She phoned her editor's secretary.

"Ray said I should let you know when I'm ready to leave."

"Yes, Miss Parker. The car and guard will be waiting."

She took the elevator to the garage, stepped out and saw the gray Town Car parked nearby. A tall no-nonsense-looking man got out of the car and held the back door open. She ignored him and walked around to check the license plate. Satisfied that she wasn't being duped, she thanked the man, and got in.

"So this is what it's like to capitulate," she said to herself. "And I hardly challenged him. I must love him more than I thought, because I certainly am not scared of anybody hurting me. I wish I knew where this was going."

"I'm Bob, Miss Parker. I'll try to stay out of your way, but I'll always have my eye on you. You're safe with me."

"Thank you, Bob. I don't doubt it one bit." What she did doubt was her ability to tolerate the loss of her freedom. "I'm going to have a talk with Ashton about this. It's more than I'm prepared to suffer."

Ashton would have preferred not to take Teddy with him to Rose Hill, but he wanted his son to know his uncles and, especially, his great-grandfather. He dressed in a tan summer suit, a white short-sleeved dress shirt, white shoes and socks, and dressed Teddy identically.

"I'm dressed like you, Daddy. Now everybody will know you're my daddy."

"They'd know that if we weren't dressed alike. Tie your shoes. You don't want us to miss the plane, do you?"

"You tie them, Daddy. When I do it, they always get loose." He sat Teddy on the bed, tied the boy's shoes, picked up their luggage and headed downstairs.

"Wait for me, Daddy. I have to find the picture I drew for Granddad."

Ashton dropped their bags at the bottom of the stairs and looked up at the little replica of himself, his reason for being. "All right, two minutes."

"I only need one, Daddy." Ashton couldn't help laughing. Teddy wanted everything spelled out, and if you didn't do it, he would. Within a minute, the boy joined him, but he still wasn't ready to leave the house.

"I have to show Miss Eartha how I look. She says I always get dirty. Am I dirty, Daddy?"

"Of course not, you just put that on. No more stalling here. We have to make that flight."

"You mean I'm flying? Gee." He ran back to the breakfast room. "Miss Eartha, I'm flying to Rose Hill. 'Bye."

Their plane landed in Frederick, and Ashton drove them on to Rose Hill in a rented Chevrolet. Anxious to see the improvements in the building and to examine the new tack, he stopped first at the Rose Hill Riding School.

"I don't have to ask who you are," the blonde said to him. "I've met Cade and Damon, so you have to be Ashton. Never saw such resemblance."

"All things considered," he replied dryly, "you're the new riding instructor. Is Cade around?"

"He went home a minute ago, but don't worry. You're safe. I don't bite."

Not sure whether he faced antagonism or her brand of humor, he said, "I rarely worry about anything. If I can fix the problem, I do that. If I can't, I accept that fact and get on with my life. What's your name?"

"Leslie Fields."

"Glad to meet you, Ms. Fields. I'll see Cade at home."

Granddad had really done it this time. Ashton got in the car and drove on to the house and, to his surprise, Teddy jumped out and raced to his great-grandfather with his arms outspread and a glowing smile on his face. "Granddad. I brought you a picture I drew for you."

Jake picked the boy up and hugged him with love glowing in his face.

After embracing his grandfather, Ashton said, "Grand-dad, I know you like pretty women, but Leslie Fields takes the cake. Can she teach anybody how to ride a horse?"

Jake ran his hands through his thinning hair. "She's really something. Yeah, she can teach, and she's quite a jumper. Cade seems taken with her."

"What? You're kidding."

"No, I'm not. If you think Leslie's a sex pot, you're in for a stunner. She's an intellectual, and she teaches physics at the university, but she loves the outdoors. So she's teaching at the riding school during the summer. In October, she'll be back at the university."

Ashton sent a sharp whistle zinging through the air. "Danged if she didn't fool me. I should have realized she had something to back up that sharp tongue."

"Oh, she's actually a very gracious woman."

"I see. If Cade's happy with her, so am I."

"Where's Miss Parker? Didn't I ask you to bring her the next time you came?"

"Miss Parker and I have to iron out the wrinkles in our relationship. If we do that to suit us both, I'll bring her."

Chapter 8

Ashton put his bags in his room and went to find his brother, Cade. "I figured you'd be out here," he said to Cade when he found him lounging beside the pool. "I wasn't prepared for Leslie Fields. I expected somebody around forty, muscular, makeup-free and flat-chested."

Cade released a sound that could be called a snicker, raised both eyebrows and then showed all his teeth in a grin, rare for him. "You're joking. Not in a million years would Granddad choose a woman who wouldn't finish in the top five of a Miss America contest. He can't tell me he picked her for her riding skills. He got lucky. The old man may be over eighty, but he still knows a woman when he sees one."

"So do you, from what I hear."

Cade closed his eyes and relaxed in the lounge chair. "She's a breath of fresh air."

"Don't tell me you sit around here talking physics and computer science with that woman. She's Halle Berry and Marilyn Monroe rolled into one."

"After a while, you don't notice it. I don't think she's aware of it," Cade said, and put on his sunglasses.

"Well, I'll be damned. You've always been unsparingly honest with yourself and candid with everybody else. Don't you want to like her? You do, you know."

"I don't know, Ash. I don't know how the hell I feel about it or about her."

The seriousness of his brother's tone worried Ashton. He sat on a nearby chair. "How does she feel about you?"

"That's one of the problems. Neither of us is the type to start a relationship in a hurry. It looks to me as if we're tiptoeing around each other, postponing the moment when we'll precipitate an explosion. It'll be like throwing a lighted torch in a gushing oil well."

"Whew! Are you planning to do anything about it?"

Cade's shoulder flexed in a shrug that didn't fool Ashton. "If she wanted an affair, she could have a dozen, and I am not jumping out on that 'love-me' limb again, brother. No sirree!"

"Too bad. You're going to be very unhappy." He thought of Felicia, how he missed her and how badly he needed her.

"Yeah. Better to be miserable because I'm smart than to be miserable because I was a fool."

"That sounds like a new kind of logic to me, but who am I to judge?"

"Right. How are things with you and Felicia? If I had a sister like her, I could discuss these problems that I'm having."

"You'd do no such thing, so can the hints. We're off-track right now, but I intend to work on it as soon as I get back to New York."

"Glad to hear it. Who's fault was it, yours or hers?"

"Ours, but I don't mind making the first move. She means a lot to me."

Cade sat up and pulled off his sunglasses. "You're in love with her? Is that what you're telling me?"

"Yeah. Now that I'm CEO of Skate newspapers, and she works for one of them, she's uptight."

"Good Lord. I didn't think about that. Whatever you do, don't get heavy-handed with her."

"I did." He told Cade about the column on dishonest congressmen and the reaction of readers. "I ordered her to use that limousine with a bodyguard, and I'm not sorry. If I can get within five inches of her, I'll straighten it out."

"Don't let it drag on. How does she get on with Teddy?"

"So far so good. Come to think of it, I'd better find out what he's doing. He'll twist Granddad around his finger."

That evening, he sat around the chrome barbecue and grill machine with his brothers, his granddad and his son. The adults talked of the changes in their business enterprise, and their changing roles in it.

"Now that Damon is taking on the job of legal counsel, what do we do about the escort service?" Jake asked. "Seems to me it's a source of civil suits against us. We've been lucky that none of the men have gotten out of hand."

"I vote we sell the business. Obviously, there's a need for it, so we shouldn't disband it," Cade said. "It's served its purpose, anyway. Without it, Ash probably wouldn't have met Felicia Parker. I say put it up for sale."

"I agree," Ashton said. "We sell the escort service, we

get a principal to manage the riding school, and another instructor to teach animal husbandry. Anything else?" When none of them offered another suggestion or asked a question, he said, "Okay. Teddy and I will be heading out tomorrow morning."

"Can I stay here with Granddad and Uncle Cade, Daddy? I won't bribe Granddad anymore. Honest."

Ashton looked at his grandfather. "Did he try to bribe you?"

"Well…he's too little for that, but—"

Ashton walked over to the grill, got a plate of food and gave it to Teddy. "Eat that, and go to bed. I'll deal with you tomorrow."

"Yes, sir."

At two-thirty the next afternoon, Ashton walked into his house, greeted Eartha, and dashed up stairs to his room with Teddy right behind him. He changed the boy's clothes, went to his own room and sat down. Cade had said, "Don't let it drag on," and he was right. The longer a problem existed, the bigger it got. He dialed Felicia's office phone number.

"Felicia Parker speaking."

"This is Ashton. I need to see you, and I'd like to meet you when you leave work today. It's important to me, Felicia." The long silence drilled an opening in the pit of his belly. He had no choice but to wait for her answer as sweat beaded on his forehead.

Finally, she said, "I…uh…have to go home. Can't we meet at my house at about seven?"

He let out a long breath, closed his eyes and gave silent thanks. "That's fine with me. Why don't I make a dinner reservation someplace?"

"Let's not go to any place fancy. How about Peter's Backyard down in The Village?"

"I haven't been there in ages, but why not. The food's great. I'll see you at seven." He hung up. Why had she decided to go home first? He hoped she only wanted to freshen up, that she wasn't concerned that her colleagues might see them together. No matter, at least she wanted to be with him.

Felicia had been expecting Ashton's call, but neither his tone nor his suggestion. It occurred to her that she would have to explain her behavior during the past three weeks, and that if she wasn't truthful, if she didn't tell him why she'd backed away from him, she could forget about him. Ashton would know if she withheld the truth. And what of the things they never talked about? Important things, like Teddy, the child's relationship with his mother—if he had one—and most basic of all, where he wanted or didn't want their relationship to go. He knew whether she suited him physically, what she was like as a lover, just as she knew he was the man for her. But other than his distaste for the publicity-seekers, and his admiration for her work, what did he really think of her as a woman? She didn't know, and it was time she found out.

The doorbell rang at seven o'clock precisely, and she dashed down the hall toward it. Stopping so short that she nearly twisted her ankle, she leaned against the wall, verging on hyperventilation. "Good Lord, I have to get myself together. I can't let him see me like this." The bell rang again, and she forced herself to straighten up and walk to the door.

"Hi."

"Hi. I thought you'd decided not to open the door."

She stared up at him. Had his long-lashed olive-brown eyes always been so beautiful and so enticing? Were they the reason she loved him so? Her gaze wandered down to his perfectly knotted yellow-and-gray paisley tie and back up to the eyes that now signaled what she needed most to see. She gripped his shoulders and the expression in his eyes nearly unglued her. He stepped inside the foyer, kicked the door closed with the heel of his foot and lifted her into his arms. Her hands went to the back of his head and he plunged his tongue into her waiting mouth.

More. She had to have more of him. A sweet and wrenching hunger settle in her. It had been so long. Lord, so long. He moved in and out of her, showing her what he'd do to her if he got the chance, and her hips began the slow dance of love. Try as she would, she couldn't control the passion that now roared out of control, and she tried to climb his body. He leaned against the wall, letting it take his weight, locked his hands on her hips and held her still.

"You'll never imagine how much I've missed you," he told her, "and as badly as we need to make love right now, we need an understanding before we get to that."

She groped for her sense of humor, hoping to add levity to what was almost an embarrassing situation. "And if you don't get any food," she said, "you won't have any energy."

His eyes sparkled with wicked glints. "If you think *you* won't need energy, you're fooling yourself."

Realizing the import of what she'd said, she leaned back and glared at him. "You misunderstood me perfectly."

Oh, how his laughter thrilled her! She tightened her arms around him and kissed his lips. "You're addictive,

Ashton. There's no other plausible explanation for this. Let's go eat."

"Me? Addictive? I'd begun to think something quite the opposite. But we'll get to that later."

A limousine pulled up in front of the apartment building as they walked out to the street. To her surprise, Bob got out and opened the back door. "Good evening, Mr. Underwood, Miss Parker."

They greeted Bob and settled into the backseat of the Town Car. "You think I need a bodyguard when I'm with you?" she asked him, a little peeved.

"I used to be pretty good with my fists back in the days when I was a teenager and used them, but I'm well out of practice. Besides," he said, making himself comfortable, "if there was a problem, I'd probably need a gun, and I don't have a license to carry one. That answer your question?"

"I told myself I wasn't going to bring that up, and I'm sorry I did. So, please let's drop it."

"Thanks," he said, and wrapped her hand in one of his. "New York is wonderful at night. Almost as busy as it is in the daytime, and far more colorful. I wonder about the night people, prowling the streets, looking for something to happen."

"Maybe they're lonely," Felicia said.

"Yeah." His voice took on a distant quality. "And this is one of the easiest places in the world in which to be lonely. And I mean lonely and alone."

Her head snapped around. "Are you telling me…I mean have *you* ever been lonely?"

"Felicia, I've been lonely. I've been alone and unhappy all at once."

"But surely being alone was your choice."

"When you didn't return my calls for three weeks, whatever I was experiencing as a result was not of my choice. Right?"

"No it wasn't, and let's eat dinner before we get into that," she said. His fingers tightened around hers, and his warmth flowed into her as a river empties itself into the sea. Her body moved itself closer to him, and he released her hand and eased his arm around her shoulder.

"Something tells me it'll take a genie to kill what's growing between you and me. Don't you sense that?" he asked her.

How could she tell him she sensed it when, although she prayed for it, her own actions worked against the chances of their having a permanent relationship? "I know there's a good basis for thinking that," she hedged.

"And I know that's all I'm likely to get out of you right now." The limousine stopped in front of the restaurant. "I'll phone you when we're ready to leave, Bob. Park in a garage somewhere, get your dinner and save the receipts."

"Thank you, sir."

"We have a crowd tonight," the waitress said. "Your table will be ready in about fifteen minutes. Would you like to have a seat at the bar?" He nodded, and she led them to the bar.

"Do you want to go somewhere else?" Ashton asked Felicia.

"Oh, no. But if I'd known I had to sit on this stool, I'd have worn a wider and longer skirt."

"That's no problem," he said, lifted her and placed her on the stool. Two men sitting nearby applauded. "Right on, man. Way to go!"

She ordered a spritzer, and when Ashton looked hard

at her, she explained, "You're going to ask me a lot of questions, and I need my full mental faculties."

He whispered in her ear, "Yes, I am."

She hadn't thought the noise at such a level that she couldn't hear him. When his breath caressed her ear, she turned to face him. "I may not be in the mood for teasing, Ashton."

The waitress came then and led them to their table. "I hope you don't mind the balcony," she said. "It's quieter there."

Felicia tried to be jocular and to exchange quips with Ashton, but that was not what she wanted from him. She needed him to love her, needed to explode with him buried deep inside of her. She wished she hadn't agreed to go to dinner, and had ordered something from one of the take-out restaurants on Columbus Avenue.

"What's the matter?" he asked her. "You're not your usual vivacious self."

"I know, and I'm sorry, but I have this awful feeling of an impending disaster."

He reached across the table and took her hand. "If you love me, what can you look forward to other than happiness? We're going to talk, because I want us to have a clean slate. After the way we greeted each other this evening, you ought to be feeling great. I am."

"You're not the one who put the skids on this relationship. I am, and I know I'm the one who has to pay up."

A grin sprinted across his face and he closed his left eye in a suggestive wink. "Yes, I know."

She gazed at him for a minute before her face slowly creased in a laugh. "You devil."

"But I'm precious, aren't I? I mean, you wouldn't

exchange me for any other man, now would you? Come on and fess up."

"I'll give that some thought," she said. "I don't like to make rash statements."

"Hmm. I see. That's a trait to be prized."

"You're laughing at me."

He poked his tongue in his cheek and made a stab at appearing serious. "Considering what I may be up against, you don't think *I'd* be that rash, do you?"

She hated to josh like that when she wasn't sure of her ground. She could banter with the best of them, provided there was no serious undercurrent. Nobody had to tell her that when they got back to her house and began to talk, there wouldn't be a smile on Ashton's face. He took his time with the chocolate cheesecake that he ordered for dessert, chewing slowly and sensuously as he looked into her eyes. She pushed away her sorbet, her taste for food gone, as her nipples tightened and tension gathered within her while she stared into the dark desire of his mesmerizing eyes. He placed his fork on the side of his dessert plate and beckoned for the waitress.

"May I have the bill, please?" He took out his cell phone and dialed Bob. "We'll be out front in about ten minutes."

He didn't kiss her in the car, and that disappointed her, though she should have known he wouldn't do that in the presence of a man who was obviously his employee. She didn't know what he said to Bob when they got out of the car, but she hoped he told the man that he'd finished work for the night.

"I'm going to make us some coffee," she told him in her apartment. She didn't especially want coffee, but having it would allow her to do something with her hands while they talked.

"All right, if you like, but please don't stay in there too long."

She made the coffee with Melita papers, poured it into an insulated pitcher, put it on a tray along with cups and saucers, milk and a spoon and was back within a few minutes. She placed it on the coffee table and sat on the sofa in front of it.

Ashton faced her in a chair, and when her surprise showed, he explained, "I want us to talk, and if I sit over there with you, talk will not be my priority. Why did you stop returning my calls?"

She realized that she had folded her arms across her middle in a posture of self-protection, and unfolded them. "I was scared, Ashton. I saw myself going through what I experienced a decade earlier, only this time, I had invested so much more of myself in the relationship. You told Miles that, although you loved me, you weren't satisfied that I was the woman for you. Did you expect me to sit around and wait for you to find a more suitable woman?"

He leaned forward and braced his hands on his knees. "And you didn't care enough to discuss it or even to find out what aspect of our relationship wasn't working for me? Don't you know that if a man really loves you—and I do— you can fix most anything that goes wrong? Anything short of infidelity, that is."

"That's what Miles said, but I was hurt. You had some shortcomings, too, Ashton."

"Of course I have, and we'll get to those as soon as we iron this out."

He wanted a clean slate, and so did she, so she wasn't

going to hold back a thing. "I agree that I should have talked with you, but I looked at that as begging to be accepted, and…well, that's not in me. I wasn't unfaithful, although I confess that I tried to be. I simply couldn't go through with it."

"I know."

She nearly swallowed her tongue. "You know *what?*"

"I've known Jeffrey Nash since college days. He told me, but he made it clear that you did nothing to encourage his feelings for you." He looked directly at her then with slightly narrowed eyes. "Sometimes I think you have no idea how attractive you are, and how alluring. Why did you try to go to bed with Jeffrey?"

"I can't stand a man who tattles," she said. "I wanted to get you out of my thoughts. I wanted to stop needing you. That's why. And, dammit, stop grilling me."

"I'm not grilling you, I need to know, and I can only find out by asking you. He wasn't tattling. He wanted to tell me that you loved me and that, if I loved you, I ought to get busy and shore up my relationship with you. He was being a friend. I had already had as much of your silence as I could take, Felicia. If he hadn't spoken to me, I'm not sure I would ever have made this move. You hurt me terribly."

"But you gave me a limousine and bodyguard. Was that a business move, or what?"

"You know it had nothing to do with business. I forced it on you because I needed to protect you."

She needed the answer to one question, and that meant raising the issue that had the potential for destroying their relationship, but she had to do it. "Why have you never invited me to your home? You're not married, and I don't think you're living with a woman. Why?"

With his elbows braced on his thighs, he rubbed his flat palms together, back and forth. "I didn't realize that that concerned you. I've never taken a woman home with me or invited one to visit me, because I don't want Teddy to see women parading in and out of my life. I also don't want him to think that having different women friends is necessarily a good thing. Most of all, I haven't wanted him to become attached to a woman, only to have her slip out of his life to be replaced by another one. I made up my mind when I was given his sole custody that until I was certain that I wanted a woman to be my life partner, I wouldn't introduce her to my son. As it happened, he met you and took to you at once."

"Did that bother you?"

"Not really. I saw it as an act of fate. Is there anything else about me that bothers you?"

"Why didn't you tell me you'd bought Skate newspapers? You spent an evening here and didn't say one word about it."

"I learned that morning that the deal went through, and I didn't want to say or do anything that might spoil the evening. I phoned you the next day with the hope that we could have lunch together, and I'd tell you about it, but you didn't answer my call then or anytime thereafter until today.

"Do you feel any resentment toward me?" Ashton asked her, and she could tell from his aura of concern and anxiety that the time had come to let go of her self-protective attitude and to trust that, because he loved her, he would not deliberately hurt her.

"Not that I recognize. I've missed you, and I confess that I didn't really understand who you are to me until I was repelled by the prospect Jeffrey Nash—a good-looking, kind and respectable man—would possess me. I think you and I asked each other to atone for someone else's sin. You're right to set a good example for Teddy and to protect him from ephemeral attachments to different mother substitutes. As I think of it, your policy in regard to Teddy is commendable."

She brushed a tear from her left eye. "I'm not crying— this eye likes to get teary." It was a time for the truth, not for posturing or withholding her feelings. If he was closer, and if he had his arms around her, maybe sharing what ached inside of her would be easier. It would have to wait for another, more intimate time.

She smiled to remove the emotional flavor of what she was about to say and lowered her gaze. "That night at the hospital…I… Teddy was so sweet. I wanted to hold him forever, and so would every other normal woman," she added as if she needed to defend a moment of weakness. "You haven't touched your coffee. I'll heat it," she said, changing the subject and, she hoped, the tenor of the conversation.

"Thanks, but I don't want any coffee. I want you, and I want us to see if we can make a go of this. Are you willing?" He was standing then, holding his arms wide, and she jumped up and sprang into them.

"There's been no one else since the first time I saw you," he said as his arms enfolded her. She stroked his cheek with loving hands, caressing and adoring him as he gazed down into her face. *Don't hide what you feel,* her head told her. *He needs to know that you adore him.*

"And there's been no one for me, Ashton."

He gazed down at her until the hot fire of desire roared through her, turning her limbs to liquid. He continued to stare at her, beguiling her with the lover's promise that raged in his eyes. She wanted to tell him to take her that minute, right there, but when she parted her lips, no words came and he plunged his tongue into her, rocking her senses. Her body recognized the touch of his fingers as they roamed over her back and buttocks, and responded to his loving. Her breasts, heavy and tight, begged for the warm tugging of his mouth, and she grasped his right hand, placed it on her left breast and sucked feverously on his tongue.

"What do you want? Tell me," he said.

"You know what I want. I need to feel your mouth on me. Honey, please!"

He freed her breast, pinched and rubbed it, toying with her while he twirled his tongue in her mouth. Frustrated by his denial of what he knew she wanted, she gripped his belt buckle, and getting no response, she slipped her hand lower and caressed him. His body jerked as if she'd sent a shot of electricity through him. He lifted her, lowered his head and sucked her nipple into his mouth, sending her blood on a mad rush to her loins.

"Ashton. Oh, Lord." He sucked vigorously as if he loved it, pulling her deeper into his mouth. She let out a keening cry. "Get into me now. I need you. I want you in me."

He picked her up and carried her to bed.

He could no longer deny it; he belonged to her as he was now certain that Felicia Parker belonged to him. He looked down into the face of the sated woman lying beneath him and knew that she was his morning sunrise and his evening shade. He'd have to learn to adjust to her public life, because he didn't see how he could live without her. Yet he wasn't ready to cross that final bridge. He didn't understand his hesitancy, and especially not after what they had just shared, but he believed in following his lights.

"I'm not going to see any other women, and I don't want you with any other man. I want us to see if we have what it takes to make a life together, and I don't mean shacking up. Will you agree to that?"

"Yes."

"And until this controversy about your column blows over, is it understood that you'll accept the car and body-guard whenever you step outside?"

"All right. It will never sit well with me, but I suppose it's for the best."

She wasn't going to like what he was about to say, but he couldn't help it. "Will you understand if I leave now? I have a nine-thirty meeting this morning, and I need to make some notes first. I'll make up for it. I promise."

With her hands at the back of his head, she brought his lips to hers. "Is everything all right between us?"

"As far as I can see. What about you?" he asked, wondering what had prompted her question.

"I'm happy. Call me tomorrow."

He was almost happy. If the uncertainty about Dream didn't pester him daily, he could coast on his achievements at least long enough to enjoy a two-week vacation somewhere with Felicia. By three o'clock that morning, he'd prepared himself as well as he could for the board meeting and by ten-thirty he was satisfied that the board stood with him one hundred percent in his fight with Barber-Smith. He adjourned the meeting and got busy familiarizing himself with the individual Skate newspapers.

He'd barely begun when his secretary brought him an indictment from a woman named Roma Jones, who claimed to have sustained a rash and other facial blemishes from use of the cream that made Dream famous and a best-seller. He sat at his desk, dumbfounded, wondering when life would stop screwing him. One day, he'd get a blessing, and the very next day, he would receive a curse.

"We'll fight it in court," Cade told him when they spoke. "Looks like there's no end to the calamities you can get in business. I just spent an hour teaching a mad-as-hell customer how to get a computer working, and while I was doing that, I lost a good half a million dollars and a new client who didn't have the patience to wait until I taught Miss Dufus how to start her computer. Have you called Damon about that suit?"

"I left a message on his cell phone. I'll talk with you later." He telephoned Felicia, knowing that her voice would raise his spirits. "I hope you slept well," he said. "I did, but my peace of mind was short-lived." He told her about the civil suit.

"Wait a minute. You're not going to take her word for it, are you?"

"What do you mean? If she's got skin blemishes, we don't know how she looked before."

"I'm sure your lawyer will tell you this. Have her take a skin test, and make sure it's administered by an independent chemist or other person. She's got to prove that. Some people will do and say anything for money."

"I didn't think of that. I'll get onto it right away. I haven't spoken with Damon about it yet, because he hasn't returned my call, but I won't wait for him. This is too important. I'm in your debt."

"No you aren't," she said. "What hurts you hurts me. Talk later. Kisses."

"I love you," he said, and hung up.

When Damon returned his call, Ashton told his brother what Felicia suggested.

"Absolutely," Damon said. "I wouldn't think of taking her word for it. Fax me a copy of the papers, and I'll get right on it."

The following morning, Thursday, Ashton opened a copy of the *Wall Street Journal* and shuddered when he saw that the value of Dream had plunged to its lowest point in months. He phoned his stock broker.

"What caused that action on Dream?"

"News travels fast, Ashton, and three papers carried the story of the Jones woman's suit against that product."

"But I only got the papers an hour and a half ago, which means somebody tipped off the papers no later than yesterday afternoon. I smell a rat."

"In this business, friend, they're all over the place."

A week later, Ashton opened results of the test and a feral expression froze on his face. He contacted a fraternity brother, a police captain, for the information he needed, got it, and phoned Damon.

"This is Ashton. I have the report, and Roma Jones is not allergic to that cream. The allergist put it behind her ears, on her neck and at her throat. No reaction whatever after three days. I want to know why she came up with that lie."

"Getting a court date takes a while. I suggest we indict her," Damon said, "and offer her a chance to plea bargain."

Faced with the prospect of a decade in jail, Roma Jones confessed that Barber-Smith paid her to make the claim and promised her that no one would know whether she was telling the truth, that allergies were temporary conditions.

At dinner with Felicia that evening, Ashton pondered his next move. "Industrial sabotage is a crime, and since I have a video of the woman making the statement in the presence of three policemen, I figure I'll get justice from Barber-Smith, but I need to get the value of that stock up."

"I think I can do something about that," Felicia said. "Send me a transcript of that tape. I'll publish it verbatim."

He stared at her. "In your column? You'd do that? Suppose your editor, what's his name, objects?"

"If he does, I'll remind him of who pays him."

Ashton couldn't help laughing. "Would you believe I hadn't thought of that?" He stroked the back of her hand, found that an unsatisfactory expression of his emotions, reached across the table and caressed her cheek. "You're precious. If you hadn't told me to have the woman tested, I might not have thought of it."

"Maybe not, but Damon would have. Can you fax me that transcript tomorrow?"

"I'll get it to you tonight."

"Then, let's go," she said. "Maybe I can rewrite my column for tomorrow. I have to fax it in by eleven."

Felicia wrote the story and ended it with a verbatim account of Roma Jones's testimony. Ashton asked himself time and again whether Felicia's work was that of a first-class journalist or of a woman in love fighting for her man. It didn't make sense that he wanted her to have done her best because of her feelings for him. Yet, how else could he explain his buoyant feelings when he read the article? A call from his broker confirmed that the column may have had a positive effect on the stock. He didn't telephone Felicia, for to do so would be to risk unloading all that he'd stored in his heart for her.

Two days later, he nearly jumped from his chair when his secretary handed him a copy of Felicia's interview with Roma Jones, in which the woman told of her meeting with Smith of Barber-Smith, her personal favors to him, and the amount he paid her to lie about the Dream cosmetic.

He phoned Felicia. "You actually interviewed her?" he asked Felicia after greeting her. "I can't believe she'd speak so freely with a reporter."

"There's more. I'm going to run this story a few more days. I see that the stock is up again today. This will teach old man Smith a lesson," Felicia said. "Roma Jones is a poor woman, a single parent, trying to care for three children. Even a few thousand dollars seemed like riches to her."

"I can imagine. Get her address, will you? Someday, perhaps I'll be able to thank you for what you're doing, but right now I can't find words that will do justice to what I feel."

"I don't want you to thank me, Ashton. It's enough that I've done something that makes you happy."

He couldn't answer, and not even telling her that he loved her seemed enough. He needed to love her, to show her what she meant to him. "May I see you tonight?" he heard himself ask her.

"I'd like that, and I'll try to get my column done this afternoon."

After he hung up, he told himself that he was on a nonstop, one-way train, and for the first time, the idea failed to disturb him.

That night, he went into her arms and into her body trembling with excitement and anticipation, overflowing with love.

The following Monday, Underwood Enterprises filed suit against Barber-Smith, charging industrial sabotage. The media picked up the story from Felicia's series of reports. And the value of Dream began an upward spiral to the financial advantage of Ashton, his brothers and his grandfather. In a call to his grandfather, Ashton told him, "Damon has done a great job with this case, but without Felicia, I doubt we'd be smiling now."

"Does she know you feel this way?" Jake asked him.

"I don't know. I tried to show her what she means to me."

"But you haven't done your best. She'll get the message when you bring her to see me, and I don't want you to wait till she's looking down at me lying in a box. I won't live forever."

"Yes, sir. I'll take care of it."

"See that you do." It wasn't the time, but he didn't tell his grandfather that. He had an important job to do and, as usual, he would not allow anything to interfere.

"I'll be in Mississippi for the next two weeks," he told Eartha several days later, "and you know that's not for publication, unless Teddy, Granddad or one of my brothers needs me." Each year, he took his turn helping to build a home for some underprivileged family. This year, the house would go to another of Katrina's victims. He kissed Teddy.

"Be good, son, and obey Miss Eartha. I'll be back in two weeks." He telephoned Felicia, but didn't get an answer at home or in her office. Disgusted and saddened, he headed for the airport and called once more when the boarding process started but, getting no answer, he satisfied himself with the notion that he'd call her from Mississippi.

* * *

Felicia couldn't know that Ashton tried but failed to reach her before leaving New York. At the time, she was speaking at a school in Chicago, and had turned off her cell phone. She didn't understand his silence and, after a week during which she experienced a feeling of alienation from him, she replaced her hurt pride with anger and telephoned him at home.

"He's out of town, Miss Felicia, and I can't reach him. His lawyer, you know…his brother, is trying to get hold of him. Something must be wrong. I'm going out of my mind. He never did this before. Teddy is worrying me to death."

"You're right, this doesn't seem like Ashton at all. If you'd like, I could go over and try to distract Teddy."

"Lord, Miss Felicia, I sure wish you would. The poor little thing is fretting so badly. This child loves his daddy. When are you coming over?"

"In about an hour." She stopped at a store, bought a building game and a stuffed tiger, and wondered what she'd do with a four-year-old boy who only wanted to see his father. Eartha opened the door, holding Teddy in her arms.

"You must be tired," she said to Eartha. "Teddy, I'm Felicia, how would you like to build a teepee? Some Americans once lived in teepees." She had his attention immediately. "Some Native Americans still live in them."

"Do you know any stories of Native Americans?" he asked her.

"I do," she said, and held out her arms to him.

"Daddy says I'm getting heavy," he told her and indicated a preference for standing on his feet. He led her to what she presumed was the family room, and said, "Tell me some stories, please."

She told him the story of Hiawatha, of Minnehaha and, when his appetite for the stories proved insatiable, she made up a few. He would laugh, slap his hands, and ask her if he could go play with the Native American children. She couldn't help but join in his infectious happiness and, after promising to visit him again, she had to force herself to leave.

At home that night, she devoted her column to an exposition of the treasure to be found in the company of a four-year-old boy. When she finished it, it occurred to her that she couldn't remember enjoying her work so much.

The next morning, she answered her phone and instead of Ashton's voice she greeted Eartha.

"Miss Parker, Teddy wants me to ask you to come back to see him, and he wants to talk to you, but I told him you were busy in your office."

"Thank you," she said, although she wanted to speak with the child. However, she thought it unwise to cross that line. If Ashton ever wanted her to develop a relationship with Teddy, he knew how to manage it. "Tell him I'll visit him again as soon as possible." She wondered what Ashton would think of her column. He knew Teddy and would guess that she'd written about him.

"Well, I can't help it if he freaks out," she said out loud. "He's the one responsible for this awkward situation."

To her chagrin, when she opened the pages of the *Brooklyn Press* two days later, keeping tabs on her competition, Reese Hall's column mocked her. She read, "Does Felicia Parker have a kid hidden away somewhere? That's not a casual relationship described in her column yester-

day. Something tells me the gal isn't what she's cracked up
to be." She folded the paper, wondering if the foolish
woman knew she had guided readers to Felicia's column.

Felicia wished she hadn't misplaced Cade's number.
She was becoming alarmed by Ashton's continued silence,
for if he didn't want to contact her—and she doubted
that—he certainly would stay in touch with his son. "If I
don't hear from him by tomorrow, I'm going to hire a de-
tective to locate Cade. She telephoned the escort service,
but the telephone had been disconnected. She whispered
a prayer for Ashton's safety.

After a day of grueling work, Ashton hitched a ride to
Jackson, the state capital, telephoned his home, spoke
with Teddy and Eartha, and read the newspapers. He
opened the paper to Felicia's syndicated column, read it
and found a seat in front of the public library where he
could sit and think. That column was about Teddy, and no
one could make him believe otherwise. Yet, neither Eartha
nor Teddy mentioned a visit from Felicia. He bought a
cone of frozen yogurt, enjoyed it and phoned Felicia.

"Ashton, where on earth are you? I've been on my way
out of my mind with worry. Nobody could reach you."

"I tried to call you before I left New York, but you
didn't answer your cell phone or your home phone, and I
knew you weren't in the office. I got down here and discovered that my cell phone wouldn't work, so for three
days I was out of contact with you and with Eartha and
Teddy. That was an intriguing column you wrote on the
joys of being with a small boy. I assume you and Teddy
got on well."

"We did. Eartha told me that he was becoming uncontrollable because he missed you, and she couldn't contact you, so I spent a couple of hours with him, and told him stories of Native Americans. He loved it."

"Thank you. I…uh…I don't like being away from him for any length of time, but what I'm doing is important. It's, uh, something I do annually, but this year, it's doubly important."

"When you want me to know about it, I suppose you'll tell me," she said, and he was sure he heard a note of resentment in her voice. He didn't do that hard work for credit or for recognition, but because he needed to pass some of his blessings on to his fellow man. Giving money would have been easy and painless, but he needed to give himself, sore muscles, blisters, splinters and all.

"I'm not doing anything unlawful, Felicia." Oh, what was he doing? She was the person closest to him after his son. "Sweetheart, when I get back, I'll tell you all about it. I've done this annually for the past five years, and I wouldn't miss it. I help build houses in Habitat for Humanity projects. I'm in Mississippi, and I'll be back after I've put in my two weeks."

"If you're calling now, why couldn't you call earlier? Did you have your cell phone repaired? Aren't there any other phones around?"

He didn't like being grilled in that tone, and said as much. "Felicia, surely you don't think I deliberately made it impossible for my son to reach me, not to speak of you. There isn't a telephone within several miles of where we're building, and my cell phone doesn't work there, as I already told you. What's the matter with you? I thought trust was more than belief that your lover doesn't fool around with other women. It's believing in him, period."

"Belief does not preclude the desire for explanations. It's enough that I believe you when you explain it."

Now, he'd stirred up her temper. "All right, sweetheart. I see I rang your bell. I suppose you have a right to question my silence, but you should—"

She interrupted him. "I trust you, and you know it. But I'm just recovering from my anxiety and fear for your well-being, and when you got testy with me, my temper shot up."

"Let's put it behind us. I love you, and I appreciate your soothing Teddy, not to mention Eartha. Whenever she gets upset and I'm not at home, Teddy loses his sense of security and shows it by being uncontrollable."

"You trust her, and you don't worry about her competence. But she feels the weight of that trust and of that responsibility," Felicia said.

"I suppose so. I hadn't thought of it that way. What about you? You're the caretaker of my heart."

"I know, and I haven't slept worth a dime since you told me. I mean, you don't have another one."

"Damned straight I don't. Handle with care."

"Sure I will, and you take care of mine."

"Not to worry, sweetheart. I've got it under lock and key. Be there for me when I get back?"

"With my arms wide open."

He hung up, stepped out of the phone booth and looked up at the clear blue sky. Maybe his ship had finally docked. If it hadn't, he was in for some rough times.

Chapter 9

Ashton couldn't miss Felicia's genuine affection for Teddy as he read her column, for her account of the child and his antics would lead one to believe that the boy was her own child. He opened a copy of the paper that contained Reese Hall's column, read it and, for the first time, found something in the woman's writing that pleased him: she, too, sensed Felicia's affection for Teddy. "I pray to God that I'm not on the wrong road here," he said, hailed a taxi and returned to the volunteers' camp.

Ashton didn't express concern about or disapproval of her visit with Teddy and Eartha so, when Eartha called her to say that Teddy wanted to speak with her, she took the phone.

"Miss Felicia, this is Teddy. I forgot all the stories you told me. Can you come over and tell me some more stories? My tiger is lonely. I think he wants to see you, too."

It occurred to her that charm might be inherited, for Teddy not only bore a startling resemblance to his father, but he also had Ashton's facial expressions and beguiling ways. "But your tiger has you," she said, testing the child's ability to make a case for himself.

"Yes, but he misses you. Honest. Can you come today? I promise to be very good. My daddy is building a house for poor children, and I don't know when he's coming home."

"He'll be home in about a week or ten days, I think, Teddy. I'll come over tomorrow, and we'll go somewhere."

"We will? Oh, I can't wait for tomorrow. I'll tell Miss Eartha. I love you, Miss Felicia."

"I love you, too, Teddy," she said, and sat down on the edge of her desk. She wasn't trying to teach Teddy to love her, and she wouldn't, but a feeling of apprehension pervaded her. Would Ashton think she'd deliberately gone behind his back and done the one thing he'd sought to avoid? Eartha was short on maternal instinct, though she loved Teddy, but the child needed more than she knew how to give.

The next day, Saturday, she packed a picnic basket and took a taxi to Ashton's home.

When Eartha opened the door for her, Teddy's squeals of delight thrilled her and, unable to contain her joy, she knelt with open arms and the child launched himself into them. She hugged his warm little body and fought back the tears when he kissed her cheek.

"Gee, you smell so good," he said.

She looked at Eartha. "I thought we might have a picnic

in Central Park. The weather is perfect, and later, we can stop at the children's zoo—"

Eartha interrupted her. "I'm already combing my hair. I'll be ready in a minute, and I'll get a blanket and a tablecloth. This is such a good idea. Teddy is getting sick of the inside of this house."

They entered Central Park at Seventy-second Street and Fifth Avenue. "Let's make a stop at the children's zoo," Felicia said, so Teddy could see the animals. Teddy's happiness proved contagious as he petted an alpaca, stroking and caressing it.

"I like this one, Miss Felicia. What is that one? Ooooooh. It's a goat. Is that a pig?" he asked, racing along the fence. "I want to play with the pig." He squatted and rubbed the Vietnamese potbellied pig, until the pig began to groan with pleasure. Teddy giggled with joy. "Can we come here again, Miss Felicia?"

She nodded. The child's excitement made her think of all she'd missed. In her drive to achieve her goals, she may have bypassed true happiness. She pulled in a deep breath and told herself it wasn't too late.

She and Eartha found a tree beneath which to enjoy their picnic. "Hot dogs!" Teddy shouted, clapping his hands. "I love hot dogs, Miss Felicia."

She poured from a thermos lemonade that she made the previous evening and chilled overnight, and it delighted her that both Teddy and Eartha approved of her choice. "Mr. Ash doesn't let him drink soft drinks. He says they're not good for his teeth. This is just perfect," Eartha said. Along with the hot dogs they ate deviled eggs, cherry tomatoes and strawberries.

"This is better than mashed potatoes, Miss Eartha. I wish you'd forget how to make mashed potatoes."

"No, indeed," Eartha said. "You want to eat French fries all the time. No way."

After they finished eating and Felicia repacked the picnic basket, Eartha produced a ball that was smaller that a basket ball but larger than a baseball and asked Teddy if he'd like to play catch.

"Maybe a little bit, Miss Eartha. Then can we go hear that music?"

Eartha's face bore a perplexed expression. "What music is he talking about?"

"Don't you hear it?" Teddy asked Felicia. She did and realized that he'd heard a jazz band from the direction of Sixty-sixth Street. After throwing the ball a few times and realizing that it held no interest for Teddy, they walked down to the Naumburg Bandshell where nine men played classical jazz. She didn't see or hear anyone that she recognized, but Teddy had already taken a seat and become absorbed in the music. It became evident that he especially liked the alto saxophone. After about an hour, Eartha announced that it was time to go home.

"I don't want to go," Teddy said. "I want to stay here."

"We have to leave now, Teddy," Felicia said.

Teddy's lip protruded and he folded his arms, giving notice that he meant to have his way. "I thought you told me that if I came to see you, you'd be very good," Felicia said. "I don't call this being good."

He looked up at her with the saddest eyes she'd ever seen. "I like the music, and I want to stay."

"We'll come another time," she said, "but we have to do as Miss Eartha says."

He stared at her as if he didn't believe her. "You, too? You're not a little boy. You're bigger than she is."

She couldn't help laughing, and she laughed so hard that Teddy soon joined her. "Teddy, adults also have to obey sometimes."

She wasn't sure he believed her, for he shook his head as if uncertain. No matter, she thought, when he slid out of the chair and took her hand.

"You must be a miracle maker," Eartha said. "Honey, when he digs his heels in, it's like that till Mr. Ash gets home and straightens him out."

"Stubborn, eh?" Felicia said.

"In a way," Eartha said. "Usually, you can reason with him. It's only when he misses his father that he gets difficult, and I can't say I blame him. Those two have a wonderful time together, but when Mr. Ash lays down the law, he means for Teddy to do as he says. He's a good man, I'm telling you."

Felicia sat in her living room that evening mending the silk case of an olive-green decorator pillow that had been cleaned too many times, glancing occasionally at a rerun of the "Cosby Show" on television, which she had tuned in primarily for company. The character, Rudy, although older than Teddy, nevertheless reminded her of him in her precociousness and seemingly innate charm. She recalled Teddy's rapt attention to the music of the jazz ensemble and his reluctance to leave it. It wouldn't hurt to determine whether he had a genuine interest in the music.

The next day, she stopped by a record store on her way home from work and bought CDs containing the music of Lester Young, Duke Ellington and Oscar Peterson.

"I don't know a thing about playing music," Eartha

told Felicia when she took the music to Teddy. "If you have time, would you please play them for Teddy?"

"That's just like the music we heard in Central Park," Teddy said, and Felicia's jaw sagged. He jumped up and down at the sound of Lester Young's alto saxophone rendition of "Back Home In Indiana."

"I like that," Teddy said.

"Did you ever hear that instrument before?"

"In Central Park. I'm going to ask my daddy to buy me a million CDs." He ran to her and hugged her. "Thank you, Miss Felicia. Gee, you smell so good."

She wondered to what extent Teddy had been introduced to music and asked Eartha, "Has Teddy been exposed to music?"

"Yes, indeedy. Mr. Ash is a terrific pianist, and Teddy loves to hear him play. He'll sit and listen as long as Mr. Ash plays."

She stared at Eartha, certain that her jaw sagged. "You mean to tell me that Ashton plays the piano that well?"

"He sure does," the woman said, in a voice filled with pride. "There isn't much that Mr. Ash can't do, from putting on a diaper to mending Teddy's clothes. This is a huge house, and I can't do everything and take care of the little one, too. So he helps me all he can."

She nearly said, *But he could hire additional help,* and was glad she didn't when Eartha looked at her and smiled. "Mr. Ash wants us to be like a family, and he doesn't want Teddy to grow up thinking somebody's around to wait on him and pick up after him. Teddy has to pick up after himself. And I tell you, he's such a sweet child. If you don't watch out, he'll wind you right 'round his little fingers." She laid her head to one side and appeared to muse over something. "Mr. Ash will do that to you, too. Sure as shootin'."

Didn't she know it! She made a mental note to discuss with Ashton Teddy's apparent interest in jazz. She'd had only modest training in music, but what she knew was sufficient to alert her to talent, and she suspected that Teddy had it. *I only hope he doesn't think I'm butting into something that's not my business.*

"Where the devil could they be?" Ashton dialed his home for the fifth time in one hour and still didn't get an answer. What if Teddy was ill and Eartha hadn't been able to reach him? "I'll call one more time, and then I'll…" He fished in his pocket until he found the little notepad on which he'd written Felicia's cellular phone number. It was his only hope, and he dialed the number with unsteady fingers, fearing that he would pass out from the pain in his foot.

"Hello?" Thank God, she answered.

"Sweetheart, this is Ashton. I can't find my family. I've been calling—"

She interrupted him. "They're fine, Ashton. I accepted Teddy's invitation to visit him, and decided to take him and Eartha on a picnic in Central Park. We also went to the children's zoo, and Teddy had a ball petting the animals. I'm sorry I didn't think to call and tell you where we'd gone."

"You couldn't have reached me. My cell phone doesn't work where we're building. Remember? I came into Jackson so I could make some calls, especially to you and to my home. So Teddy and Eartha are okay?"

"Yes. They're fine. Teddy loved the animals and…

Ashton, he heard jazz music and wanted to get closer, so we stopped at the band shell, and he didn't want to leave. I gather he loves the saxophone."

"Really? If so, it's the first I heard of it. Maybe he just wanted to stay in the park."

"Maybe, but that isn't the impression I got."

"Look, I…I'll call you back. I have to take care of something here." He hung up. "Just a minute, Doctor. I have to call my son. He's only four, and he gets upset if I'm away for long periods without contacting him."

He called his house and listened to Teddy's tale of his afternoon in Central Park. "Daddy, I'm going to ask Miss Felicia to come see me again. Why can't she stay here with me, Daddy?"

"She has to stay in her own home, son, but I'm sure she'll visit you when she can."

"But I want her to stay with me, Daddy."

"We'll discuss this after I get home." He wanted to speak with Eartha.

"Daddy, can we go listen to the music in the park? I liked it, Daddy. I'm going to ask Miss Felicia if we can go back."

"All right, but remember, she works, so don't use up all of her time. Do you understand?"

"She won't mind, Daddy. She loves me."

He'd like to know how a child that age judged love, because his granddad always said that children and dogs were better judges of people than adults were. After he hung up, an orderly helped him into a wheelchair, and he grimaced from the pain that the movement caused him. "Take it easy," the orderly said. "In a few minutes, you won't feel a thing."

"Yeah. That's what I'm afraid of." He'd been so concerned about Teddy and Eartha that he'd become careless and dropped a two-by-four plank on his left foot, injuring it.

"I'll have to set this bone," the doctor told him, "and I don't think you can handle it without a sedative, so I'm going to give you a shot that'll probably keep you out for three or four hours, depending on your tolerance for it. But first I need the name of a contact."

Ashton gave the doctor Cade's name and phone number and added, "Don't call my brother unless it's absolutely necessary, because he'd be here in a few hours."

"This is merely a matter of policy. I don't expect to call anyone. Now, take a couple of deep breaths and relax. I'll get some X-rays, put this baby in a cast, and you'll be as good as new."

However, when he awakened three hours later, he did not feel as good as new. His foot pained him, and he didn't like having to lie on his back, his least comfortable sleeping position. With effort, he raised himself to a sitting position, rang the bell and asked for his cell phone.

"You aren't allowed to use it," the nurse told him.

His stern expression could have been aimed at a recalcitrant child. "Miss, I am a single parent of a four-year-old who is at least five hundred miles from here and doesn't have any idea what the hell's going on with me or where I am. Hand me that cell phone, please."

"Yes, sir."

After speaking with Eartha and explaining to her the details of his accident and his present predicament, he talked with Teddy, who continued to rave about the jazz music.

"I'll take you to a jazz concert as soon as I can find a suitable one," he told Teddy.

"What's suitable, Daddy? Does it mean I have to grow up first?"

He couldn't help laughing. Teddy thought that all problems were solved by being grown. "No, son. It means I have to find a place where they play jazz."

"Oh. When are you coming home?"

"I'm not sure, but it won't be long." He hung up and reflected upon Teddy's interest in jazz. The child loved music and had since he was a few months old. And though he loved hearing him play the piano, he hadn't seemed enraptured by it...or had he? Perhaps he should pay closer attention to Teddy's musical interest.

He telephoned Felicia, and she entranced him with her account of Teddy's delight in the jazz CDs that she gave him. "What amazed me," she said, "was his ability to relate the CDs to the music we heard in the park. They contain the identical kind of music. The saxophonist in the park wasn't as good as Lester Young, but the style was very similar. No doubt he inherited this passion for music from you."

"He's been exposed to it since birth. It's a part of who he is, but I'm going to pay closer attention to the way in which he reacts to different kinds of music. Sweetheart, I can't tell you how much I appreciate your bringing an extra dimension to Teddy's and Eartha's lives. I know their happiness revolves around me, and that's one reason why I dislike being away from them."

"When are you coming home? I miss you."

"You can't be missing me half as much as I miss you. I'll be home soon, because...well, I can't finish the job, and I hate that. The part of the house for which my group and I are responsible will have to wait till next year."

"Why? Why can't you finish it?"

"I got careless. As we speak, I'm lying here in this hospital with my left foot in a cast. I dropped a plank on it, and I can't hobble around there on a crutch. I need my arms."

"Oh, dear. Ashton, I'm so sorry. Does it hurt badly? I wish I was there with you."

"I wish you were, too, and I wish I could finish this job."

"Honey, I don't know a thing about building houses, but if somebody will show me what to do, I'll try to finish it for you. Rosalind Carter builds them, and Reba MacIntyre does, too."

"Are you serious?"

"Of course, I am. I haven't had a vacation in ages, so I can tell Roy I need a couple of weeks, and if I write half a dozen columns between now and Sunday, I could leave here Sunday. Where is it, and how do I get there?"

He couldn't imagine that beautiful, sophisticated woman building a house, trudging over unpaved roads, negotiating mud puddles and mosquitoes, sleeping in a tent, and sharing a makeshift outhouse and bath with strangers. "I appreciate your offer to help," he said, "but this isn't for you." He described the circumstances in which the volunteers lived and worked on that particular project and added, "It's totally unglamorous."

"And you think I can't exist without a Jacuzzi, a chrome kitchen, a king-size mattress and air conditioning? Is that the kind of woman you think I am?"

"Look, I didn't say that." He imagined she'd poked out her chin and raised her feathers like a little Bantam rooster prepared for a fight. "But I know what it's like down here, and I wanted to protect you from the discomfort."

"If that's your only reason for objecting, tell me how I

get there." He gave her the information and added, "I'll tell
the crew leader. Someone will meet you at the airport, and
I'll stay here and give you the benefit of what I know. Be
sure and bring thick cotton clothing, mosquito repellent,
sunscreen, brogans and a cotton or straw hat. The sun's
merciless. Send me an e-mail to the address I gave you to
let me know when you're coming."

"You're not upset that I want to do this?"

"No, I'm not. I'm deeply touched. You astonish me.
Kisses."

"Kisses to you, love."

He hung up and remembered that he hadn't told her he
loved her. She'd nearly sent him into shock. "I'll see where
it goes. Somehow I can't envisage those delicate fingers
with their perfectly manicured nails laying tile on a floor
or, for that matter, banging a sixteen-penny nail into a
two-by-four plank. If she manages to do it, this won't be
the first surprise she's given me.

"What the hell! I'll soon see her, and right now, that's
what matters most. If she gets into trouble here, I'll take
her home." He closed his eyes, submitted to the groggi-
ness caused by the sedative, and slept.

If Ashton worried about Felicia's ability to finish the
work he had started and to endure the hardships that faced
her, Felicia did not. After remaining up for most of two
nights, she completed enough columns that, if interspersed
with several old ones, would satisfy her readers for the next
ten days. With her editor's permission and blessings, she
left work early and headed to Macy's where she bought
what she needed. For the brogans, she went to a shoe store
that catered to men. With her bags packed and her ticket

in her pocketbook, she telephoned her brother, Miles, and told him what she planned to do.

"Is there any way that I can dissuade you?" he asked her. "You could kill yourself down there."

"Ashton won't let that happen. He'll show me how to do it. I can bang a nail as well as the next person, and I'm capable of learning how to do anything else that's needed."

"Well, hell, Felicia. If the work's so dangerous that he's laid up in the hospital, why do you think you'll just breeze along there like a flower swaying in the wind?"

"I don't think that, Miles. Anyway, I called because I always want you to know where I am and what I'm up to."

"Take care, sis. I can't see how Ashton Underwood allowed you to do this."

"He tried to dissuade me, but I'd made up my mind. Don't worry. I'll be safe."

She called a taxi, headed for La Guardia airport and, at three-ten that Sunday afternoon stepped off the plane in Jackson, Mississippi. She'd never thought she'd make a footprint in Mississippi, but she was there, and she intended to do her best.

"Is Mr. Underwood out of the hospital yet?" she asked the crew member who met her at the airport.

"Yeah, but his foot's in a cast. He's in the car. Ready?"

"I'm ready," she said, afraid to trust her voice as jolts of anticipation flashed throughout her system. In a few minutes, she'd see him even if he couldn't wrap her in his arms. She had pulled her hair straight back, braided it and made a small knot of the braid in the back of her head. She had also filed her nails down until they were almost even with her fingers and removed the nail polish. She didn't wear makeup, but she wondered what Ashton would think of her without lipstick.

"Tough," she said to herself. "Nobody would wear lipstick in the kind of place he described to me."

"It's pretty rough out there, miss. We're building a new community almost, and it'll be great when we finish, but right now there aren't any amenities."

"I know, but if the rest of you can take it, so can I."

"Well, we're sure glad to have you, miss. Losing Underwood was going to mean we didn't make our quota. There're a dozen of us, and we work together someplace every year. We've gotten to be friends. I'll get that." He lifted her bag from the carousel. "All set? The car's right out there."

She didn't know what she had expected, but she'd been unable to envisage Ashton disabled, for he was to her strong and capable both mentally and physically. A man who wore his masculinity the way falcons wore their great wings. They stepped out of the terminal, and she saw him leaning against the car, his arms folded and a grin covering his face. With great effort, she controlled the impulse to run to him. At last she stood in front of him.

"Hi," she said when she saw that he wouldn't embrace her in the man's presence.

"Hi. You are a sight for sore eyes. Do you want the back or the front of the car? I have to sit in the back to rest my foot as much as possible. You're welcome to join me."

Before she could say she'd join him and at least get a chance to hold his hand, the crew member who was their driver said, "You might prefer to sit up here, Miss Parker. That way, I can show you all the sights as we go along. We're going to pass a couple of historic plantations."

She glanced at Ashton, and noticed his disappointment, but the man was already opening the front passenger's door, and she saw no choice but to ride in the front. She hardly saw the plantation homes, the endless fields of high cotton or the numerous marshes fed by the Mississippi River. Her thoughts and her focus dwelt on the man sitting behind her as she wondered how long she'd have to wait before she'd be in his arms again.

"You sleepy?" the driver asked her. "To most people from up your way, this region is like a foreign country. I grew up in Alabama, and I'm used to this. Have you always lived in New York?"

"Why, no," she said, realizing that she must seem unsociable. "I was born in North Carolina, but I grew up in Washington, D.C., and neither is anything like this. I'm…uh…just taking it all in."

"Why do you want to do this?" the driver asked. He hadn't bothered to introduce himself.

Apparently he didn't mind asking personal questions, but she'd answer as she saw fit. "Some very personal reasons," she said, not bothering to look in his direction. "And my parents raised me to help those who can't help themselves. I try to do that to the extent that I can." She turned her back to the door so that she could look at Ashton. "How's that foot? Does it pain you very much?"

"It's mean enough, because it's past time I took the painkiller the doctor prescribed."

"Then why don't we stop so you can get some water and take it?"

"We wanted to be back at camp before dark," the driver said.

"I shouldn't think five minutes will make an important difference," she said through her teeth. "Here's a café. Please stop, and I'll go in and get a bottle of water." Maybe he wasn't accustomed to taking commands from a woman, but she couldn't care less. If Ashton needed water in order to take a pill, it was the man's place to stop and get water.

"I'll get it," the man said, but she was opening her door, jumped out, turned and looked toward Ashton. "Do you need or want anything else?"

"A bag of popcorn, if you don't mind. I'm starved."

She bought three orders of fried chicken, candied sweet potatoes, string beans and sweetened ice tea, got napkins, knives, forks and spoons and a bottle of water and went back to the car.

"That took a little longer than five minutes," the driver said.

"What's your name?"

"Matt."

"Well, Matt, that man in the backseat said he was starving and, being a female, I'm a nurturer. I'm also logical. I have no idea what I'll find when I get to camp or how long it will be before I get there, and I, too, am hungry. So here's your food, Matt. She handed him a foam plate, passed one to Ashton and then opened her own. "Let's eat. We'll get there when we get there."

She heard the long breath that Matt released before he said, "I was worried that you might not be up to the job, but I see I wasted my concern. I expect we'll finish that house after all, Ashton."

"Wouldn't surprise me one bit," Ashton said, and she didn't miss his amused tone of voice.

Ashton knew all along that Felicia was a determined person, that she set her cap for something and worked hard to achieve her goal. He also knew that she did not allow anyone to trample on her or even to come near it. Matt made the mistake of deciding that a woman wasn't to be taken too seriously, and Felicia had just taught him that he'd better take *her* seriously.

"You'll never know how much I appreciate this food, Felicia," Ashton said. "I had hardly any breakfast, and we didn't have time to stop for lunch. Matt thought you'd panic if you arrived and didn't find anyone waiting for you. I didn't bother to tell him that the chances of your panicking about *anything* were practically nil."

They arrived at camp well before dark, as he'd known they would, but he'd gotten used to Matt's exaggerated concerns about practically everything, so he hadn't voiced his thoughts about getting back before dark. Matt parked a few feet from Felicia's tent, took her bags and bedroll there, and gave her a typed list of rules and instructions.

"We breakfast at six," he told her. "I hope you won't have a problem with that. Also, if you're threatened in any way, ring this bell four times, pause and ring two more times. Each of us has a different ring. You can get supper in the mess tent from six-thirty to seven-thirty and not a minute later. I hope you enjoy your work with us."

"I'm sure I will, Matt, and thanks for everything."

Matt got into his car and left them. Ashton leaned against the post at the door of her tent and looked at her, a sweet and lovely vision from another world. "You shortened your nails," he said, and thought how foolish that must sound to her.

But her smile invited him to say and do whatever he liked. "You said there was nothing glamorous about this work, and I took you at your word. I'd better unpack before dark, so I can set up my lighting system."

"First, would you please come over here and kiss me?"

"We'd better not do much kissing, hon, because I don't believe I can think about you and bang nails simultaneously without mashing my fingers. So, don't pour it on. Oh, Ashton. I missed you terribly."

She sprinted across the small tent, threw herself into his waiting arms, and his heart hammered out an erratic rhythm as she locked herself to him. Her sweetness and her soft and yielding body were his. Shudders ricocheted through him when his libido signaled its arousal. He grabbed her buttocks with one hand, wrapped his other one around her shoulders and lowered his head. She parted her lips and took him in, and he thought he would incinerate as she gave herself to him. He looked around for a place to… Good Lord, he couldn't do that. With her head against his shoulder, he inhaled deeply time and again until he had himself under control.

"I thought you said don't pour it on. With that kind of loving, you could make a man lose his head," he told her. "These tents are reasonably secure, but they can't be locked. If I could have locked this thing, I'd be making love to you right now."

"I know, and I wanted it as badly as you did."

He hugged her, stroked her back and longed for privacy. Every cell in his body begged for relief from the sexual tension that gripped him. "It's not past tense with me, sweetheart."

"Me, neither." She moved out of his arms.

"Are you here because you didn't want me to be disappointed or because you believe in helping others? I need to know."

Looking him in the eye, she said, "Both, but I can find other ways to help people."

He stared down at her, uneasy in the presence of her extraordinary calm. "So you are here because of me. If it's that and that alone, I want to know it."

"I'm here because of you. Period."

"The more I know you, the more you mean to me. I didn't want you to come because I feared you'd get hurt, but you're here and I'm glad. Don't overextend yourself. If anything happened to you, I don't think I could bear it." He let his hand drift slowly down her cheek in as intimate a gesture as he dared. At that moment, he felt as if he would burst with love for her.

"I'll see you at supper," he said. "Turn left from your tent, walk straight up the road, and you'll see the food tent. It's the big yellow one. Always carry your bell and flashlight." He leaned over, kissed her nose and hobbled off with the aid of his crutches.

Inside his tent, three doors from Felicia's and next to the food and service tent, Ashton moved as quickly as he could to wash up, light his kerosene lamps and his citronella candles and head to the food tent. Felicia was not aware that she'd be the only woman in the camp and, although he hadn't worried about that aspect of her being here, it occurred to him that he didn't know these men personally. If any of them was short on morals, he could have a problem on his hands.

When Felicia arrived for supper, it pleased him to see that she had deglamorized herself to the extent possible. Nonetheless, she received appreciative stares from several of the men, married ones among them. At that moment, he knew he had to let them know that Felicia was off limits. She looked around, saw him and hesitated, so he beckoned for her to join him.

"Hi," she said. "Am I the only woman in this crew?"

He nodded. "Right, and I've just decided that I'd better let them know you're off limits. If I had full use of both legs, I wouldn't worry, but I don't have, and I don't want to have to kill anybody."

"Oh, you needn't worry about that. I know how to dust off a man. Trust me."

"Oh, I would if you were in New York City, but out here…" She could figure out the rest of the thought.

He stood and rapped a fork against his glass. "This is Felicia Parker. Felicia is a columnist for the Skate newspaper chain, but she's here to help me finish my share of the work on house two-thirty. Felicia Parker is also my significant other." He heard a couple of groans, but ignored them. "I tried to persuade her not to come, but she can be stubborn. She's a hard worker, and I'd appreciate it if you would all welcome her."

Gratified by the enthusiastic applause, he gave the group a thumbs-up sign, sat down and focused on his supper. "At least they know where they stand," he told Felicia. "If any of them steps out of line, he'll get it from me. If I'm not around, report any problems to Matt."

She wrinkled her nose in a flirtatious frown, a gesture he hadn't previously seen her exhibit. "What if it's Matt who's the problem?"

"It won't be. Matt's as straight as a born-again-Baptist preacher."

"Which is your tent, Ashton?"

"The one next door to this food tent heading in the direction of yours," he said. "Why? Planning to visit me when nobody's looking?" he asked, and thought for a minute that she'd sock him.

Her glare slowly faded into a grin behind which there seemed to be the beginning of desire. Quickly, she banished it and he marveled at her self-control. "Don't put ideas into my head. I thought you said these tents don't lock."

"They don't, but if I try, I can make it impossible for anybody to enter it without tearing it down. Give me a reason, sweetheart, and for you I'll move mountains." He didn't mean that as a light comment, but having said it, he mused about it for a bit. Wasn't he moving closer and closer to ending his days as a bachelor, and wasn't he increasingly less reluctant to do that?

"What are you thinking?" she asked him, then held up her right hand as if to halt his words. "If you're not thinking about me, I want to know who she is."

He hadn't realized that his facial expression reflected his feelings and said as much. "Not to worry. You're queen of this castle. I'm ready to turn in. Don't forget that we have breakfast at six, and start work at seven. I'll walk you to your tent."

"You don't have to do that. I can see how difficult it is for you to move around on those crutches."

"I'll walk you to your tent, Felicia." However, he didn't go in, for he knew that because of his announcement they would be the center of attention. "Good night, sweetheart." He leaned down and kissed her lips, as much for any onlookers as for them. "See you in the morning."

Felicia slept fitfully, unaccustomed as she was to the night sounds. The sound of crickets, the croaking of bull frogs, the cracking of sticks and dry leaves caused, to her mind, by human or animal feet, kept her awake much of the night. Nonetheless, she got up around five o'clock, hastened to the bath tent, hung out the "occupied" sign, washed up, brushed her teeth and hurried back to her tent. At six o'clock, she walked into the food hall and sat at the table she occupied the night before.

"What kind of column do you write?" a male voice asked her, and she looked up just as the man placed his tray on the table at which she sat.

"A political column," she replied, "and I also report straight news. Oh, here's Ashton. Hi, darling. Sit down and I'll get a tray of food for you. What do you want this morning?"

He sat down, placed his crutches against the empty chair, leaned over and kissed her lips. "Hi, sweetheart. Orange juice, grits, rope sausage, scrambled eggs and three biscuits, please."

"Am I interrupting something?" the man said.

"Not at all," Felicia replied. "Ashton explained our relationship at supper last night. We're all here for the same good cause. What's your name?"

"Jack. I wasn't sure he was serious."

"Oh, I was serious, all right. I announced that so every man here would know precisely who this woman is. She isn't looking for a man. She's got one, and I'm he."

Jack showed his perfect teeth in a wide grin. "I got the message, brother, but you can't blame me for getting it straight."

"Do you have a family, Jack?" Felicia asked.

"Who hasn't? One's at Howard, and two are at University of Michigan. In a couple of years, I'll be able to buy a new car." He laughed, and she didn't believe he thought it amusing.

"Where's their mother?"

"She's home. She'd never do what you're doing. My wife has to go to the hairdresser every Thursday, the manicurist every Tuesday, the matinee every Wednesday, and so on, ad infinitum."

"In this case, I'm sure you came to this table because you wanted to talk with *me*," Ashton said, looking the man in the eye.

"Touché," Jack said. "I play, but I've got my first time to follow through. If things don't get better at home, who knows?"

"They won't get better starting here," Felicia said. "So keep it between the lines, Jack. I have everything I need."

Ashton finished eating, leaned back in his chair and sipped his coffee, slowly and deliberately. "Is everything clear, Jack?" he asked after a few minutes of silence.

"Clear as clean crystal."

"I'm glad to know it," Ashton said. He looked at Felicia who enjoyed her sautéed salmon, scrambled eggs and grits as if she were dining on it in Buckingham Palace. "If you'd like, I'll show you where we start this morning."

She picked up a biscuit, buttered it and smiled. "This food is off the chain. I'm going wherever you take me—otherwise, I'll get lost."

"If you stick with me," he said, "you'll never get lost and you'll never lose. I'll always be there for you." He didn't smile, because he meant every word.

"I know that very well," she said as if Jack wasn't present.

"And I hope you never forget it," he said, and reached for his crutches.

Jack looked at Felicia with narrowed eyes. "You sure you're Underwood's girl?"

Felicia finished chewing her food, took a few sips of coffee and drank the remainder of the water in her glass. Then without saying a word she stood and, to his astonishment, she reached up, opened her lips over his and gripped his shoulders with both hands. Shock reverberated through him and, without giving it a thought, he plunged his tongue into her waiting mouth and locked her body to his. As easily as she started the fire that raged inside of him, she squelched it, moved away and looked at Jack.

"If you need more evidence, pal, I'll move into his tent." To Ashton, she said, "Let's go, hon. I'll only be here ten days." Ten days that he prayed would be uneventful.

Chapter 10

When the crew stopped for lunch—or dinner as Southerners called it—Felicia thought she had half a dozen muscles in her arms and shoulders that she hadn't known existed. "How do you feel?" Ashton asked.

"Great," she said, and that was true. She had used a plane to smooth a door, and her coworkers had congratulated her on a job flawlessly done. She'd also made a window that hung straight, and she'd had no trouble banging the nails. What a great way to release stress and tension, she'd said to herself, as she'd hammered the tenpenny nails into the door frame.

"Ashton, I have such a wonderful feeling of accomplishment."

He rested an arm around her shoulder. "And you should have. Don't forget that you can rest whenever you feel you need it."

"I'll do that," she said, but she had no intention of stopping until the remainder of the crew stopped. She figured she was younger than at least half of them and, for that reason alone, she could hold her own. She ate a lunch of Swiss steak, mashed potatoes with gravy, string beans cooked with smoked ham hocks, baked corn bread and for dessert, the best apple pie she'd ever tasted.

"This cook deserves a medal," she said to Matt, who joined them at the table.

"He sure does. The food is always first-class. You surprised all of us, Felicia. Mind if I call you Felicia? The men told me to ask if you'd care to join the crew as a regular member. We only do one project a year. If you join, it might encourage some of our wives to do the same." He looked at Ashton. "It must give you a lot of satisfaction to know she supports you in something that's so important to you."

"You can't imagine how much. When I saw her measure for that window, put it together and hang it, I was prouder than I was when I received my M.B.A."

"You have a right to be proud. I meant to tell you, Felicia, you'll probably need a hot shower after we knock off. Would five-fifteen suit you? If so, I'll reserve the time for you."

"Thanks, Matt. I'll take whatever time is available. And thank the guys for inviting me to join the crew. I appreciate it, and I'll give it serious consideration."

"Five-fifteen, it is, then. Well, I want some cheddar cheese to go with my pie. Either one of you want some?"

Felicia shook her head. "I've had enough calories, thanks. What are we doing after lunch?" she asked Ashton. "Do we start on the roof?"

They discussed plans for the afternoon's work, but she had a feeling that his thoughts were elsewhere. "What is it, Ashton? You're not with me."

"You amaze me. I'm…admiring the way you jumped into this as if you'd done it for years. Don't you feel sore?"

"A little, but I haven't stretched myself, Ashton. I'm going to enjoy that hot shower, though. And Matt made an everlasting friend of me when he mentioned it. I'd been wondering how I'd get one."

"How do you like sleeping in the tent?"

"I told myself I'd get used to it, and enjoying sleeping on the ground will happen before I get accustomed to those crickets and things chitchatting all night."

"It's weird, all right."

After supper that evening, Felicia and Ashton strolled over to the little river that promised to make the settlement attractive and inviting to those fortunate enough to occupy the houses. Ashton leaned against a huge magnolia tree and propped his crutches against its trunk.

"What's that?" she asked him as she watched their reflections in the water, clear as a picture in the moonlight.

"I think it's a mockingbird, but I'm not sure. I heard some of them last night."

"It must be," she said. "Oh, Ashton, this is so idyllic. Imagine what this will be like after the houses are painted, the roads paved, flowers everywhere and children laughing and playing. It will be a heavenly oasis." She looked up at him and gasped, for she had caught him with his feelings bare, naked and vulnerable.

"Do you want children?" His question stunned her, and her words came out as a stammer, honest and revealing.

"M-more than anything in this w-world."

His big hands gripped her waist. "Do you want my children?" he asked in a voice muffled with emotion.

"If you give them to me willingly. Yes. I want yours and only yours, but I'll take what I can get."

His fingers pressed the edges of her breasts. "You'd have another man's child?"

"I want to be a mother, and I don't want to wait until I'm fifty."

"I don't want another man near you. You're *my* woman, and your children will be *my* children." He wrapped her in his arms, lowered his head and, with his lips an inch from hers, he gazed down at her with stormy, passion-filled eyes. She tingled from head to foot waiting while the expression on his face changed to that of a man anticipating a feast. She eased her hand up to his nape, and his mouth came down on hers strong and sweet. Possessive.

He gripped her buttocks with one hand and her shoulder with the other and shoved his tongue into her mouth. She welcomed him, greedy for the feel of him inside of her. He stroked and squeezed her buttocks and her back while he tortured her with the thrusts of his tongue, intentionally reminding her of the way she felt lying beneath him helpless while he stormed inside of her.

Without thinking of what she did, she widened her stance, pressed her pelvis to him and began to rock. Suddenly he put her away from him. "What's that?" he said, his left arm tight around her waist and one of his crutches in the other hand. "Who's that?" he repeated. "Don't move," he whispered. "It may be a wild animal, and I don't know what kind live here."

She marveled at her lack of fear. The night before, she shuddered at every sound, and that night was full of strange sounds, but even with his limited capacity, she knew that whatever came, Ashton would deal with it. The sound of steps approached them, and Ashton released her, braced himself and prepared for whatever adversary appeared. She looked around to note the position of his other crutch; if a problem arose, she didn't intend to let him fight it alone.

She stared at the sight of a white-tailed deer and the little fawn that followed close behind. "Well, just look at that," Ashton said when the doe looked around before nudging her fawn to the stream. They drank and then walked on, evidently unaware of their audience. "What a sight," he said. "It could have been a wildcat or some other fierce animal, so I think we'd better get back."

She wished she could hold his hand as they walked. When they reached her tent, he said, "I'm not going to tempt myself or punish myself, but I'll wait here until you look around carefully and then secure your tent. I'll see you at breakfast."

She searched the area with a flashlight, called good-night to Ashton and secured her tent for the night. If she stayed here long enough, she would get over her craving for midnight snacks. Without a refrigerator to raid, and with her meager supply of miniature Baby Ruths rapidly dwindling, she was about to experience a bout of enforced self-discipline.

She needed something, anything, to distract her from her longing for Ashton and to move her mind off the night around her and its strange creatures. If only she had a window and she could see the moon and the stars as they were when she walked earlier with Ashton and as she had never seen them before. Silent and majestic on a clear summer night when not a single leaf moved on the trees. She put on a pair of pajamas—not daring to sleep in the skimpy teddies that she usually wore to bed for fear that she might have to get out of the tent in a hurry—and got into bed.

She didn't ache, although her body told her that it had been well used. After an hour of twisting and turning, crossing her legs in frustration, and trying to ignore the jabbering of the night creatures, she began counting white-tailed fawns. When her clock alarmed at five o'clock, she crawled out of bed, washed her face in the basin of water she put in her tent the night before, brushed her teeth and dressed. On the way to the food tent, she stopped at the lavatory and gave thanks that it was unoccupied.

"Did you sleep well?" Ashton asked her when they met near the entrance to the food tent.

"No, but I might have if you had minded your own business."

"Me? What did I do?"

"The problem was not what you did, but what you didn't do."

He looked down at her and closed his eyes. "I'm not going near that right now, but I promise you that won't be a complaint when I get you back to New York City."

Ashton hadn't slept well and for the same reason that she hadn't, although he at least was not afraid of sleeping alone in a tent in a half-wild area. Felicia seemed to tire as the morning wore on, and he counseled her to rest, though she paid little or no attention to that request.

"I want you to sit down here and rest for ten minutes," he said to her around two o'clock that afternoon. "You may not be tired, but after dragging that bag of cement over here, I am. Let's sit here for a minute." He knew she was tired, but that she didn't want to be a drag on the crew, so she didn't stop. He reached out and took her hand. "I know we shouldn't be affectionate in the presence of others—though you made a show of it at breakfast the first morning you were here—but I need you close to me right now. I need to feel that you need me."

"I do need you," she said. "I need to share things with you, to laugh with you. I love the way you laugh and the way your eyes sparkle. I need you when I'm not happy, too, Ashton, and I need you when I'm lonely."

He wanted to wrap her in his arms, hold her and protect her. "I don't want you to be lonely," he said, "and if you'll let me, I'll try to prevent it as much as I can."

"I know," she said, but she looked beyond his shoulder at something in the distance. "We'd better get back to work, hon. Before you know it, it will be time to...to knock off."

He stood, tried his weight on his foot and decided against pressuring it further. At the end of the working day, he figured that their share of the work had progressed almost as much as if he weren't handicapped. "You needn't worry about the walls," he told Felicia. "They're the least of our problems. A professional plasterer does that after we finish the exterior."

"Is he a volunteer?"

Ashton nodded. "You bet."

After supper, he walked Felicia to her tent and kissed her quickly. Lingering over a kiss would only add fuel to the furnace that already raged inside of him. He needed more, so much more. Impulsively, he hugged her to him and held her for a minute.

"See you at breakfast," he said in deep guttural tones

that he hardly recognized as his own voice. Her smile seemed to him as false as thirteen gongs from a grandfather clock, but if he didn't ignore it, they could find themselves in an embarrassing situation. He went to his tent, lit his kerosene lamps and citronella candles, and prepared to read for a few minutes before going to sleep. He got into bed, put the lamps nearby, turned to page one fifty-six of Robert Fleming's *Fever In The Blood* and began to read. At eleven o'clock, he forced himself to put the book aside, dimmed the lamp and went to sleep.

"What the..." He rubbed his eyes, turned up the lamp's wick and sat up. What the hell! Felicia! What on earth? Quickly, he calmed himself. "What is it, baby?"

She said nothing, and he watched her move a chair, put down her bedroll and bedding, get in bed and go to sleep. He wanted her in there with him as much as he wanted to breathe. Surely he must be hallucinating. He considered getting up and shining the light on her face to be sure he wasn't dreaming, and thought better of it. For whatever reason, she was here with him, and he wasn't about to look a gift horse in the mouth. He got out of bed, secured the tent—something that he rarely bothered to do, but did now to protect Felicia—returned to bed and looked at his watch. Two-thirty. He wondered what caused her to come to his tent.

"I'll know in a few hours," he told himself, dimmed the lamp and went to sleep.

Felicia awakened at five o'clock, dressed and went to the lavatory tent to take care of her ablutions. She didn't spend time wondering about Ashton's reaction to her moving into his tent in the middle of the night. She did know that she wasn't sleeping anywhere else as long as she worked on that project. "I'm through with punishing myself," she said out loud as she walked toward the food tent. "I finally had two and a half hours of solid, undisturbed sleep for the first time since I came here. I don't care what these people think, from now on, I'm bunking with Ashton."

Ashton arrived for breakfast promptly at six o'clock, and it delighted her to see that he walked with only one crutch. Instead of going immediately to the table at which she sat, he got in line with his tray, got his food and then joined her.

"You're welcome to sleep in my tent," he began without bothering to say good morning, "especially since that's where I've wanted you to sleep all the time. But would you mind telling me why you joined me at two-thirty in the morning and without so much as a glance in my direction? I'm glad to have you with me, and I promise that you may sleep there undisturbed, if that's what you want. Humor me, Felicia. I want to know what happened."

"I was scared. I heard footsteps. Somebody walked back and forth in front of my tent half a dozen times. Before that, I had already had enough of that hooting owl and those other things that make noise all night—"

He stopped eating. "You heard somebody walking in front of your tent—a somebody who, out here, could only have been a man, and you went outside not knowing who it was or what he wanted. Have you lost your mind?"

His remark was not unexpected. She sipped her coffee, rested the cup on the table and said, in the tone of one talking to a mentally challenged child, "Was I supposed to wait till he came into the tent, where I wouldn't stand a chance? No one would have heard me if I screamed. I got outside because I knew there aren't many men in this camp who can outrun me, and if I screamed, everyone, including you, would have heard me. No point in getting upset, Ashton. Until I leave here, I'm sleeping wherever you sleep. Period."

He stared are her with an expression of incredulity. And then his face transformed itself into a thing of beauty as he grinned from ear to ear. Her lower lip dropped, and she gazed at him. Mesmerized. Unable to shift her glance. Sometimes she forgot what a good-looking man Ashton Underwood was, mostly because he seemed unaware of it. Thank God, he was decent and respectable; if he were different, she'd be in real trouble.

His eyes sparkled with mischief. "Sweetheart, let me assure you that you may sleep with me as often as you like. Twice a day wouldn't be often enough for me."

She managed to recover her aplomb, dragged her gaze down to her food and said, "I hope you noticed that I brought my own bedroll."

"As a matter of fact, I did notice it. How were you going to run while you were carrying that thing?" Suddenly his jocular mood faded, and his gaze roamed the food tent. He didn't have to tell her that he was looking for the man who might be watching their table. "I'm glad you're with me, Felicia, and I'm also glad that whoever the fool was, he had the sense not to pursue you. My foot is in a cast, but there is absolutely nothing wrong with my two fists."

"I wouldn't want you to get into trouble because of me. You have a reputation to protect."

"I have a woman to protect. That's what's important here. By the way, would you like to ride into Jackson with

Matt and me tomorrow? It's Saturday, and I want to call my family."

"I'd love to. Thanks." She hesitated, lest he think she had a reason for asking. "Eartha is very dear to you, isn't she?"

"She is, indeed. I know she's limited in some respects, but she takes good care of Teddy. She's honest and caring, and Teddy and I are her whole life. She doesn't have a family, and if she didn't live with us, she'd be completely alone. She loves us, and we love her." In other words, Felicia understood him to imply, "she comes with me and my son."

Ignoring the implications of his remark, she said, "I've thought that you are indeed fortunate to have this woman to care for Teddy. There's a simple decency and honesty about her, and I've wondered if she was like that when you hired her or if she grew into the person she is."

"Some of both, I guess. Once she realized that I considered her a part of my family, she began to treat us as if we were her family. You are a very perceptive woman. We work half a day today, and we're off tomorrow." She knew he'd deliberately changed the subject.

She didn't want him to hobble around the city of Jackson showing her the remnants of Antebellum Mississippi. She'd seen enough slave quarters, whipping posts and plantation mansions built with the blood and sweat of slaves. Two hours there would be enough for her. "Do you think we can get Matt to join us in a game of cut-throat pinochle tomorrow evening when we get back? If he doesn't know the game, I'll teach him," she said.

He shrugged. "If it's a card game, Matt plays it. Let's

go. I'd like us to get the front steps in place this morning. Two of our group made them earlier."

Now that she no longer faced the night alone in that tent, she felt like skipping to work. "Gee, this air feels great," she said, and headed for the house that she, Ashton and three other volunteers hoped would be perfect when they left the camp four days later.

"Why are you sitting out here, man?" Matt asked Ashton after supper one evening. "If I had in my tent what you have in yours, damned if I'd be cooling my heels out here."

He wasn't in the habit of explaining his personal affairs to anyone, but Matt was becoming a friend, and he didn't feel like dusting him off. "She's in my tent because some jackass or other who's in this crew frightened her one night by hanging around her tent. We don't live together in New York, and it didn't occur to us to shack up here. I respect her feelings about this. She was scared, so she came to me, as she should have. She's out of there before I get up and she's in bed before I enter that tent in the evening. It's difficult for both of us, but I want her to be safe, and I don't want to have to commit a crime in order to insure her safety."

"But if she's your…your woman, what's wrong with it?"

"Not a thing. This is the way she wants it, and I respect her wishes."

Matt took off his baseball cap and fanned his face. "Whew! I'm not sure I'd have your self-control. That's a beautiful, feminine woman."

"Thanks."

Matt rested his back against the post that would someday support an electric or telephone wire, stretched out his legs and said, "I'm curious about what you do when you're not volunteering with Habitat for Humanity. You're different from most of the guys here, and it isn't just the way you talk."

Trust Matt to ask a question, personal or not, if he wanted the answer. "I manage some companies with the help of my two brothers. I began with nothing. My parents could have paid my university tuitions, but I worked and paid my own way, and they encouraged me. I don't mind hard work, and I believe in helping those who can't help themselves. That was my mother's creed, now it's mine, and that's why I'm here."

Matt drew up his knees toward his chest, wrapped his arms around them and appeared satisfied, as if he'd worked out a puzzle. And maybe he had for he said, "I've got it. It isn't your height or your bearing, it's the polish that sets you apart. And it's so much a part of you that you don't even know you have it. Way to go, man."

If Matt could get personal, so could he. "What about you, Matt? I confess that I'm curious about you, too. I told Felicia that if she had a problem here and I wasn't around, she should go to you because you're as straight as the crow flies. What's your background?"

"Thanks for the vote of confidence. I'm a seminarian. I haven't yet been ordained, and I'm wondering if I should settle for teaching theology at a university rather than preaching. Either way, I want a career as a theologian. Does this surprise you?"

"Not really. I would only have been surprised if you'd told me you did manual labor. I've looked at your hands, and they're not the hands of a man who uses them to earn a hard living."

"Neither are yours," Matt shot back.

Ashton observed Matt from the corner of his eye. "How far do you live from New York City?"

"Twenty minutes via the Path train. I live in South Orange, New Jersey."

"Then I hope we'll see each other from time to time. I've enjoyed your company here."

"And I've not only enjoyed your company, Ashton, but I've learned some important things from you. I'd like very much to see you from time to time. And I'd like you to meet my girl."

"It would be my pleasure. Is she the reason why you'll probably be a university theologian rather than a priest?"

"One of them. My conscience tells me that it's service that matters, not the capacity in which I give it."

"You're so right," Ashton said. "I think I'll turn in. Good talking with you."

She was not in bed and covered from her neck to her toes as usual, but sitting in a chair, fully clothed, with her knees crossed and an expression of displeasure on her face. "What's with you?" she asked. "Anybody would think that an armed bandit was waiting for you in here. If you'd rather I moved out, say the word. Anybody else in this camp will welcome me in a second."

He must have looked like an idiot staring at her with his mouth wide open. She stared right back at him. *She's asking for it, and she's going to get it.* Why did women get testy instead of just saying they wanted you to make love with them? She set the rule, and her rule said no, not here. Now she was acting as if he ignored her because he wanted to. He closed the tent, secured it, walked over to where she sat, leaned down and covered her mouth with his own. Immediately, he got the reaction he wanted when her breath quickened and her lips parted. He slid his tongue into her mouth, and she grasped it like a drowning person grabbing at a rope. Handicapped by his wounded foot and unable to pick her up and stretch her out on her bedroll, he settled the issue by yanking her blouse over her head, unhooking her bra, leaning down and sucking the nipple of her ample left breast into his mouth.

"I didn't tell you you could do that," she said, panting as if she'd run a marathon. He raised his head and grinned at her. "Oh, but you did. You want me to stop?"

She grabbed his right arm. "You know what I want. I'm starved for you. I—" He returned to his feast at her breast, and the excitement that her muffled groans created in him nearly sent him over the edge.

"Honey, if you keep that up, I'll scream. I can't stand this. I don't need all that teasing, I want you to get inside of me. Ashton, I'm burning up."

"Then why didn't you say so instead of being mean to me when I walked in here? I'd waited outside to give you privacy." He threw his shirt over to his own bedroll. "I should tell you no, because I'm hurt," he said, wanting to tease her into showing him how much she wanted him.

Ready to give as good as she got, she said, "Do that, and everybody anywhere near here will sympathize with you." She slipped out of her slacks and kicked off her loafers. "If I didn't love you, I'd walk out on you."

"Yeah," he said, unable to banish his humor, "after you got straightened out."

"Now, you—"

His kiss stopped her words, and he locked her nude body to his own. "I'd give anything if I could pick you up and put you on that bedroll. Lie down over there, sweetheart. I want my place inside of you. I've sweated for seven straight nights listening to you breathe, hearing you turn over, and wanting you so badly, I thought I'd go mad. If I didn't love you... Oh, never mind."

She stretched out on the makeshift bed, raised her arms to him in a gesture as old as Eve, and desire rioted in him. With as much care as he could muster, he knelt to her, covered her with his body and began his assault on her senses.

"Please," she moaned. "I'm ready. I was ready before you walked in here. I just want to... Oh, Lord," she said when he flicked his tongue over her nipple. He had to watch it, because he knew that if he loved her the way he wanted to, she'd scream and bring every man within three hundred yards to his tent. He slid his right hand slowly down her body, past her navel until he reached his goal. He wanted to taste her, but that would have to wait till they had more privacy. She spread her legs and the perfume of her sex nearly sent him over the edge. He stroked her gently and, within seconds, the evidence he needed flowed over his fingers.

"Take me in," he said after shielding himself, and then her fingers grasped his penis, fondled and played with it until he croaked out, "If you don't stop it, I'll spill it. Sweetheart, *stop!*" She slid down and guided him into her welcoming body, and he thought he'd lose it. She started rocking, and he shifted his hips and took them on a fast ride to ecstasy.

He longed to collapse and simply give in to the sweet

oblivion in which he was engulfed, but he couldn't let her take his weight. He braced himself on his forearms and gazed down at her. It hit him then with the force of a locomotive slamming into the night. He couldn't let her slip out of his life, and he'd better stop telling himself otherwise. It was up to her. She held the aces, because she had his heart, she met his needs, and Teddy believed that she loved him.

His lips brushed hers in a gentle kiss, and she smiled. "Were you angry with me when I came in here this evening?" he asked her.

"I was hurt and that's the way I showed it. Until you mentioned it, I didn't realize that you always waited until I was in bed before you came in."

He tweaked her nose. "Tell the truth. You wanted what you got, and you were tired of waiting for it, so you got testy. Level with me now, because I want to know how to read you in the future just as you have to know how to read me. There's want, and then there's need, and we have to recognize the difference."

"Yeah. I was pretty hungry," she admitted, and he liked that. He had no patience with coyness. Although he found it cute in little girls, he had no tolerance for it in women.

"Hungry? I was starved. I can now boast that I'm a man capable of rigorous self-control."

"Good," she said, "because this is it for now. I don't want to get used to sleeping with you every night."

"Why not?"

"You can easily become addictive, and I've already developed a taste for you," she said, and lowered her left eyelid in a long, lusty wink. "You know what I mean."

He couldn't help grinning. When she was sassy and

impish, he felt as if he could love her senseless. "Behave yourself, woman. You are totally vulnerable, and if you're not careful, I'll have you begging for mercy."

"Go ahead," she said, stretching and purring like a satisfied feline. "I'm shameless."

Lord, how he loved her!

Felicia didn't want Ashton to move from her. She wanted him to stay where he was, buried deep inside of her. But she knew that neither of them would rest, and a day of laborious work faced them.

"I don't want to put my weight on you, but what I need is to relax in your arms. You're one sweet woman."

"You won't be too heavy. I love holding you like this."

"If you encourage me, I'll probably wear your out," he said, and she could feel him hardening within her. He gripped her hips and her shoulder and drove her to climax, and when relief came, he dragged from her everything, including that little treasure of herself that she had always retained, even with him. Her limbs had turned to rubber, and her willpower was nonexistent.

Exhausted from her emotions, tears trickled down her cheeks. No more. She wanted no more teases of what it could be like to live with him always.

"You're crying?" he asked, his voice trembling with obvious concern.

"Yes, but I'm not sad, or I think I'm not. I'm just… shook up. It's as if I don't have anything left of myself."

"You're not alone in that feeling, sweetheart."

"Have you thought about what will happen when we leave here?" She knew the question would drive a wedge, however small, between them, but the thought haunted her and she had to ask, even at the expense of cooling his ardor.

"Is it worrying you?" he asked her.

She answered truthfully. "I don't know how I'll feel not seeing you every day or eating my breakfast and dinner with you. I think I got used to you."

"Is that good or bad?"

She didn't feel like emptying her mind for his benefit, much as she loved him. Her soul was her own, or it had been. "It just is," she answered, knowing that that wouldn't satisfy him.

"Are you suggesting that we live together? I thought you said shacking up—as you phrased it—was out of the question."

"It is. I don't believe in make-believe marriage, or in trial marriage which is foolish 'because total commitment isn't here.'"

"I couldn't agree with you more."

She didn't want to talk about their future, she realized, because she didn't know what she'd say if he proposed marriage. She loved him, and she knew she would love Teddy, but was she ready to be a mother? She wanted children in the worst way, but shouldn't she stay home with them? She knew she wasn't ready to be a housewife. Each time, Ashton had been careful to protect her from pregnancy. Had he done that for her or for him?

"What's the problem? What is it? You seem so...so concerned."

She tried to smile. "You're messing up my mind."

He ignored the comment, as if he knew it was a sham. "Will you go home with me to Rose Hill to meet my family?" he asked her, staring down in her face and reading her every unvoiced emotion. What on earth made him ask her that?

"If you want me to," she heard herself reply. "I don't think I can go within the next ten days, because I'll have some catching up to do."

He held her closer, almost possessively. "I want you to meet my folks, and I can fly us there and back one Sunday if that's all the time you have to spare."

Don't screw up, girl. This man is talking business. You know you'd lose it if he walked out, so let him know how you feel. This is it.

"I hope we can at least spend the night there," she said, and she could feel his body relax in her arms.

"Let's plan to go weekend after next. I have a board meeting next Friday, so next weekend is out, and I suppose that, after ten days away from home and work, you'll need that time for a variety of things. I'm hoping that Cade and Damon will be home that weekend."

"Should I be nervous about meeting Cade? When I talked with him I got the impression that he can be formidable."

He inclined his head slightly to the right and appeared thoughtful. "Cade's a real pussy cat, unless you're stupid enough to yank his tail. Then you're on your own. But why should you worry about *him?* I'm your man."

"He's important or you wouldn't want me to meet him. Who's bigger? You or Cade? I noticed that Damon is about half an inch shorter that you."

"Cade and I are about the same height, but he's around five pounds heavier. What Cade thinks is important to me, because he's my brother and I love him, but his opinions aren't gospel to me by a long shot. My family is warm and loving, Felicia." He separated them and lay on his left side. "Since my parents died, my brothers and granddad have been my family. Granddad will love you, because he adores pretty women."

She couldn't help laughing at that. "Still?"

"Absolutely. But he also likes women who are intelligent and accomplished. He was deeply fond of my mother because he didn't have a daughter, and when my dad married her, Granddad accepted her as his child." He rolled over on his back and locked his hands behind his head. "I miss my parents' warmth and the loving environment they created for us. I want that for myself."

The words seemed to fall lightly from his lips, but she wasn't fooled; he'd just told her something that was of singular importance to him. "You're blessed, Ashton. My father remarried the day his divorce from my mother became final. His philandering behavior did not encourage me to have confidence in men. Miles isn't like him, thank God. He's always been my cornerstone."

"I'm sorry to hear that. It's too bad that the first man you became involved with proved to be just like your father."

"Right," she said, "except that he also lied about his marital status. Tell you what, I'll bake your granddad a cake and bring it with me to Rose Hill," she said without thinking, for she wanted to change the subject as quickly as possible. "Or maybe he'd rather have some cookies."

"If you take him a caramel cake, he'll be your slave forever. I can find a recipe if you want one."

"Thanks, but I can almost make one with my eyes closed."

"He's going to be a happy man," Ashton said, then leaned over and kissed her. "I know it's cramped, and you said you didn't want to get into the habit of sleeping with me, but I want to sleep with you in my arms." He fell over on his back and pulled her on top of him. When she spread her legs, he eased into her, and she put her head on his chest and went to sleep. Minutes after she awoke the next morning, she exploded into orgasm.

Two weeks later, at home and fully recovered, Ashton dressed himself and Teddy in light gray suits, gray shirts and yellow ties. He'd have preferred to travel in a pair of jeans, but Felicia was their guest, and he figured the best way to teach his son was by showing him. He parked the rented car in front of the apartment building in which Felicia lived, tipped the doorman to watch it and, a few minutes later, rang Felicia's doorbell.

She opened the door, and Teddy shrieked, "Miss Felicia, I didn't know I was coming to your house."

Ashton gazed in astonishment as she knelt and Teddy dashed into her arms. "Miss Felicia, I told Daddy I wanted you to come stay with us, but he said you couldn't."

He wanted to say, "Don't hold him so tightly," but Teddy obviously enjoyed her embrace and hugged her just as tightly.

"I'm not jealous, dammit," he said to himself, "but they could at least acknowledge the fact that I'm here." She attempted to stand, holding Teddy as she did so, but the child was too heavy, and he leaned down and raised her to her feet. He didn't know why he did it, but he enclosed both of them in his embrace and kissed Felicia's lips. Teddy looked from one to the other, turned and duplicated his father's act.

"I love Miss Felicia, Daddy. Can she go with us to see Granddad?"

"She can, and she will," he said, easing Teddy from her arms. "You're too heavy for her to hold, son."

"I like it, Daddy."

"Who wouldn't?" he said under his breath. "I certainly do."

Chapter 11

In the backseat of the limousine en route to La Guardia Airport, Teddy sat between Felicia and his father, but Ashton couldn't help noticing that the child leaned toward Felicia. *Damned if I'm not going to have to sit by myself on the plane. I can see Teddy raising a ruckus if he can't sit with Felicia.*

"What is it about you that's so attractive to Underwood men?" he asked her, half serious and half teasing. "My son is enamored with you."

Her smile held that enigmatic quality that made the *Mona Lisa* famous. "We were attracted to each other from the get-go," she said. "I think we simply fell in love with each other."

He turned and gazed down at her. "Who do you mean? You and him or you and me?"

She laid her head to one side and let her gaze peruse

him. "Him and me. I thought you came into our relationship kicking and screaming." Her face had the look of one totally innocent of what she was, or was about to be, accused. She patted his hand, soothingly, as a mother would a child. "But you got your act together, didn't you?"

"You pick a fine time to get fresh with me," he said. She had a way of yanking his chain at times when he couldn't give her her comeuppance, like now with Teddy sitting between them. "If you don't want it spread around," he said to her, "don't let *him* hear it."

"Gosh, I guess that takes some getting used to."

"It definitely does. Even speaking in code doesn't help. This is what I call the rubber sponge age when kids absorb everything. It's also a great time to teach them."

"Daddy, is Miss Felicia going to stay with us at Granddad's house?"

"Yes, she is."

"Gee. Can I stay with her? You can stay with Granddad or Uncle Cade."

"We will accept whatever arrangements Granddad makes."

The limousine arrived at La Guardia Airport, and the driver got out and opened the door for Felicia and Teddy. "If your plans change or your plane is late, sir, just give me a call. I'll be here when you arrive."

"Thanks, Bob. See you Sunday," Ashton said. For the last seven years, he'd been what anyone would consider very wealthy, but he had yet to take for granted the numerous conveniences available to him, and he didn't want a woman whose principal sport was lolling in luxury. He wanted a woman who... He nearly lost his breath. He wanted Felicia, and he wanted her for the rest of his life.

He looked back, thinking that Teddy dragged behind, and shook his head in amazement when he saw that the boy walked hand in hand with Felicia.

He thought about that as he drove the rented car from Frederick Municipal Airport to Rose Hill. The quiet in the backseat gave him license to let his mind roam, and roam it did. After watching Felicia do a man's job for ten days, he'd come to terms with her popularity and the fame-seekers who trailed her, because he now knew that it wasn't a part of her, that she neither needed nor sought it. She said she wanted children, and he believed her, but to be sure that she meant it, he would ask her each time if she wanted him to use protection. From the rearview mirror, he saw that Teddy was asleep in her lap with his head on her breast, and on her sleeping face was the most serene expression he'd ever seen on a woman. He parked in front of his family home, turned and feasted his eyes on the sight of his child asleep in the arms of the woman he loved.

"Planning to sit here the rest of the day?"

Ashton jerked his head around at the sound of Cade's voice, got out of the car and embraced his younger brother. "You're looking great, man," he said. "I'd better wake them up."

Cade's eyelid dropped in a signifying wink. "Yeah. That picture back there is enough to make a man think. I gather Teddy's in love with her."

"Looks like it." He walked around to the side of the car on which Felicia sat with Teddy in her arms. "I can't imagine Teddy sleeping during midday," he told Felicia. "Neither Eartha nor I can get him to take a nap. He'll just lie in bed and play with his toys or the computer. You've got magic, woman." He held Teddy in one arm, and put his other one around her.

"Cade, this is Felicia Parker."

"So I gather. I'm happy to meet you at last, Felicia. Welcome to our family home." He kissed her cheek, turned and looked at Ashton, his face covered with a rougish smile. "Man, is Granddad going to love this woman!"

"And I'm delighted to meet you, Cade. Why is your grandfather going to love me?"

Cade's grin broadened. "Well, he likes good-looking women, and he especially likes brainy and accomplished women. You're the perfect package."

"Thanks."

"I sure hope you're right," Ashton said. "By the way, how's Leslie getting on?" He looked around and didn't see Teddy. "Wh—"

"He ran inside," Felicia said. "I felt as if I'd been deserted."

"Not to worry," Cade said. "Teddy knows where to get ice cream."

"You didn't answer my question," Ashton said to Cade. "I assume she's still here."

Cade ran the backs of his fingers over his hair. It was a strange trait, and no one in the family could understand why he did it. "Oh, yes," he said. "She's very much here." He fell into step beside Felicia, and they walked up the walkway to the house. "You'll meet her this evening, Felicia."

"I'll look forward to it," she said. "Uh…I have a feeling that Leslie is important to you. Is she?"

"I think so, but I haven't sorted it all out yet. Maybe you and I can talk about this another time."

"Yes, of course. If you'd like," she said, and Ashton knew then that his brother had been waiting for an opportunity to talk with Felicia about Leslie. He wondered what the problem could be, but he didn't intend to bring up the subject. If Cade wanted his advice, he only had to ask.

Holding Teddy's hand, Jake opened the door as his two grandsons and Felicia walked up the steps of his modern, five-bedroom home. He often said he'd get lost in the house if he hadn't worn a path from the master bedroom, where he slept, to the kitchen, dining room and front door.

He stood tall and erect with his right hand on his hip. "Well. It's high time I met you, Felicia," he said, opened his arms to her, and she walked into them and hugged him. "I'd begun to wonder if my elder grandson had any sense at all," he said with his arm still around her. His grin, so like Ashton's, eclipsed his face. "You're as beautiful as you are smart, and from what Teddy tells me, you have a way with little boys."

"I'm happy to meet you, too, sir," she said. "I hear you've got a sweet tooth, so I made you something."

Jake hugged her. "If my grandson doesn't get his act together, I'll throttle him." He opened the box. "Felicia, I'd turn somersaults for this." His joy at receiving the cake spread over his face in a brilliant smile. With a grin still shining on his face, he embraced Ashton. "Thank you for bringing Felicia to me. How are you, son?"

He didn't know why, but he felt the way he did all those years ago when his professors examined him for his M.B.A. degree. "I'm well. There're one or two things outstanding, but they ought to straighten out in a week or so."

"Barber-Smith?"

"That's the fly in the ointment, but I'm doing my best to stave them off."

"Good. Let me know if I can help you further." Cade and Teddy left Jake and Ashton and took Felicia with them. "She's more than I hoped for, son. She isn't merely beautiful and brainy, she's a warm, sweet and feminine woman. Take care with this relationship."

"I'm trying to, Granddad. My only reservation now is that fame-seekers follow her hoping for mention in her column, and even that's becoming less important in view of her other assets. But, gosh, it's impossible to have a peaceful dinner with her in a reasonably good New York restaurant. I got fed up with it."

"If she doesn't encourage it, you can't blame her," Jake said. "And you don't have to eat in Twenty-One. Find some good restaurants in Westchester or Queens. Is that all? Do you love each other?"

"Oh, yes. That, we do."

Jake patted Ashton's shoulders. "Then don't waste time. Teddy's crazy about her, and in matters such as this, children are not easily fooled. You have my blessings."

At seven o'clock, Ken, who cooked and kept house for Jake and Cade, announced that dinner would be ready in half an hour. Felicia hadn't thought that suburbanites dressed for dinner, so she'd brought a red silk jumpsuit to wear at the evening meal and was glad she did. Leslie Fields, the riding instructor who seemed to have captured Cade's heart, arrived in a green one, albeit of a different fabric and style. She liked Leslie at once, for it was obvious that the woman didn't waste time competing with other women either for attention or for the favors of men.

She created an opportunity to speak with Leslie, pretending that her zipper seemed caught. "This is a wonderful environment," Felicia said to Leslie. "It seems a century from New York with its noise and stress."

"Yes," Leslie agreed. "In a way, I'll be sorry when the summer ends and I have to go back to the university. Sometimes, I've a good mind to stay here. Until I took this job, I'd never heard a mockingbird sing, never seen a firefly, had a squirrel eat from my hand, or felt water running over my feet in a brook."

"Does Cade have anything to do with this nostalgia?"

"Of course, he does," Leslie said, showing a disdain for coyness. "He's a wonderful man, and we tiptoe around each other as if we're avoiding land mines, but both of us know the day will come when we'll get together, and believe me, it will be a powerful explosion."

"What's holding the two of you back?" Felicia asked her.

"I think it's because we're a lot alike. Both of us need to be certain, because we know that once we start it, it will never go away."

"Would you be upset with me if I told Cade this?"

"Good Lord, no, I wouldn't. I'd be happy if you did. I need to know whether I'm misplacing my feelings for him, and I—I need him." She looked at her unpainted, but well-buffed fingernails. "You and Ashton are in love." It was statement, not a question.

"Yes. We are, and that's why Ashton brought me to meet Cade and his granddad. I've met Damon."

"Let's go back in there. Maybe you and I will see a lot more of each other. I sincerely hope so," Leslie said.

Felicia stopped. "Do you have any more reservations about your relationship with Cade? I mean, is there more that you need but aren't getting?"

"A lot," Leslie said, "but I can't send that message by you, if you get what I mean."

"I do, and I'm sure that, given the opportunity, you'll take care of that. Sometime, you have to shake them up. If you have to wait too long, *make* the opportunity. Come on."

"Do you have any little boys for me to play with, Miss Leslie?" Teddy said as soon as they sat down at the table. "Miss Felicia doesn't have any."

"No, I don't, darling. I wish I did."

"Maybe my daddy can get some for you. Can you, Daddy?"

"I know he's clever," Cade said, "but I'd rather he wasn't *that* clever."

"Do you want to go to the zoo with me again sometime, Teddy?" Felicia asked the boy, hoping to distract his attention. She wasn't accustomed to Cade's candidness, but the other adults at the table showed no surprise. Both Ashton and Leslie smiled their thanks for her intervention.

"Oh, yes," Teddy said, "and can we take Miss Eartha?" She assured him that they could.

After supper, Cade went over to Felicia, spoke softly and then said out loud, "Brother, you don't mind if I take a short stroll with your girl, do you? I haven't had a chance to talk with her."

They walked out to the garden, and it didn't surprise her when he stopped at a place where they would be in full view of the other adults. "Do you love my brother?" he asked without preliminaries.

Taken aback, but understanding that the man was forthright and plainspoken, she answered truthfully. "Yes. I love him."

"I ask because I can see that he loves you, and deeply, too. I won't ask what your intentions are, because you may not have told Ashton, but you're the woman for him. He knows it, too, because he's never brought another one to this house."

"Somehow, I suspected that," she said.

"What about Teddy? He's a part of the deal, you know."

"I know. If he weren't, I'd have a hard time respecting Ashton. Teddy comes first with him, and that's as it should be. He's such a precious child."

"Then you're satisfied with Ashton, even though you'd have to share him with Teddy?"

"Cade, I love Teddy and he loves me. I will love him no matter what happens between Ashton and me."

"Ashton is a lucky man. I'm happy for him."

"You could be just as lucky."

Cade's eyebrows shot up. "What do you mean?"

"Leslie cares for you, and she's perplexed that you don't make a move, although you want her. Do you fear loving someone? Don't be afraid, Cade. I never knew who I was until Ashton held me in his arms. I walked alone, lived alone, and then I saw *him*. When he held me, his touch was so intense, so electrifying like…like the sight of the sound of thunder and…and the sight of lightning streaking through the sky. It's an unbelievable feeling to hold and be held by the one you love. I bloomed like a flower opening to the morning. Don't let it pass you by, Cade."

"Did she tell you she felt something for me?"

"Yes, and when I asked her if she minded my telling you, she said she wanted me to tell you."

"She's in my mind twenty-four-seven. She's… Do you like her?"

"Very much, indeed, or I wouldn't have mentioned her to you."

Suddenly he showed his teeth in a grin that quickly covered his face. "I told Ash that what I needed was a sister. It's time he gave me one. Let's go back."

"Where's Damon?"

"He'll be in sometime tonight."

"I wish you blessings with Leslie."

"Thanks.

They joined the others, and she noticed Jake's attentiveness to Leslie. He spoke directly to Cade. "Son, do you realize we're going to lose Leslie at the end of September when she goes back to the university? I don't see how we can run the riding school without her."

Cade took a seat beside Leslie and draped an arm across her shoulder, an act that obviously surprised her. "Ever wonder why the weather forecasts miss the mark half the time, Granddad? It's because mankind is unable to predict the future with accuracy. So let's not get into the matter of Leslie's leaving here."

Let that be a lesson to you, girl, and never forget it. Even the strongest, most self-assured man needs encouragement from the woman he wants. She remembered her seductive behavior that brought Ashton's mouth in contact with hers for the first time, and cautioned herself not to forget that a man needs to know that his woman wants him.

"I'm going up to put Teddy to bed," Ashton said, looking at her. "Want to come along?"

"I want to sleep with Miss Felicia, Daddy," the boy said as they climbed the stairs to the room in which they would sleep.

"You're too big a boy for that, son, so you stay with me tonight."

"Aw, gee whiz. Can she sing something to me, Daddy? Miss Eartha can't sing."

"You're trying to postpone going to sleep," Ashton said, sat Teddy on the side of the bed and began removing his shoes and clothing.

"I'll sing one song for you, and then you have to close your eyes and go to sleep," Felicia told him.

Teddy dived into bed and looked at Felicia. "Now, you can sing," he said. She sat on the edge of his bed and stroked his cheek while the soft sounds of Gershwin's "Summertime" flowed from her throat. At the end of the song, she leaned forward to kiss his cheek, and his little arms encircled her neck in a gripping hug. "I love you, Miss Felicia," he whispered.

"I love you, too," she said, pulled the sheet up around him, got up and without glance in Ashton's direction, almost stumbled out of the room. He caught her before she reached the stairs.

"What's the…" She turned into his arms. "You're crying. What is it? What's the matter? You've got to talk to me right this minute." He guided her into the guest room where she would sleep and sat with her on the side of the bed. "Talk to me."

"I… It's dangerous to love somebody else's child, when that child can be t-taken from you in a second."

"Don't forget that it's equally as dangerous for him. He loves you, and he would be devastated if he lost you. He doesn't feel the same for Eartha as he feels for you. Don't worry. I'm not planning voluntarily to separate the two of you."

"I should ask what that means, but I won't. When you want me to know, you'll tell me."

"I brought you here, because I wanted you to meet my family and for them to get to know you. How'd you make out with Cade? Did he interrogate you?"

"We got on fine. He asked questions, and I answered them. We also talked about his relationship with Leslie. I think he loves her, and I doubt he could find a finer woman."

Ashton grabbed her shoulders and gazed down at her. "Do you mean that? Then why can't they get together?"

"Because they're both alike. She's crazy about him, but he doesn't make a move, and I told him so. And she loves it here so much that she's dreading the time when school opens. She admitted that her love for the place is bound to her feelings for Cade. If he finds her warm and loving, I'd say she's for him."

"Well I'll be damned. I thought she was a serious professor who couldn't see past the back of a horse. Oh, she's friendly, but—well, since I knew Cade was interested in her I haven't talked with her much. Granddad thinks the world of her."

"That ought to tell you something. He's a discerning man. We'd better go back."

They found Jake sitting alone. "Felicia," he said, "since you, Ashton and I have some privacy, I hope you and my grandson will make a life together. I'm happy that my grandson has a woman like you. He's blessed. He's a fine man, but don't let him get used to you. When a man and a woman are in love, they should get married. Relationships don't stand still. Next time I see you—"

"Granddad, you're about to overstep your bounds."

"Well, I didn't raise you boys to be so slow. Cade couldn't get a move on until he saw how things are with you and Felicia. They left here practically locked together. We may not see him again in a year." Ashton laughed out loud. "Well," Jake said, obviously on a roll, "she's been here two months and I'd swear he's never had his hands on her. Tonight, he put his arm around her shoulder, and she almost jumped out of her skin. Minutes later, they leave here all hooked up to go off someplace and howl at the moon."

"I think you got that wrong, Granddad. Cade's been baying at the moon alone for the past two months, but he won't be howling tonight."

"Humph," Jake said. "He'd better not let that fine woman get away."

Felicia patted Jake's hand, one that had been in use so long that every vein impressed itself upon his skin. "He won't let her get away, Mr. Underwood, and she doesn't want to get away."

"Humph. I'll wait and see. I'm also going to be watching you two."

Late Sunday afternoon, he was preparing to board a Piedmont Airlines plane at Frederick Municipal Airport with Teddy in his arms and Felicia's hand held tightly in his own. He wanted to take her home with him to spend the night, but he had to think about his family's reactions to finding her there Monday morning. Moreover, he didn't think that Felicia, with her strong sense of privacy, would like the idea. All right, she bunked with him in Mississippi, but circumstance drove her to it and, even then, she slept with him only once.

"Is Miss Felicia coming home with us, Daddy?"

"Don't you remember that we went to her home and got her? Well, we have to take her back home."

When Teddy's bottom lip protruded, he knew he had a problem. The child folded his arms and refused to get on the plane. He didn't want to let Teddy's behind feel the palm of his hand, but he did not tolerate disobedience from his child.

"Listen, son," he said as gently as he could, "you get up and walk into that plane or Felicia and everybody else in this airport will see my hand go to your behind. Is that clear? I am ashamed that you would let Felicia see you behave so badly."

Teddy got up and walked over to Felicia, but he spoke to his father. "I wouldn't be bad if you'd take her home with us. I want her to go home with me."

"Some other time, but not now. I do not reward you for bad behavior. Do you understand?"

"Yes, sir. Come on, Miss Felicia." Teddy took her hand, and she looked to Ashton for some guidance.

"Go ahead, you two," he said, aware of her split allegiance in her desire both to give Teddy motherly love and to please him. "She'll have to get used to it," he told himself. "Teddy could be a handful."

"I'd give anything to come back to you tonight," he told her as he stood at her door holding a sleepy Teddy in his arms, "but by the time I get him to bed, it will be late. Your going with me to meet my family this weekend means more to me that I can express right now. When we speak, I'll try to tell you what your talk with Leslie has meant to Cade. After this weekend, well… I think he's besotted with her, and he's happier than I've ever known him to be." He leaned forward and kissed her as best he could with Teddy asleep in his arms. "Don't forget that I love you."

"I won't forget anything about you. And you remember that I love you." He tweaked her nose and walked off with a smile that began in his heart.

Still in a state of euphoria from her weekend with Ashton, Teddy and their family, Felicia sailed into the offices of the *New York Evening Journal* that Monday morning singing softly and anxious to start her working day. Within minutes her editor managed to prick her balloon.

"John Underwood is in another fight with the Barber-Smith people over ownership with his company, Dream. Something screwy's going on there, and I want the inside scoop. Get it from anybody willing to give it, except Underwood, of course."

"What? How do you know this?"

"I don't have to know it," Ray said. "The story will sell papers."

"Forget it. I will report the truth or nothing. You want me to ruin my reputation by fabricating a story that every financial media will pick up and carry? No, sirree. And, Ray, have you forgotten that Underwood owns this paper?"

"Sure. I know he bought the chain...as if he didn't have enough money already. My brother used to own this paper. Old man Skate bought it out from under him, but he let him stay on as manager and me as editor in chief. Underwood wants to run the thing himself."

Her back stiffened, and the bile of irritation coiled inside of her. "Surely, he doesn't plan to edit this paper."

"No, but he intends to keep his muddy fingers in the running of it, right down to handling the payroll from his office. I want a juicy story on that merger, and I'll edit it myself. I don't demand approval of your column, but I will approve this one."

She decided not to confront him, but to submit her column and, if he altered it to distort the facts, she would speak to Ashton about it. She warned Ray, "I'll write a column on the merger, and if you distort the facts, I'll go over your head, Ray. I like working with you, but if you sink this paper to the level of a supermarket tabloid, I will expose you."

"You'll go over my head, eh? To whom?"

"Just please don't make me do something that we could both regret. Is that all?"

"No. I want the article for your Thursday column."

She hung up and began wondering where, other than Ashton, she could find information on the Underwood/Barber-Smith tug-of-war. As she was about to check out some Internet blogs, her phone rang.

"This is Ashton. How's my girl?"

"After that wonderful, relaxing weekend, I'd feel sorry for myself if I wasn't looking forward to seeing you this evening. I am, am I not?"

"You bet. Would you be willing to go with me to Hobart and Buffield's annual garden party? It's an event for the board of directors, which includes me. Will you go with me?"

Taken aback, she stammered her agreement. It hadn't occurred to her that he'd be on the board of such a high-powered firm. "I'll be delighted. Is this a wide hat and billowy skirt affair?"

"Wide hats and gloves, but I don't remember any billowy skirts. Most years, they've looked sleek and sexy to me."

"Okay. Just tell me what you're wearing."

"White tuxedo."

She'd probably faint if she saw him in that getup. "What time?"

"I'll pick you up at a quarter after five. It shouldn't take us more than fifteen minutes to get to there."

"Doggone," she said after she hung up. "Now I have to find a long, sexy, chiffon dress and a hat to match. Those rich dames are not going to shame me."

After work, she headed for the East Village and a shop that sold expensive "antique" clothing and found precisely what she wanted—a peach-colored silk chiffon sheath and matching wide-brimmed hat. White, elbow-length gloves would have to do.

On the day of the garden party, she got home at about five o'clock, hung the dress in a closet, and headed for the shower. While the water cascaded over her naked body, in her mind's eye she envisaged Ashton's hands replacing the stream and trembled with anticipation of the evening to come. Ashton's granddad had warned her not to let Ashton become complacent with her, and she didn't mean to let that happen, but it seemed like years since she'd felt him storming inside of her. When her mouth watered and her nipples puckered, she turned off the water, and as she dried her body, frissons of heat fired her libido. She could think of nothing but the minute when she would feel his mouth all over her body.

She slipped into her scant, peach-colored bikini pants and demi-bra, eased into the evening dress, zipped it up and gazed at herself in the mirror. "He's got the self-control of a heavenly angel if he gets out of here tonight without making love to me," she said to herself. She stuck her feet into a pair of silver sandals, rolled her hair into a French knot put on the hat and admired the effect. Just as the doorbell rang, she pulled on her gloves, got her silver lamé evening bag and opened the door.

His sharp whistle was all the approval she needed. She stepped back and stared at him. "Cary Grant and Duke Ellington would have to genuflect to you," she said as marbles battled for space in her stomach.

"If I did what I feel like doing," he said, "we wouldn't leave this apartment."

Her left eye closed in a slow, seductive wink. "There's always later."

Flames seemed to jump in his eyes, and she could see him battling his will, but she did nothing to help. His Adam's apple worked furiously, and his breathing shortened. He closed his eyes briefly, and then forced a smile. "Where are your keys?" She handed them to him, stepped out into the hall and watched while he locked the door.

"One of these days, I'm going to make you holler uncle."

She knew her smiled encompassed her whole face. "I can't wait."

He grasped her arm and walked more swiftly than she would have liked to the elevator and, later, to the waiting chauffeured limousine. She spoke to Bob, got in with as much grace as her long sheath would allow, and leaned back. "I'm glad you no longer see the need for me to have a bodyguard," she said.

He bunched his shoulders in a shrug, but that didn't fool her. And well it shouldn't have, for he said, "I just don't pester you about riding with him, but Bob trails you. I figured that your absence from the scene while you spent two weeks in Mississippi would cool off any likely predators." She clenched her teeth and said nothing, for she didn't intend to ruin her evening with him.

"If I thought you looked beautiful wearing fatigues, a baseball cap turned backward and brogans, you may imagine that the way you look right now has me strung out. You make a man feel important."

"Thanks. You *are* important. I wasn't exactly prepared for the way you look, either. I'm proud to be with you, and not just because of that elegant tux."

"That's one of the nicest thing you've said to me. A guy likes to know that his woman is proud of him, and I'm not talking about the way he looks."

"If I wasn't wearing lipstick, I'd kiss you."

"You can do that later," he said with a grin. "I think you alleged that possibility when we were leaving your apartment. If you haven't already discovered it, you'll find that I have the memory of an elephant."

"I'll give you something to remember," she said beneath her breath.

"I heard that, and you can bet I intend to give you the opportunity." He leaned over to kiss her cheek just as the limousine turned the corner and, instead of her cheek, his lips claimed her mouth.

"Please don't do that unless you have plenty of time, Ashton. I'm not in the mood for a tease."

"I wasn't teasing." His hand rested on her thigh. "I was attempting to communicate something to you."

"I know," she said, stroking his right cheek.

The limousine rolled to a stop in front of a town house on Eighty-third Street between Fifth and Madison. She deliberately showed no interest in the furnishings, for she didn't wish to appear awestruck—the black gal agape at such a measure of wealth. She surmised that she'd been in wealthier homes. From the balcony, she saw that her choice of attire couldn't have been more perfect and, with so many white, pink and blue dresses, it pleased her that she hadn't worn either.

They walked arm-in-arm down to the garden, and her gaze landed on Kate Smallens, the mistress of Julian Smith, co-partner in Barber-Smith, Inc. She whispered to Ashton, "Don't look toward that trellis right now, but the woman in pale blue is Kate Smallens."

"What? Get outta here! She doesn't belong in this crowd, or does she?"

"I don't know, Ashton, but she's paying us a lot of attention."

"Really? Then let's go over and greet her."

"I don't know, but if you say so." With an arm around her waist, he was already headed that way, and Kate Smallens suddenly appeared uncomfortable.

"Hello, Ms. Smallens," Felicia said. "How nice to see you again. Allow me to introduce John Underwood, CEO of Dream. John, this is Kate Smallens."

"This is certainly a surprise, Ms. Smallens," Ashton said, aware that in letting the woman know he connected her to Dream and, thus, to Julian Smith, he knocked her off balance.

Felicia had never seen a human being shrivel up so quickly. "Uh…glad to meet you," was all she said.

"I wonder what she's doing here," Ashton said as they walked on.

"She may be related to our hostess."

"That's right. I have to find Martha and introduce the two of you."

"Well," Martha Buffield said to Felicia, "it's time somebody slowed Ashton down. I've introduced him to

four women, and not once did he invite one of them out.
I can see why. Bring her to see me, Ashton. I'd love to
arrange a small dinner party for her." She appeared to
scrutinize Felicia. "You *will* come, won't you?"

"Thank you for the invitation," she said while failing
to give the assurance that Martha sought.

"You response was perfect," Ashton said later. "Would
you like a drink?" he asked Felicia.

"Thanks, but this hat and this dress require that I nego-
tiate with a level head. I'll have a drink when I get home."

He raised an eyebrow. "Alone?"

She raised one right back at him. "I wasn't planning to."

His adrenaline kicked into high gear, and the heat of
desire raced through him. She looked as cool as a woman
could look, but beneath that veneer of seeming indiffer-
ence was a hot woman who could open her arms and
send a man into the stratosphere. He closed his eyes in
a futile attempt to erase from his memory the sight of
her writhing beneath him in orgasm after orgasm. The
light touch of her hand on his arm brought him back to
the present.

"What's the matter?" she asked. "Do you want to leave?"

"As soon as I locate our host in this thicket of human
flesh we can leave. I dislike cocktail parties, and the fact
that this one is out of doors in a garden doesn't make it
more palatable."

He accepted the handshake of an older man. "Good to see
you, Underwood. I understand we're in for a fight with
Barber-Smith, but the board's behind you. Still, we have our
work cut out for us." He looked at Felicia. "To be honest, I
stopped to have a closer look at your charming companion."

"Gordon Ellsworth, this is Felicia Parker."

"Not *the* Felicia Parker. I hope you give 'em pure hell about their latest tricks."

"Glad to meet you, Mr. Ellsworth. What tricks? It's dangerous to make such statements to a reporter."

"I was hoping you'd say that. If you're planning to do a story, here's my card. I hope to see you both again soon." The man shook hands with Ashton and walked on.

"I think he knew who you were," Ashton said. "Ellsworth is a cunning man, and I suspect he knows something about Barber-Smith or one of its partners."

"I wonder what it could be," she said.

Ashton found Mark Buffield of Hobart and Buffield, thanked him for the party, and escorted Felicia to their limousine. "If you don't mind, could we put the hat in the trunk of the car and let's get some dinner. We can't go to Subway with you wearing that dress. What about Plaza Athenée? It's upscale, the food is delicious and the clientele aren't likely to annoy you."

"Wherever you may be, I'll follow you," she sang the song in a subdued but honeyed tone.

"Be careful. Those words may come back to haunt you."

"Not unless you decide to take me somewhere." With his hormones galloping out of control and his testosterone at flood level, he was in no mood for three hours of foreplay, starting with her ability to seduce him with words.

After an elegant meal that began with Margueritas and ended with Crème Courvoisier, he was more than ready for what she had teased him about during the past four-and-one-half hours.

As they headed out of the elegant restaurant, Felicia patted his left arm. "Excuse me a second, please." In the ladies' room, she brushed her teeth, freshened her lipstick and dabbed some Fendi perfume in strategic places. "He's been sending me signals all evening," she said to herself, "and I hope he got mine."

She stepped out of the women's room just as he emerged from the men's room. "If we didn't have the limousine, we could walk," he said, taking her arm.

"You want me to use up my energy walking?" she asked him. "I wouldn't have thought it."

He missed a step. "When I first met you, you weren't so fresh."

"When you first met me, I didn't know as much about you as I do now."

Bob held the door while she slid into the car and Ashton followed her. "I hope you're choosing your words carefully," he said, leaning back with a grin on his face. "Because you're going to pay for this."

She eased closer to him so that her thigh was snug against his. "Will I enjoy it?" she asked him

"I'll do my best to see that you do." This time he didn't smile, and she knew she'd carried the joking as far as he would permit. Remorseful for having joked about something sacred to them both, she grasped his hand and rested her head on his shoulder. "I'm sorry, but you're all I've thought about all day and I…I need to be with you."

His arms went around her. "I know. I need you, too, more than you can imagine."

He remembered to take her hat out of the trunk of the limousine, walked over to Bob and spoke softly, but she heard the words, "Good night," and her heart began to thump madly in her chest. *No point in acting cool, girl. You started this.* Yes, she had, but courage was easily come by when there was no possibility of following through. At the door of her apartment, she handed him her key and asked, "Would you like to come in for a drink?"

"Yes. I'd like that a lot." He opened the door, followed her into the living room and took a seat on the sofa. "I like this room," he said. "It's uncluttered, spacious and these colors are warm and inviting, like you. Soft, autumn colors. But your bedroom is lavender and a dark shade of pink. It's beautiful, but so unlike the living and dining rooms. I've wondered about that."

She didn't want to talk about the colors in her apartment, and she doubted he did. She smiled to hide her nervousness. "Would you like wine, scotch or vodka and tonic?"

"Vodka and tonic, please, and try not to stay away from me too long. I may get lonely." She wondered at his sober expression and tone, but didn't articulate her thoughts. He was here, and before he left her, he would be hers once more. She brought the drinks and a dish of toasted pecans, placed them on the coffee table and sat beside him.

He lifted his glass, and she did the same. She thought he'd say some kind of a toast, but he merely clicked her glass and sipped his drink. Finally he said, "Felicia, I've never stayed out all night since I had Teddy, but I want to spend the night with you. I also want to be home before he gets up."

She mused over that for a minute or so, glanced at him and realized that he was waiting for her response. "I can set the clock to alarm. Is six o'clock too early?"

She'd swear that while she gazed at him, storm clouds gathered in his eyes. "It would be perfect," he said, as if passion hadn't gripped him. "What are you drinking?"

For an answer, she put her glass to his lips and let him taste the gin and tonic. She rarely drank hard liquor, but for this night, she was in a mood to let it all hang out. Even though she knew she shouldn't drink it fast, she put the glass to her lips and drained it. Almost at once, the gin made its presence known in the pit of her stomach, and she rested her head on the back of the sofa.

"I'd put my head on your shoulder," she told him, "but I don't want to soil your white suit. Lord, you look great in this thing."

He put his glass on the table, pulled off his jacket, threw it across the arm of the sofa and pulled her into his arms. "I'm not wearing the jacket now."

"No, but you're wearing this silk shirt," she said, and began unbuttoning it. She looked up, found him gazing at her with his heart in his eyes, and sucked in her breath. "Oh, darling, hold me. Love me. I—"

His mouth came down on hers fierce and possessive, and his arms tightened around her. As if frustrated, he lifted her onto his lap, and kissed her eyes, face, neck, ears, throat and her lips, while his hands stroked her arms and her back.

"Take this off me. I want to feel your hands on my body." He unzipped her dress, lowered the bodice and sucked her nipple into his mouth. She let out a keening cry for more, and he stood and carried her to bed. At last, he was storming inside of her, moaning her name, driving her to climax after climax. "You're mine," he said. "Do you hear me? You belong to me."

"And you are mine," she breathed. "Mine alone."

Suddenly he became still, pushing back the relief for which she reached so desperately. "Tell me you love me. Only me. I don't want you with anyone else. You're all I want. All I need," he said.

"I love you. I'll always love you," she whispered. He locked her to his body, found the place that she loved to have him stroke and took them both to the sweet oblivion of ecstasy.

When the clock alarmed at six o'clock, he separated their bodies, kissed her and left her bed. A few minutes later, she heard to front door close and automatically lock. He'd done and said everything but ask her to marry him. It was time she asked him about his intentions.

Chapter 12

Taking the stair steps two at a time, Ashton hurried to Teddy's room, opened the door softly, peeped in at the sleeping child, and breathed deeply in relief. Whenever he was away from the boy, even for a short while, he didn't rest until he saw him safe and unharmed. He went to his own room, got out of his white tuxedo, showered, dressed and went downstairs. When he realized that it was too early for Eartha to have started the breakfast, he made coffee, toasted a bagel, smeared raspberry jam on it, and sat down to eat and read the previous evening's paper.

His glance caught a boxed item in the lower right-hand corner of the front page, and he nearly spilled hot coffee on his trousers. Readers were told that Underwood Enterprises was in for the fight of its life against Barber-Smith, and that a full accounting would appear in Felicia Parker's Thursday column.

What the hell! I don't believe this. She was with me for twelve hours and didn't see fit to tell me she was writing about something this important to me. She had the perfect opportunity when old man Ellsworth told her he had information she could use for her next column about Barber-Smith and invited her to telephone him.

He read the financial section word for word, but could find no other mention of the upcoming story or of his battle with Barber-Smith. "How could she?" He fumed. *She swears to love me, and last night she practically hypnotized me. I could hardly make myself get out of that bed and out of her and come home.* He rubbed his forehead as if confused. *Just when I'd convinced myself that I couldn't live without her, that she would make a good mother for my child... I couldn't have been that far off. We've been through a lot together. Hell! I was going out today, buy a ring and ask her tonight if she'd marry me.*

"Good morning, Mr. Ash," Eartha said, rubbing her eyes. "Why you in here so early? No, don't get up. I can have you some scrambled eggs and bacon in ten minutes, and I only have to warm the biscuits."

"I have to make a call. No. Never mind. I'll do that later." He sat down, having decided to bring up the matter while he was looking at her. He sat there pretending to read the paper, but he didn't see words, only his dream slipping away from him.

Within a few minutes, Eartha put his breakfast on the table and topped off his coffee. "Why you so somber, Mr. Ash? Anybody would think you'd be grinning from ear to ear this morning."

"What do you mean?"

She hurried back to the stove and busied herself. "Well, since this is the first time you ever stayed out all night when you were right here in the city, I was hoping you'd found...uh...you know what I mean."

He didn't answer her but forced down his breakfast as quickly as he could. "I'll be in my office."

"Yes, sir. Me and Teddy are going to the supermarket soon as he gets up and eats his breakfast."

He telephoned Felicia. She was probably still in bed getting her Saturday morning rest, but he couldn't help that. He knew he'd better call her before he developed a hardened attitude, and did the unthinkable, for if he didn't call her after having spent the night in her arms, and her body, she'd have every right to think him a scoundrel.

"Hi." Her voice was that of a warm, sleepy and sated woman.

"Hi. I take it you're still in bed."

"I am," she said. "How are you?"

"I'm on my way to my office. How about dinner around seven-thirty? I can't make it earlier, because I'd like to sit with Teddy while he eats."

"Sounds good to me. Couldn't we go someplace where he can come, too?"

"Hmm. Some other time, maybe. See you at seven-thirty."

"Okay," she said. "Love you."

Before he could reply, she hung up, and he knew she detected the coolness that he tried without success to hide. "Why didn't she tell me? She knows what Dream means to me."

"You talking to me, Mr. Ash?" Teddy came barreling down the stairs, and he didn't have to answer Eartha.

"Daddy, ask Miss Felicia if we can go to the zoo today. I want to pet the little pig."

"Not today, son. If it doesn't rain tomorrow, I may take you."

He stared, disbelieving, when Teddy's bottom lip protruded, and he dropped himself into the chair at the table beside his father. "I want Miss Felicia to take me."

"You're either going with me, or you're not going. That's that."

The child looked up at him with a pained expression. "Then can she come over to see me?"

What did he say to that? Teddy needed Felicia's softness and her sweetness. He knew that, even when she reprimanded Teddy, she did it with a softer hand than he used. He had to teach the boy to be a man, but she taught him how to feel and to express affection and caring. *Why the hell did she neglect to tell him?*

"We'll sort this out tomorrow, son. I have to go to the office now. Be a good boy and don't give Miss Eartha any trouble."

"I don't bargain with her anymore, Daddy."

Teddy walked with him to the front door where he lifted the boy and hugged him, probably tighter that he should have, for Teddy looked at him with an inquiring expression and said, "I'll be good, Daddy. Honest."

Alone in his office that Saturday morning, he struggled with thoughts as to what he should do about that story. He owned the paper, and he could put a stop to the publication in the *New York Evening Journal* of that or any other item with one phone call. But he didn't believe in censoring the news simply because he didn't like its content. Moreover, he didn't see himself doing anything to hurt

Felicia, not even if her column contained something unfavorable to him.

He answered his cell phone. "This is Damon. What the
hell does Ray Gilder think he's doing? Has he forgotten
who owns that paper? Or did you give Felicia permission
to write that story?" Damon demanded.

Just what he needed. An irate brother to deal with. Any
minute, he'd get calls from Cade and his grandfather
blasting Felicia. "I'm dealing with this, Damon. One way
or the other, it will work out all right. Cut me some slack
here, please."

"I suppose you know that Ray's brother formerly
owned that paper, and Skate got control of it."

"No, I didn't know that. Thanks for telling me. Leave
this to me, Damon. I'll handle it. I saw that notice about
an hour ago, and I haven't talked to Felicia about it yet. I
have to see what she says."

"Yeah. Maybe Ray hasn't told her he's giving her the
assignment."

"God willing. I'll be in touch."

The day sped by much too swiftly, for he dreaded the
moment when he would see her and, knowing himself, he
wouldn't greet her as a man greeted a woman he loved and
who, twelve hours earlier had been his eager lover.

"I can't pretend what I don't feel," he said to himself,
"but I'm going to try my best not to hurt her until she's
had her say."

He needn't have worried. Felicia also saw the notice
in the paper and guessed the reason for his coolness. She
had planned to interview him for the article, but that was
insufficient excuse for not having mentioned it to him,

and especially since Ray wanted a story that would incriminate Ashton.

She dressed in a lavender-colored, cotton-pique sheath, sleeveless with a scooped neck, and told herself to expect the worst. He rang the bell at seven-forty, evidence that he hadn't knocked himself out to be punctual, as was his style. She opened the door and looked up at him. She'd guessed right; his entire demeanor mirrored his anger.

"Hi," she said, grasped his left hand, reached up and kissed his cheek. "I see you've had a rough day."

"That's an understatement if I ever heard one." She locked the door herself and put the key in her handbag. "Where're we going?" She didn't usually ask, but she needed the sound of something other than that of her shoe heels clicking on the tile as they walked.

"Lydia's on Columbus Avenue. It's walking distance." Where was the man who asked her opinion about everything that concerned her and some things that didn't, who forced a bodyguard on her because he had to know that she was safe, and who had a man trailing her for the same reason though he deemed that the bodyguard was no longer necessary? That John Ashton Underwood was no where in evidence.

She ordered a simple meal of shrimp *diable,* spaghetti and a green salad. And although he ordered veal Marsala, mashed potatoes and sautéed spinach, he hardly tasted it. They talked very little while eating. Later, sipping espresso, he looked her in the eye and said, "Why didn't you tell me that you're doing another story on Barber-Smith's attempted takeover? Did you learn something new? Is that why you're doing it, and behind my back yet. What's the secret? And after meeting you in my company, what's

Ellsworth going to think was your reason for not admitting to him that you're writing the story? In this case, you're either with me or against me. There's no middle ground."

"Ray demanded that I write a story unfavorable to Underwood Enterprises, and I told him I wouldn't do it. He has no new information about Barber-Smith, but he wanted me to write a column fabricating something. I'm terribly sorry that I didn't tell you, Ashton, but since I had no intention of writing it, I didn't mention it to you."

"Good for you. But you damned well should have told me. Ray may know something. If you don't write it, he may get another reporter to do it. You even gave Ellsworth the impression that you didn't know what he was talking about when he asked if you were going to write another piece on Barber-Smith. Maybe there is something brewing. You know what this means to me, and you had plenty of time to bring it to my attention. Didn't it occur to you that I might be able to take some strategic steps on my behalf?" He ran his fingers through his hair, punishing his scalp. "If Ray prints a lie in that paper, he can look for another job."

"I knew I wasn't knowingly going to write anything that I couldn't verify as being true, so I didn't take it all that seriously."

He stopped himself just before he banged his fist on the table. "*You didn't take it seriously!* You know how important Dream is to me. You say you love me, but you don't concern yourself with my interests. Hell, Eartha wouldn't have withheld such vital information from me as you did, and we know she's limited."

She bristled at his attack. "If you've finished berating me, I'm ready to leave."

"What do you have to be upset about? I risk losing almost half of my income, and you didn't take it seriously." His lips quivered, and she didn't know whether from anger or some other emotion.

If she knew anything about Ashton, it was that, when it suited him, he could be intransigent. He hadn't listened to her explanation, but was so immersed in his disappointment, that he couldn't see the logic in her explanation.

"I said I was sorry, and I am," she told him, pained and no longer able to look at the eyes she adored, but which held no warmth for her now.

"Thanks for dinner." Without realizing that she would do so, she whirled around and walked out of the restaurant. "I love him, and maybe I was wrong in not telling him. I'm sorry, but I'm damned if I'll give my blood to placate him." She flagged a taxi and went home. So much for that. It was a great ride while it lasted.

Ashton didn't allow his gaze to follow her; it was sufficient that the clicking of her heels sounded increasingly softer as her anger took her farther and farther from him.

"Would you like something else?" the waitress asked him.

"Another espresso, please."

"And one for madam?"

He shook his head. "Cancel that, and bring me the bill."

At home, he checked his answering machine and found that he'd had calls from Cade, his grandfather and Gordon Ellsworth. He phoned Ellsworth first.

"I don't think the press has this yet," Ellsworth said. "I got an inside tip, and I hear it's going to be an uphill fight against Smith, though the board members are with us. We need more shares if we're going to bury them. Why would

Smith go to such trouble for Kate Smallens? She'll spread for any pair of trousers that has a pocketful of greenbacks."

"Beats me. I appreciate your support, and I'll be doing everything I can to keep the company."

"Attaboy. I expect you'll make it."

So this was something that not even Felicia's editor knew about. He sat beside the phone for nearly half an hour before he called his grandfather. "How are you? I just got in."

"A movie company wants to shoot a feature film here. If we allow it, I want them to bring their own horses, build the fences, houses or whatever, and leave the property as they found it. Cade wants all that and more in a contract."

"Cade's right. Tell Damon to draw up a contract and to charge them by the day, so they won't stay there forever."

"Sure will. I hadn't thought of that."

He hung up, phoned Cade and heard more about the probability that a feature film would be produced on their property. Thank God, neither of them had seen the paper or heard the latest rumor, and neither had spoken with Damon.

After hanging up, he went to the kitchen, got a bottle of pilsner beer, took it out to the deck at the back of his house and sat down. Stars nearly covered the sky, and he didn't think he'd ever seen the moon so brilliant. It was not a night for being alone, but he was, and he probably would be for the rest of his life. He drank a swig of beer from the bottle, and rested it on the floor. It should have been the happiest day of his life, for if fate hadn't intervened, Felicia would be wearing his ring. He closed his eyes and exhaled a long breath. Maybe she wouldn't have.

He tossed the bottle into a bin. Surely this overwhelming, almost stupefying love that he felt for her couldn't be one-sided. It hurt. It hurt like hell, but it was best that he know now, rather than later. The best thing for him to do was get on with his life. He went inside, got ready for bed and, when he could no longer postpone it, he lay down and began counting sheep.

Felicia didn't welcome the call from Miles; she knew he'd tell her that Ashton had a right to be annoyed with her, even to mistrust her for not telling him about her boss's proposal. "You mean to say that you didn't tell Ashton what your editor planned to do? I thought you said Ashton owns that paper."

"He does own it, and that's one reason why I didn't tell him. I don't ask him to solve my problems, and I knew I wasn't going to write a bunch of lies about Ashton, his company or anything else, so I didn't bother to mention it. But Ray obviously didn't believe me, so he printed that notice on the front page. He thinks I'd be afraid of losing my job. You see, he doesn't know that Ashton and I are friends, or were."

"No matter. You should have told Ashton, because your editor can always give the story to another reporter if you refuse to write it."

The weight of that possibility hit her, and she sat down on the edge of her desk. "That's what Ashton said. Well, what's done is done. He no longer trusts me, and I walked out and left him sitting alone in the restaurant. It's over."

She heard Miles pull air through his teeth, something that their mother had always frowned on. "Don't be ridiculous. Patch it up, for goodness' sake. And don't be stubborn. That man loves you, and right now, he's hurting.

The longer you let it go, the deeper his pain will be. Have you ever been lonely, Felicia? Let me tell you, it will hit you like a scud missile when you need him, really need him and he isn't there for you."

"I know. But he's so stubborn."

"So are you. Get over it, and do what you have to do. I'll be routing for you."

She phoned the paper's financial columnist. "Ray wants me to write another column on Dream and Barber-Smith. I'm not anxious to do it, because as far as I know, there's nothing new since I last wrote about it."

"I'm not so sure about that, Felicia. This is a relatively small company. Why is Ray so interested in it?"

"Beats me. What's going on with Barber-Smith?"

"Kate Smallens just bought a chunk of stock in Dream. So did Smith's wife, which surprises me, because they used different brokers. My spies say something is about to happen. Kate Smallens didn't even earn enough to pay income tax last year. So where did she get the money to buy seventy thousand dollars' worth of stock? Get my drift?"

"I do, indeed."

She hung up and called Miles. "How much Dream stock can you afford to buy?" she asked him. "You can sell it back next week after the board meets."

"I own some of it, and I can add to that. Now, you're using your head."

"By the way, give me your votes. I need it in writing."

She sold her shares in the paper and bought more stock in Dream. She didn't want to call Ashton and receive an icy, impersonal greeting for her trouble, but she had to tell him what she'd learned.

"Underwood speaking." He knew from his phone's Caller ID that it was she, but he chose to identify himself as if she were a stranger. So be it.

"Ashton, this is Felicia. I'm calling to tell you that our financial columnist has discovered some unusual trading in Dream. Both Smith's wife and Kate Smallens bought huge chunks of the stock this morning."

"What? Thanks for letting me know. I—I appreciate this."

"You're welcome," she said. "Goodbye." She hung up before he had a chance to respond. She knew he wouldn't engage in small talk, and she didn't want to hear it, anyway. What she needed to hear was his acknowledgment that he'd misjudged her, that he was sorry and that he loved her. But she didn't expect him to leave his cocoon of self-assurance and tell her that he'd erred in judgment. Oh, heck. Maybe she was being unfair, but no matter how you sliced it, he had wronged her.

Now, who could that be? "Hello?"

"Miss Felicia, can you come over and see me?"

"Teddy? Honey, how did you get my number?"

"Miss Eartha gave it to me. When can you come? I'm going to have a birthday soon, and I'll be five."

"Teddy, I can't visit you, because I'm going out of town, but I'll see what I can do as soon as I get back. Okay?"

"Yes, ma'am. See you." He hung up, and she made up her mind then, that she would not abandon her relationship with Teddy unless Ashton forced her to do so. She left work at three, and was at the airport in time for a five o'clock flight to Chicago. At eight o'clock that evening, she stood behind a podium at the Carter G. Woodson Library lecturing on the obligation of African-American youths to involve themselves in the country's politics.

"You can't complain about what you get in this life," she told them, "if you don't work to make things go your way." Later, as she luxuriated in the applause and the expressions of appreciation, a chill shot through her when, as if some otherworldly character spoke, she heard out loud the words, "physician, heal thyself." Then, she remembered Miles's advice. But could she make John Ashton Underwood see the light?

Two days later, she telephoned Teddy when she knew that Ashton would be in his office. "I only have a few minutes, Teddy," she told him, "but I can visit you during my lunch hour for a few minutes. Remember, I can't stay long." His squeals warmed her heart. "Let me speak with Miss Eartha."

"Mrs. Clarke, I thought I'd visit Teddy for a few minutes during my lunch hour today. Will that inconvenience you? If not, I should be there about twelve-thirty."

"No, ma'am. If you're willing to eat a hamburger, you can have lunch with us. He's been worrying his little heart out because he doesn't see you."

She heard Teddy's laughing delight when she rang the doorbell, and as Eartha opened the door, he launched himself into her arms and smothered her with kisses. "Come on and let's eat," he said. "You're in a hurry." She held him and kissed him, disbelieving the joy she felt with that child in her arms.

"I tell you, I do hope Mr. Ash is going to do something about this," Eartha muttered, walking toward the breakfast room ahead of Teddy and Felicia. "This child is gone head over heels about you. I never saw the like of it."

Eartha's hamburger was accompanied by potato salad,

sliced tomatoes and a pickle, after which she served the three of them pistachio ice cream. "If I ate here regularly, I'd be three sizes larger," she told Eartha after complimenting her on the meal, kissed Teddy and left.

She knew that Teddy told his father about her visit, and she rejoiced that Ashton hadn't called to tell her not to visit the child again. That Monday morning, she dressed for the board meeting in an avocado linen suit with black accessories, including a flattering black straw hat. She didn't have the money of those Park Avenue women, but she had the class, and she meant to display the outward trappings of it.

She walked into the grand ballroom of the St. Regis and, to her astonishment, Cade, Damon and Jacob—Jake—Underwood sat on the front row at the left aisle. She had her brother's certificates in her purse and, with them, the right to cast his vote as well as her own. She waved to the Underwood men and sat on the front row at the right aisle. She didn't sit with Ashton's family, because she didn't intend to give Ashton the impression that she was sucking up to his family. When Eartha Clarke arrived and sat beside her, she relaxed; Ashton had done his homework. And so had she.

She had managed to impress upon her editor the importance of having at least an accurate basis for the story on Barber-Smith and Dream, and had promised to write it as soon as she could do adequate research. In fact, her motive was the postponement of the story until after the board meeting.

Before Ashton could speak, Julian Smith took the floor, asked for the board's confidence and received scattered applause. Gordon Ellsworth rose and asked if the news that Smith hoped to give Dream to Kate Smallens had any merit and was rewarded with a roar of laughter.

Ashton walked up to the podium and when his glance fell on her, she thought he tried but failed in an effort to smile. His dispirited demeanor saddened her, and she gave him the thumbs-up sign.

He addressed the group. "I have managed this company with integrity and skill. Not since this stock has been on the Exchange has there been a period in which shareholders did not receive dividends, and some of the biggest companies can't lay claim to that. Starting with nothing, my family and I have made this into a thriving company, and we did it with hard work and imagination. I don't think Miss Smallens could do as well. I want a vote by ballot."

Nearing the end of the balloting, she saw how close the vote was and stood, lest some of those who had voted for Ashton should change their vote in order to be with the majority.

"I cast thirty-seven hundred votes for Underwood Enterprises," she said, and gasps could be heard throughout the ballroom. Ashton stared at her, seemingly unable to believe what he heard.

The accountant rapped the table. "Considering the few remaining legal votes to be cast, Underwood carries. According to our by-laws, Barber-Smith must wait seven years before another attempted buyout."

Still staring at her, Ashton closed the meeting. "Thank you for your confidence." With that, he jumped from the rostrum, picked Felicia up and twirled her around and around, all the while laughing with unrestrained joy. The other Underwood men crowded around them, as did

Eartha Clark, who—with her gaze toward the ceiling—said, "Lord, I sure am glad this is over."

"Sweetheart. Oh, sweetheart," Ashton whispered, locked her to him and seared her lips with his own. "Can you ever forgive me for not believing in you?"

"I told you so," his grandfather said. "Didn't I tell you that this woman wouldn't do anything to hurt you? Have you seen anything else about this in your paper? No you haven't, 'cause I've been reading it every day."

"We have to celebrate," Cade said.

"Yeah, but can we postpone that?" Ashton asked them, looking from one to the other. "I've got some fence-mending to do."

"Yeah," Damon said, "and make sure you do a good job of it." He hugged Felicia. "We're all in your debt."

"No you aren't, Damon. What hurts Ashton, hurts me, and maybe I can get him to understand that."

"Don't be too hard on him, Felicia. He's being hard enough on himself," Damon said. "He told me that you went to his home and had lunch with Teddy while he wasn't there, because you didn't want to see him, and that, in spite of the coolness between the two of you, you called to alert him to Barber-Smith's latest sally. He's been trying to find a way to…all right, he should have called and apologized, but—"

"But he was being Ashton. I love him, Damon, but I need some evidence that he believes in me."

"Look," Ashton said to them. "I'll be in Rose Hill Friday night, and we can talk. Right now, I need some time with Felicia."

"Bring her with you," Jake said. "It's time you two cut out this nonsense."

"Yes, sir. I'll ask her."

"I'll see you at home, Mr. Ash," Eartha said.

"Can we have lunch together or...or whatever?" Ashton asked her. They walked out of the hotel onto Fifth Avenue.

"All right, but I'd like something light, and I don't feel like going to a fancy restaurant."

He looked down at her as if trying to gauge her mood. Then he said, "What if we get some hot dogs and a cold drink from that guy on the corner over there and eat in the park? You've got a blouse on under that jacket, haven't you? It's rather warm." He bought the hot dogs and two bottles of lemonade, and they reached the park before she realized that they were holding hands and behaving as if they had never had a misunderstanding.

"If you forgive me, I give you my word that I'll always listen to what you have to tell me, and I'll listen with an open mind and heart."

"What happened? It was so unlike you," she said. "Ray wanted me to fabricate something, and I said no way. By printing that, he hoped to get my readers to lean on me for the story."

"It hasn't come out yet," he said. "Do you know what happened?"

"I stalled for time, because I didn't want him to give the assignment to another reporter until after today."

"One more thing. I didn't know you owned such a big block of Dream."

"I don't." She explained to him how she bought the additional shares and that she also cast her brother's votes.

"You did that for me in spite of my pig-headedness. I

was so hurt when I read that announcement. You see, I had planned to ask you to marry me at dinner that evening, and seeing that was like a blow to the solar plexus. My emotions got the better of my head, Felicia. Intellectually, I'd swear that you wouldn't do anything to hurt me."

"All the same. I should have told you and left it up to you to manage your affairs."

"Can we bury this issue? Have dinner with me tonight. Will you?"

"What time?"

He stood, lifted her to her feet, and kissed her quickly, just enough to make him long for more. "I'll be at your place at seven, and please be ready, because I'm not going inside."

"Why not?" she asked with a raised eyebrow.

"Because I don't want to risk not leaving there."

She opened the door to Ashton at precisely seven o'clock, and he seemed unable to still his gaze from her as it roamed from her head to her feet. "You are so beautiful," he said in a soft voice. "At least to me, you are perfect." She had dressed her best in a short red-silk-chiffon sleeveless dress, fitted to the waist and flared with multilayers from the hips down.

She wasn't sure what she should say to that, so she handed him her key and stepped out into the hallway. "Thank you. You look wonderful," she said of his Oxford-gray striped suit, pale gray shirt and red-and-gray paisley tie. "You always look great."

"Thanks. I enjoy pleasing you."

"It's a nice night for walking," she said, but she'd decided that she wasn't going to ask him where they would eat.

"Yes it is, but we'll take the car tonight." The driver held the door while Ashton assisted her into the limousine. "Don't you want to know where we're dining?"

"I don't really care," she said, "as long as we're together."

"Keep that up, and I'll have a big head. I love that kind of talk," he told her.

When the car turned into Riverside Drive, she caught her breath. Was he taking her to his home at last? The car stopped in front of his house, but she didn't let herself breathe. Maybe he'd forgotten something. He got out, assisted her out of the car, walked with her up the stone steps and opened the door.

"Miss Felicia! Miss Felicia!" Teddy cried, jumping up and down. She knelt and brought him into her arms. "My daddy said he was going to get you. We're going to eat now. Come on, I'm hungry."

Ashton took Teddy by the hand. "We have to give our guest time to settle down and relax. You're not that hungry."

"No, sir. I ate some potato chips, but I want Miss Felicia to see what Miss Eartha cooked. Daddy, can I play my CDs for Miss Felicia?"

"If she wants to hear them, yes." Teddy looked at her with an inquiring expression.

"I'd love to hear some jazz, Teddy." He showed her a CD. "That would be very nice." She looked at the boy and realized that he was dressed precisely like his father. "Teddy, you look wonderful, and I notice that you and your father are dressed alike."

"I like to look like my daddy," he said. "You look so pretty, Miss Felicia, and you smell so good. Doesn't she, Daddy?"

"Like father, like son. She definitely does, son."

Eartha came into the living room, "Good evening, Miss Felicia. Dinner's ready, Mr. Ash." Teddy grasped Felicia's hand and walked with her to the dining room.

Felicia's hand went to her chest, and she stifled a gasp at the elegant table, it's beautiful place setting complemented by yellow and red roses and tall yellow candles. "This is beautiful," she said when Ashton lit the candles and dimmed the electric lights.

Teddy said the grace and, an hour later, having dined on a seven-course meal worthy of any five-star restaurant, she'd been seduced to putty. As they left the table, Ashton kissed her in the presence of Eartha and his son and walked back to the living room with his arm tight around her. Her adrenaline began pumping, and she couldn't help wondering what else he had in store for her. Surely, he wouldn't allow their perfect evening to end with her in her bed and him at home in his.

"Good night, Miss Felicia. My daddy said I have to go to bed now. Will you come stay with me?"

"I'll come again soon," she said, leaned down and hugged him.

"I love you, Miss Felicia."

"I love you, too, Teddy. You're so precious."

When she raised her head, her gaze caught the naked love in Ashton's eyes. "I'm going to put him to bed, and I'll be right back," he said, tipped up her chin and flicked his tongue over the seam of her lips. Frissons of heat shot through her, and her heartbeat accelerated, and she thought it tumbled down to her belly. *Control yourself, girl.*

"Good night, Miss Felicia," Eartha said. "It sure was a

pleasure to prepare dinner for you. I hope I get to do it on a regular basis."

Well, that couldn't have been plainer. "And thank you for that wonderful dinner. I can't imagine why Ashton would ever eat out."

"You know a man has to do his thing. I just go with the flow," Eartha said. "Good night."

Ashton came into the living room. "I'm ready to go when you are." How strange that he didn't wait for her to decide when she wanted to leave!

As if he read her mind, he said, "I can't wait to get you alone."

The limousine awaited them, and within fifteen minutes they arrived at the building on Central Park West in which she lived. The second that he stepped into her apartment, he had her in his arms. His hands roamed her body, and she could feel the hot blood shooting to her loins. He lifted her to fit him, and she parted her lips for his kiss. Hungry. Starved. Like a glutton, she sucked his tongue into her mouth and he pressed her back to the wall, letting her feel his desire for her. Trembling, she took his hand and rubbed the nipple of her left breast.

"Do something," she said. "You've been teasing me all evening."

"What do you want? Tell me. Anything. I'll do anything you want. I want to please you."

"Kiss me. I want to feel your mouth on me." He feasted on her nipple until her moans filled the air. She pressed her hands to his bulging sex and stroked and squeezed until he shouted.

"Stop, baby. If you don't, I'll lose it." He lifted her, carried her to her room and continued his onslaught upon her senses, rocking her while he unzipped her dress. He knelt and pulled off her shoes. "I want to love every inch of you, kiss every bit of you until you can't ever want any other man."

"I only want you," she said, panting for more of him.

He stripped himself quickly and joined her in bed. "Tell me you love me the way I love you," he said.

"I do love you. You're everything to me, but don't tease me. I'm aching to get you inside of me." Shivers snaked through her as he kissed her throat, sucked her nipples and licked his way down to her belly, kissed the inside of her thigh until every nerve in her body stood on end.

"Ashton, please. I'm…I'm… I'll die if you don't get in me." The thrust of his tongue into her vagina brought a sharp, wanton cry from her lips. He worked at her until she thought she'd die if she didn't explode, but he wouldn't let her.

"Please," she moaned. "I want you to get into me now."

He made his way up her body, looked down at her and smiled, and her heart turned over. "Take me in, sweetheart."

She grasped his penis with loving hands, raised her hips, brought him home and he sank into her. With a hand beneath her hips, he positioned her, and began storming inside of her. She let herself go. Lord, it felt so good, and so awful as he brought her to the brink time and time again, only to postpone the moment she longed for.

"Please, Ashton, let me have it. I can't stand this."

"Is it good to you?"

"You know it is. If only I could burst wide open."

"All right. Be still, and I'll take you there." He rode her furiously, and when the pumping and squeezing began again, he accelerated his moves. She thought she'd die, and then she gave in to it and to him. He hurled her up and then down until she thought she was dying. And then, it came. Blessed relief came as he drove her to ecstasy, collapsed in her arms and spent himself.

"How do you feel?" he asked her.

"Wonderful. Where're you going?"

"I'll be back in a minute." He strode to the chair over which he had draped his jacked and came back to the bed. She couldn't believe it when she realized that he was on his knees. "Will you marry me, Felicia? I'll be a good husband to you and a good father to our children. I will love you and care for you for as long as we both breathe. Will you be my wife and the mother of my children?"

"Yes. Yes. It's what I want. I'll be a good wife and a good mother to Teddy and our other children."

"I know you need to work for your own feelings of self-worth, and that's fine with me. We can have all the help you want."

"What will we do with my apartment?" she asked him.

"We'll keep it. If we want some privacy, we'll go there and have time for ourselves."

He took her hand and slipped a two-karat white diamond on the third finger of her left hand. "Will you marry me soon? I'm tired of living without you."

"Give me two months. Felicia Parker-Underwood. How does that sound to you?" she asked him.

"Fantastic. It's my dream come true."

Dear Reader

During the past months, I've met many of you at conferences, book signings and online chats, and I look upon you as members of my extended family. Since my own family is very small, you may imagine that I cherish the caring and warmth that come to me from each of you. I've received so much mail from those of you who read McNEIL'S MATCH, that I haven't been able to answer every letter, but I hope to do so eventually. Unfortunately, meeting manuscript deadlines has to have first priority. Many of you said that you fell in love with Sloan McNeil. He's one of my favorite heroes.

Ashton Underwood is my second single-father hero. Some of you will recall Rufus Meade, a journalist and the father of four-year-old twin boys who he was raising alone. That story, SEALED WITH A KISS, was my first novel, and Kimani Press has reissued it along with my second and third Arabesque books, AGAINST ALL ODDS and ECSTASY complete in one volume. It is entitled UNFORGETTABLE PASSION. ECSTASY won the first of a number of national awards that I have received for fiction writing. If you're new to my work, I sincerely hope you will have a chance to read those stories.

I also write for Kimani Press, so look there for ONE NIGHT WITH YOU, which was issued in March 2007, and for FORBIDDEN TEMPTATION, due out later in the year.

I like to receive mail, so please write me at: GwynneF@aol.com, P. O. Box 45, New York, NY 10044.

Join my book club:
GwynneForsterBookClubOfFansAndReaders-subscribe@
yahoogroups.com.

For more information, please contact my agent: Pattie
Steel-Perkins. E-mail—MYAGENTSPLA@aol.com.

Gwynne Forster

ALWAYS
Means
FOREVER

DEBORAH FLETCHER MELLO

Despite her longtime attraction to Darwin Tollins,
Bridget Hinton rejects a casual fling with the notorious
playboy. But when Darwin seeks her legal advice,
he discovers a longing he's never known.
How can he revise Bridget's opinion of him?

*Available the first week of June
wherever books are sold.*

Can she handle the risk...?

daring
devotion

ELAINE OVERTON

Author of FEVER

Andrea Chenault has always believed she could live
with the fear every firefighter's wife knows. But as her
wedding to Calvin Brown approaches, she's tormented
by doubts as several deadly fires seem to be targeting
the man she loves.

*Available the first week of June
wherever books are sold.*

KIMANI
ROMANCE

www.kimanipress.com

KPEO0220607

From five of today's hottest names
in women's fiction...

CREEPiN'

Superlative stories of paranormal romance.

MONICA JACKSON
& FRIENDS

Alpha males, sultry beauties and lusty creatures confront
betrayal and find passion in these super sexy tales of the
paranormal with an African-American flavor.

**Featuring new stories by
L.A. Banks, Donna Hill, J.M. Jeffries,
Janice Sims and Monica Jackson.**

Coming the first week of June
wherever books are sold.

KIMANI PRESS™

www.kimanipress.com

KPMJ0600607

Acclaimed author

Adrianne Byrd

BlueSkies

Part of Arabesque's At Your Service military miniseries.

Fighter pilot Sydney Garret was born to fly.
No other thrill came close—until Captain James Colton
ignited in her a reckless passion that led to their short-
lived marriage. When they parted, Sydney knew fate
would somehow reunite them. But no one imagined it
would be a matter of life or death....

"Byrd proves once again that she's
a wonderful storyteller."
—*Romantic Times BOOKreviews* on
THE BEAUTIFUL ONES

Coming the first week of June
wherever books are sold.

ARABESQUE®

www.kimanipress.com

KPAB0120607

A brand-new Kendra Clayton mystery
from acclaimed author…

ANGELA HENRY

Diva's Last Curtain Call

Amateur sleuth Kendra Clayton finds herself immersed in
mayhem once again when a cunning killer rolls credits on a
fading movie star. Kendra's publicity-seeking sister is pegged
as the prime suspect, but Kendra knows her sister is no
murderer. She soon uncovers some surprising Hollywood
secrets, putting herself in danger of becoming the killer's
encore performance....

"A tightly woven mystery."
—*Ebony* magazine on *The Company You Keep*

sepia™

*Coming the first
week of June
wherever books
are sold.*

www.kimanipress.com   KPAH0440607

tangled
ROOTS

A Kendra Clayton Novel

ANGELA HENRY

Nothing's going right these days for part-time
English teacher and reluctant sleuth Kendra Clayton.
Now her favorite student is the number one suspect in a local
murder. When he begs Kendra for help, she's soon on the road
to trouble again—trying to find the real killer, stepping into
danger...and getting tangled in the deadly roots of desire.

"This debut mystery features an exciting new
African-American heroine.... Highly recommended."
—*Library Journal* on *The Company You Keep*

*Available the first week of May
wherever books are sold.*

KIMANI PRESS™

www.kimanipress.com   KPAH0680507